Crossing Borders:

A Narrative Journey Into
the Middle Eastern World

CROSSING BORDERS:
A NARRATIVE JOURNEY INTO
THE MIDDLE EASTERN WORLD

Copyright © 2015 by Rula Quawas

Published by
The Champlain College Publishing Initiative
Burlington, Vermont

Printed in the United States of America
ISBN-13: 978-0-9904592-7-9
First Edition: August 2015

Cover design by Jocelyn Sargent

Dedication

To all the educators, who always believe, dream, and dare.

"When you open your life to the living, all things come spilling in on you.
And you're flowing like a river, the Changer and the Changed. . .
Filling up and spilling over, it's an endless waterfall."

Cris Williamson, "Waterfall"

Contents

Acknowledgements

It is always a joy to thank those who have been of help in the task of birthing this book. First and foremost, I am grateful to my students at Champlain College, whose inspiring voices have created a mosaic of narratives which, I hope, will leave readers in a place of discovering new possibilities and new ways to unsettle dogmas and to disrupt prevailing arrangements and relationships of power in the Middle East. Of course, Champlain College, which will always be an important part of my journey as an educator, has given me more than I can possibly acknowledge.

I would also like to thank Kim MacQueen, the Managing Editor of Champlain College Publishing Initiative, for her skills in taking care of the necessary publication details and for her careful and rigorous attention to every detail in the production of this book. Additional thanks go to Jocelyn Sargent for layout and design.

I am also eternally indebted to Samia Doany, who has agreed to read the stories very carefully and to review them with enthusiasm and with wisdom. I have enjoyed our continual intellectual exchange and our interactions throughout our process of evaluation and revision.

My sincere thanks must also go to Fulbright and to the Council for International Exchange of Scholars, who made it possible for me to spend my sabbatical year at Champlain College. Their sustained support will always be remembered and appreciated.

Editor's Note

The selection of stories written by my students at Champlain College over one academic year (2013-2014) followed a rigorous process of critical evaluation and revision. Every single story was read by me and by an external Arab-American reader who is a long-standing educator and an author herself. We read the stories independent of each other and wrote a brief evaluation on each. We then started sharing notes and ideas, an act which helped me in choosing the stories that embody this book. Evidently, the choice of the stories is my sole responsibility.

The selected stories demonstrate a wide range of modes of expression. While some students question embedded patterns of dominant ideology and prescribed behavior in the Arab world, others work toward building and validating a new order. No matter which mode of expression they follow, the students, through their own words, reject imposed patterns of thought and breach walls of silencing and shaming. By affixing their names to their narratives, they eradicate namelessness and celebrate their original voices, which tell the naked truth and unlock the door to the inner workings of the human self. Their unflinching stories, which are indicative of their engagement with and revision of the Middle East, call for readers as construers of meanings, interpreters of value systems, and suppliers of bridges over gaps in signification. Indeed, the students write like no one but themselves, and everything they write seems crisp, pointed, bright, and bold.

This book aims to open the Middle East to different futures and realms of possibilities than the ones envisioned now by defenders of the status quo. There is nothing like this book in print, nothing that raises from within American classrooms the tough questions that need to be considered about the limits or lack thereof and the perceptions or misperceptions of liberal concepts of emancipation and women's empowerment for understanding non-Western women. Some of the stories refuse to be polite about the challenges faced by Arab women in the Arab region; they believe that the future of dialogic interaction depends on acknowledging and addressing those challenges.

It is evident that the authors of these stories transcend the struggle of what Marge Piercy has called "unlearning to not speak" and through their creative act they teach us, arouse us, please us, and nourish us. They are valuable as individual writers, not only because they present interesting points of view of Arab women's lives and roles, but also because they tap into the human experience.

I have organized the stories within a deliberately alphabetical framework, which is based on the family name. It should be noted that the students have agreed to the publication of their stories by signing a consent form.

Foreword

I had the good fortune to meet Rula Quawas in the summer of 2008 when, as a new dean at Champlain College, I traveled with a group of faculty to Amman, Jordan. Rula was already an active partner in our Global Modules network, and I recall being eager to meet her, having heard many stories of her exuberant personality and riveting intellect. I was transfixed sitting at lunch with her and a group of her students at the University of Jordan, listening in as they discussed Kate Chopin's The Awakening and themes of women's sexual liberation, motherhood, and the hard choices women make in their quest for the freedom to be. I appreciated at once the gift for transformative teaching that Rula possesses, and so when Champlain College decided to apply for its first Fulbright Scholar-in-Residence, Rula immediately sprung to mind.

In 2013-14, Champlain was selected to host a Fulbright scholar. Rula arranged for a sabbatical, and we began to prepare for her visit. We offered Rula a small cottage on campus and she quickly made it her home-away-from-home, entertaining new friends with chocolate-covered dates and other Middle Eastern delicacies. She attended countless dinner parties and learned her way around her new city, figuring out all the best walking and bus routes. She took particular pride in purchasing a fur-lined hat with ear flaps and otherwise readying her wardrobe for the cold Vermont winter. Always cheerful, she seemed to relish the bracing single-digit temperatures and the sharp wind off Lake Champlain, which she called "fresh." She did committee work, joined reading groups, and spoke at statewide meetings.

But mostly Rula taught. During her year at Champlain, Rula offered several sections of Arab Women Writers, a course of her own design intended to complement our interdisciplinary general education curriculum. Students registered for the course not knowing what to expect and completed the course having read and discussed powerful literature with a first-rate feminist scholar from an Arab country. And as the work in this volume testifies, the students did not merely read and discuss; following Rula's lead, they were inspired to respond, to "talk back" to the texts with their minds and their hearts.

Explicating the social, political, cultural, economic, and gendered realities of Arab womanhood in the company of four sections of engaged and increasingly passionate Champlain students, Rula eschewed the research paper approach and challenged her students to craft their own fictional accounts of Arab womanhood. Thus they experienced a very different kind of learning -- synthesizing, integrating, imagining, and ultimately making their own meaning. They took intellectual and creative risks. Rula Quawas and her students, as the work in this volume demonstrates, exemplify Champlain's motto: Audeamus -- Let us dare.

I'm very proud to invite you to sample these stories, a daring collaboration between American students and their visiting Jordanian professor. As you read the stories, you may find yourself shedding previously-held stereotypes and recognizing a deepened sense of shared humanity. You may find yourself transported and transformed. One of Rula's student's wrote at semester's end, "I would travel to Jordan just to take another course from Rula." This volume provides that opportunity. Insha'Allah ... Enjoy!

Elizabeth Beaulieu, Ph.D.
Dean, Core Division
Champlain College
Burlington, Vermont

Introduction

Let us not abandon our songs. Let us sing louder.
Naomi Shihab Nye

"Woman, rise up from behind your veil/ Woman, refuse this hold on you/
This force that annihilates you/ Woman, make your voice which is only the hint of a
trembling heard/ Because, for the moment, your voice is like a violin of desert nights/
It must unite with other voices of veils/ With other morning hands/ And all these
hands and all these voices shall take up the sword and/ transform it into a rose,
into earth and into a garden"
Evelyne Accad, The Excised. *Translated by Miriam Cooke*

During the academic year 2013-14, I spent my sabbatical year as a Fulbright scholar-in-residence at Champlain College[1] in Vermont. Throughout my stay at the CORE Division in this college, I met many professors who shared with me their educational experiences and their keen insights into the politics of teaching. I will always be indebted to the Champlain community, faculty, administrators, and students, for their unstinting support, love, and always good cheer.

This book is born out of the amazing teaching experience I had at Champlain. It is not only about my journey of exploration and growth as an educator, but it is also a celebration of the inspiring, engaging voices of my beautiful students at the college. This book speaks to my Champlain students' creative minds and educational progress, and to their aspirations and dreams as young men and women who hold the present in their hands and who envision the future with their eyes. Journeys, whether along paths of critical inquiry or through introspective meanderings, bring us into different worlds of cultures and into different domains of knowledge. They nurture our being-ness and help us to tap into an array of rich experiences that inspire and sustain our becomingness.

Before I embark on my Fulbright journey at Champlain, it is wise to start at the very beginning and address my enduring relationship with Champlain College. This relationship started in 2005 when I received a blanket email message from a Professor of History at Champlain College, Gary Evans Scudder, Jr., inviting me and all professors in the English Department at the University of Jordan[2] to be part of the Global Module program. It took me some time to

1   For more information on Champlain College, check their website at www.champlain.edu. Also, for details on the Council for International Exchange of Scholars, check their website at www.cies.org.

2   For more information on the University of Jordan, check the website at www.ju.edu.jo.

respond to the email sitting in my inbox, but when I finally did, I was intrigued by Scudder's proposal, and I wanted my students to partake in the wonderful educational experience of the Global Module, which is, among other things, a gateway to inter-cultural communication. Communication between people who come from different cultures is essential for the building up of character and for starting up conversations and debates that help to open students' eyes to new ways of seeing the world and to new ways of thinking, knowing, and mean-ing-making.

In 2003, Scudder had thought it would be a great idea to connect his senior class on world issues with foreign students, and thus, the Global Modules program was born. The Global Modules are organized according to subjects and themes covered in the course of Champlain's General Education CORE curriculum. The concept of the Global Module is simple. For four running weeks during a semester, students at Champlain and a partner institution overseas address shared readings and discuss the material online by raising big questions and by addressing these questions through their different lenses and through their diverse perspectives. The focus is usually thematic, with topics as varied as globalization, the universality of human rights, education, the sense of self, the politics of various nations, and women as "the Other." The universities involved were in countries like India, Jordan, Australia, Morocco, Kenya, Austria, and the United Arab Emirates.

My three-year experience with the Global Module program was enriching, not only for me, but also for my Jordanian students. The model of teaching I used was different for one important reason, which is obviously related to the fact that I had for the very first time ever integrated technology in the form of the Global Module platform into my courses. I am fully aware of the fact that ICTs (Information Communication Technologies) are no panacea for public education, but they do help support and enhance the classroom in the sense that that they promote collaborative and democratic learning modes. Dale Spend-er writes that in the age of electronic information, "the relationship between teachers and students will enter a new phase: one where cooperation rather than hierarchy sets the terms."[3]

The model of teaching I used was also different for another reason that is vitally important. It is the promotion of a sense of a community of learners who hail from two different countries, each of whom bears responsibility as both writer and reader. It should be noted that the role of the student is not only to read assigned materials, but also to respond to them. The students on both the Jordanian and American end were required to post their comments on certain representational texts and to read other students' posts and to comment on them with constructive and critical feedback, while observing all forms of netiquette rules. Students received points on their assignments according to how thorough-

---

3   Dale Spender, *Nattering on the Net* (Melbourne, Australia: Spinifex, 1995), 115.

ly they responded and engaged in an interactive and dialogic discussion. Their role as commentators was as important as their performance as writers. The whole exercise of reading, writing, and evaluating not only encouraged students to think of their writing and interpretive processes in relation to those of their peers, but it also allowed them to learn from one another as a group. It is true that, in some instances, the students were left with ambivalence, but they were also left with the pleasure of communication with their American peers, the pleasure of being part and parcel of an expanded repertoire of critical skills, of a newfound sense of power to have an active relationship to cultural texts and to deconstruct dominant ideology.

The Global Module was a safe space for students to explore personal as well as analytical responses to assigned reading texts. Students had profound reactions to the texts and their responses and became aware of issues raised in the discussions, for example, roles of women in different countries. The Global Module platform provided an alternative forum in which the instructors were not the sole authority figure and in which students perceived a greater ability to express themselves openly and deliberately. Professor Debra Picchi, a Professor of Anthropology and Coordinator of the Global Citizenship Certificate Program at Franklin Pierce of New Hampshire at Rindge, who ran the Global Module project with me at one time, told me in an email in 2007 that "she has so enjoyed [my] students and has gotten to know [her] students in ways [she] would not have but for their entries."[4] Clearly, a sense of bonding has made the Global Module experience a more personal experience than others.

Then, in 2012, another email from Champlain College landed in my inbox and this time it was from the Dean of the CORE Division, Professor Betsy Beaulieu. There is a story behind every email, and this time the story was about Champlain and myself. I have been invited by Champlain to come and teach for one academic year as a Fulbright scholar-in-residence. I was, of course, ecstatic and willing to embark on a new adventure in connection with Champlain, but this time not through ICTs, from a virtual distance, but through full embodied presence. Champlain has always had a special place in my heart, and now I would be traveling to be in the heart of Champlain. Sometimes we linger on our journeys for a while before getting to our destination, and, I am glad to say that, my lingering on my virtual road to Champlain had finally and unexpectedly led me to Champlain itself, where my journey continued. As Tolkien has once said, "Not all those who wander are lost."

The main scope of my introduction here is to highlight the importance of becoming aware that as human beings, we are embedded in a web of relationships. Despite the Western focus upon independence and individualism, our world actually revolves around and functions on interdependence. Because of this, consciously choosing to dialogue with diverse people, and therefore "voices,"

---

4   Debra Picchi, email message to author, March 25, 2007.

we come into contact with would allow us to get closer and closer to being able to hear and see "wholeness" through our interconnectedness.

The concept of interconnectedness reminds me of the Dalai Lama, who contends that "The theory of interdependence allows us to develop a wider perspective. . . . With a wider mind, less attachment to destructive emotions like anger, therefore more forgiveness. . . . We're not talking about the complete removal of feelings like anger, attachment, or pride. Just reduction. Interdependence is important because it is not a mere concept; it can actually help reduce the suffering caused by these destructive emotions."[5] Indeed, interdependence is not a mere concept only. It can be viewed as a cultural and intellectual tradition, which is a distinct set of ideas and concepts that students come to learn through coursework and through other learning experiences.

Thus, by being open to listening to my Champlain students' inspiring voices as they crossed my path during my stay at the College and by reading their multiple and diverse stories embedded with their own experiences, I have often found validation for my own ideas or a clearer way of seeing them, while at other times I have been challenged in my thinking. At all times though, being receptive to others and to their written creative work or by engaging in dialogue with them, has resulted in my perspective becoming wider and wider. I have, therefore, come to realize that at any point in time what I "see" and think of as "the big picture" is really only ever a part of it, as it is a dynamic picture that is constantly shifting and growing. What to begin with might be simply a personal experience or an inkling of how something might unfold, as we extrapolate from what we have learnt and heard from others, can become increased perceptiveness that gains significance through the similarity of shared experiences.

Living relationships amongst people who come from different geopolitical spaces are everything in life. As Stephanie Pace Marshall points out, to be alive is to belong to a complex network of relationships: "Life is naturally interdependent. There is simply no such thing as an independent living entity. Without the cooperation, partnership, and reciprocity of the other, the self will simply not survive. The co-creative process of life cannot support isolation. The self-regulatory capacity and sustainability of a living system is inextricably connected to the density, diversity, and intricacy of its interlinked and interactive networks and feedback loops."[6] Marshall adds that the "self is best understood, expressed, created, and re-created in relation to others. Although life continually asserts its self, it never stops seeking connections to other life. . . . We simply must be connected and in partnership with others in order to continue to learn."[7]

5   Dalai Lama and V. Chan, *The Wisdom of Forgiveness* (Sydney: Hodder, 2004), 117-18.

6   Stephanie Pace Marshall, *The Power to Transform: Leadership that Brings Learning and Schooling to Life* (San Francisco: Jossey-Bass, 2006), 26.

7   Ibid, 114.

It is the open-ended and informal nature of dialoguing that allows for creativity to be nurtured within us. Dialoguing with others is certainly akin to the notion of dialogue that Mikhail Bakhtin puts forward, maintaining that "To 'be' means to communicate. . . . Life by its very nature is dialogic."[8] The type of communication Bakhtin envisions unfolds in open dialogues and encounters where we could express our ideas, both individual and cultural, and by noticing the shades of differences and similarities of these, work toward more harmonious and kinder ways of living together.[9] Unfortunately, we are seldom reminded of how important and valuable our inner strengths are in relation to the people we meet and start a dialogue with. Our inner strengths are amplified by learning how to communicate and commune with each other.

Dialoguing with people requires openness, a positive attitude to the new, acceptance of diversity, a willingness to see the value in that which is not "standard," and an absence of the desire to suppress that which challenges conformity, and therefore by extension also authority. One of the important ways to dialogue with people is through asking questions. Ready-made answers tend to divide people and limit what can be accepted; they are definite and exclusive and they set up boundaries that are very hard to either cross or obliterate. Questions, on the other hand, allow us to further our dialogues as we come to discover each other's way of thinking and our perspectives as they transform and evolve over time. We can unify individuals and nations together through questions, not answers. As we move through time, our perspectives are also in motion, moving along with us. They are never fixed or transfixed; instead, they are always dynamic and ever-flowing. Each one of us has a unique lens through which we look at things or matters and these lenses are never exclusive. Nobody can ever "be" in exactly the same place as anybody else. We inhabit or share different realities and every single reality has its own unique meaning or perspective.

Another way to dialogue with people is through story-telling, which is, in more ways than one, all about soul telling. I am a storyteller who believes in the power of words and communication. I believe that telling stories, or *el-hekayat*, fills the emptiness of our silences. Robert Atkinson is absolutely right when he says that "Story is a tool for making us whole . . . a tool for self-discovery"; stories tell us new things about ourselves that we would not have been as aware of without having told the story. Writing ourselves is a way to make sense out of life and give meaning to it. Atkinson tells us that "Our stories illustrate our inherent connectedness with others. . . . In the life story of each person is a

---

8   James Zappen, trans., "Mikhail Bakhtin (1895-1975)," accessed July 27, 2014. http://www.rpi.edu/-zappenj/bibliographies/bakhtin.htm.

9   James Zappen, trans., "Mikhail Bakhtin (1895-1975)," *Twentieth-Century Rhetorics and Rhetoricians: Critical Studies and Sources*, eds., Michael Moran and Michelle Ballif (Westport, Connecticut: GreenWood Press, 2000), 7-20.

reflection of another's life story."[10] Thus if we can accept and "see" what has been said by so many for so long—that we are each of us unique, then we will realize that everybody's life, each individual life, has a contribution of original knowledge to make. Simply by being and by living, one flows and has a chance to share this knowledge and this experience, which, in many instances, contributes to the wholeness of humankind.

As we all know, creative expression and writing is an expression of someone's totality of self, the whole warp and woof. Writing, in general, is all about communicating an experience, an idea, a feeling or a beat of heart, a thought, or a discovery. And although there are many mediums through which to communicate, writing is all about getting the message across, thus it is reasonable to suppose that clarity might be seen as one of the most important factors in writing. But writing is not the only skill that matters. Reading and writing, more often than not, go hand in hand. Creative "wreading," a term cosily borrowed from Emily Carr, offers interactive and reactive responses to assigned texts as the grounds for subsequent critical interpretations.[11] Evidently, self-expression happens from reading as well as from experience. It is said that we cannot interpret what we do not experience. "Wreading" thus implies not only a merging of the acts of reading and writing but also, and more importantly, an investment in experiential learning. As I need trust to write, similarly much trust is needed in reading—a suspension of disbelief and judgment, and a willingness to receive.

At Champlain College, I used my 330 CORE courses, which I have designed to be on and around Arab Women Writers, some of whom are labeled as innovative, oppositional or avant- garde, as the perfect spaces for creating engaged learning opportunities in which students can experiment with self-expression and creative writing. Here students approach stories as a process rather than a product. Here they can find and hold on to a voice. Here they can develop a point of view and problematize that point of view elegantly, persuasively, and effectively. In sum, while they are still in dialogue with the whole world, they learn how to dive into a completely different culture, a Middle Eastern one in this case, submerge themselves into its running waters, and swim through its whirlpools through inquiry, opinion, wonder, and doubt. Admittedly, some of the students at first showed reluctance to participate actively in the process of creation. Not surprisingly, students are comfortable in their role as consumers; their initial responses to the task of participating in the production of signification thus involved anxiety and frustration; however, I am glad to say, a shift happened midway through the courses I taught. With time the students felt liberated to create and innovate.

The insistence by the educational system to exclusively scaffold teaching and

10   Robert Atkinson, *The Gift of Stories* (Westport: Bergin and Garvey, 1995), 3-4.

11   Emily Carr, "The Wreading Experiment: Performative Strategies for Teaching Women's Innovative Poetries," *Feminist Teacher* 20 (2010): 183-203.

learning into a series of steps accompanied by detailed instructions does not, in my opinion, create a classroom that is an imaginative site where students find freedom within the constraints of a certain text. Learning is a creative process and students should not be made to methodically and repeatedly practice and explain the individual steps with the aim of specifically mastering them, rather than harnessing creative "wreading" and reconnecting feeling and intellect, which is vital for the promotion of creativity and which leads to some kind of a tangible product like a work of art. Learning emerges from discovery, not directives; a sense of excitement and adventure, not fearfulness; reflection, not stringent rules; potential possibilities, not prescriptions; creativity and curiosity, not conformity and dogma; and diverse meaning, not rules and mandates.

My students at Champlain College have engaged in critical self-reflection and cultivated new stories from a harvest of continuous reading and learning of Arab women writers. They have interpreted certain situations and acted in them. They have examined their own privilege, their own assumptions, and the part they have played in broader systems of interlocking oppressions. They have remembered texts written by Arab women writers so as to form a whole that subsumes its artifice. They have also untangled the competing discourses at play and excavated the political and ethical commitments at stake in the act of revision. Their creative or innovative stories, which are a living testimony to new perspectives and new worlds, and which cradle their emboldened vision about Arab women who live in diverse cultures and worlds, are activists, revisionists, and interventionists. Their self-authored stories are not conventional, univocal, or plain-spoken. In fact, they come to raise a lot of big questions that are intellectually and emotionally engaging, questions that deal with sexuality, gender issues, hegemonic discourses, masculinism and patriarchy, Arab cultures and their traditions and social norms, constructions of femininity and masculinity, self and community, voice and authenticity, ownership and body.

This book embodies a multitude of stories written by my Champlain students, students who step outside their comfort areas and expand their sense of community. Their stories are nurturing and encouraging pieces that inspire community, empowerment, and teaching and learning processes. They include voices that call for inclusion of a wide variety of perspectives and that support our inner sense of what is right and wrong. Even if there is nothing the students can do about a particular situation, knowing that what is really going on involves gender power relations and power politics at times means that they are well informed and ready to connect to the world as well as to other people and to enact positive and effective engagement with diverse populations. One person matters. Each one of us is one person until we come together for a common "wreading," and that can facilitate active engagement and activism in its many forms and that can evoke positive social change. Sometimes big changes begin with our students who think creatively and critically. Sometimes big changes come when we change ourselves and our perspectives about other people and other cultures.

Through inquiry, opinion, wonder, and doubts, my Champlain students wander through, around, and over texts written by Arab women writers while in dialogue with the world, a new "glocal" world characterized by the politics of language that is made of the loudest of silences. Through innovative, active, and reactive acts of reading, these same students take up the challenge of speech, come to learn how to sound back to the discourses that supersaturate their lives, and create a space for self-making or self-invention. They position themselves as negotiating subjects who negotiate their visions against their actual world limits and who position and reposition themselves as thinking, feeling, and writing subjects so that they can create a space for influencing change. Of course, the possibility of this happening is only when active learning, teaching, and student-ing become not only a vital platform to learn, teach and share stories that weave in and out of social change but when they also create a creative location for imagining and thinking through alternative responses to social injustices.

Within my Champlain classrooms, American students come to learn to look through a self-reflective lens which mirrors their re-visions, their re-flections, and their re-creations. These students affirm their speaking positions through addressing gender trajectories and through confronting bare-footed Arab women as they are represented in Arabic fiction. They demonstrate to the whole world their rights to justice, dignity, and a way of living empathetically across differences. In the act of speaking, they make stories and they invite others to do the same. In the act of speaking, they have led me to many awakenings. I am grateful to them, to Champlain College, and to Fulbright and the Council for International Exchange of Scholars for helping me conceive and birth this book. I hope that this book will point readers in useful directions; at most it will offer only a first step in the long journey to engaged teaching and studenting and to living. For me, it is the need to believe, despite all evidence to the contrary, that literature and storytelling have something to teach us about how to fashion multiple knowledges, how to live empathetically across differences, and how to open our hearts and minds to others' humanity. Telling a story is an imagining not only of "what was" but also of "what is" and thus also of "what will be."

Free To Save
Dylan Birdsall

Today, our nation marches. Security forces are just ignored. The people want to topple the regime. I woke up to the smell of tobacco complimented by mint. My father only smokes before stressful occasions. Mother is quiet, warming her body with the hot cup of lentil soup before she places it on his plate. The unease comforts me. I have been stuck at home for months, as protests come closer and more often. My father, and brother, Anubus, have been very busy lately, meeting with friends and staying out late at night. They say that Mubarak will fall and the Brotherhood will rise. They speak of a future free from oppression and poverty. I ask: If we are fighting for the people of Egypt, why can I not come?

"Shush, Mafuane, protest is no place for a girl."

I cannot stand the days with my mother.

"School was only distracting you from your work," she tells me.

"No man is going to want you if you cannot run a house."

She never talks about her childhood. She is like a wall, only able to stand and appear supportive. She holds the house together, but remains rigid. She is an exterior, unable to speak of emotion or from the heart. We only share our inability to feel love, which drives us further apart.

As we were beginning to prepare lunch, we hear Anubus off in the distance. He came running home screaming and crying in disconcert: "Baba! Baba! Mubarak shot Baba! He died in the streets!" He fell into my mother's arms, bloody and out of breath.

Then, he began questioning what happened, frantically, which soon turned to tears of dismay. I asked where he was, and was questioned by both my brother and mother.

"Shush, Mafuane, this is not the time for asking your questions!" my mother sharply said. "Get in the house!"

That is when I lost it.

My home is a prison. Inside its walls I cannot breathe. My thoughts cannot explore. How can I lie dormant while the world around me is moving so fast? How can I stay inside when my father is dying outside? Why must I be shushed when there is so much to be said? Pressure collected in my head, and my throat turned to stone. I had nowhere to turn, so I ran. I ran towards where I last remembered being alive. I ran straight to the sea.

When I was a child, my father used to bring me here. We would sit and watch ships sail by. We would sit and listen to the water crashing on the shore. I was allowed to run and play and I was happy. I closed my eyes and thought about him.

The more I thought, the more enraged I became. Since the last day that I was here, years ago, my father has not been there for me. He keeps me locked up at home. He tells me he is fighting for our freedom, but I have become his prisoner. My mother, complacent, reiterates his mentality with little thought. I started to feel the pressure again. Everything I knew was constructed to lead me to a complacent life. I stripped off my clothes and walked into the sea for the first time.

I floated, ears silenced by the water below, with my eyes transfixed on the sky. For once, the world was silent. The water supported me, flowing over and under my body. The sun kissed my skin and warmed my heart. Freedom, I knew I was not going far, but the thought that I could enticed me. I've never felt so alone and so alive. I did not know how to swim, but I wasn't worried. I felt closer to Muhammad than I have ever before. I could die here. I held my breath and began to sink to the bottom. This was it—an end and an escape.

While I was sinking, an image appeared on the surface of the water. Muhammad came, and I heard his voice: "The strong person is not the good wrestler. Rather, the strong person is the one who controls himself when he is angry."

Islam is not running from your problems, but being able to face them. Egypt needs her children for support.

My father died fighting for what he believes. I cannot take my own life before I figure out what to believe. I went to swim back to the surface, but I was not moving. I couldn't swim. I kicked, and I thrust but water began to fill my lungs. Motivated by all the negativity, I was fueled to life. I clawed my way to the surface. Reaching the shoreline I climbed my way to the sand and caught my breath. I redressed, prayed, and went back to my house.

My family needs me. From this point I learned that there is a higher meaning. We need to work to save Egypt, through the oppression and hypocrites. My house can no longer imprison me, for my mind will forever have a greater plan.

Oh, To Have a Choice
Tana Blazek

The sun shone bright through the cracked window-pane in my room; the sound of birds singing, perched on the tree right outside, was like music and the sweet mountain air sneaking through the open window filled my lungs. My mother's delicate voice reached my ears, calling me to my daily chores, but I continue to lie here. I let the sun shine on my face just for a few minutes more, soaking it all in. The boom of my father's voice fills the house, bellowing out a tune he's sung since I was a child. It comforts me, and I lay my head back onto the pillow, but I know I must get up or my little brothers will be more than delighted to run into my room to wake me up with their giggles. I can hear their footsteps pattering down the hall. I drag myself out of bed finally, letting the sun kiss my face one last time before pulling my shirt over my head, ready for the day.

The smell of spices fills my lungs, coming from the kitchen where my mother is humming a tune with my dad, a smile on her face. She was always at ease when cooking, always humming a little tune and offering samples of her creations to whoever is nearby. I kiss her on the cheek, and rustle my little brothers' hair; she handed me a basket and motioned towards the door simply saying, "We are having a guest tonight, please go gather eggs and milk," handing me the wicker basket and shooing me out the door. Just as I was passing out of the door, I saw my father come in, trying to talk to my mother about something, but she seemed upset. "Mohammad…" but as quick as he had come in, he left to his study, dismissing her with the wave of his hand, leaving her in silence.

We didn't have much, just a house with enough rooms: one for my parents, a room for my brothers to share, and at the end of the hall was my little room with two windows, a squeaky floor board, and the crack in the wall—but it was all mine. Outside we had a small chicken coop where we got our eggs, while the next-door neighbor had a cow we were allowed to milk. It wasn't much but we were happy. I'd lived in this place my whole thirteen years of existence, and never wanted to leave.

I let my little hands scoop up the eggs, being careful not to drop them, placing them delicately into the woven basket fixed around my arm. The breeze swept through, blowing my hair around me like leaves in the wind, encasing my face, teasing my cheek, blowing to and fro with the wind like I was a part of nature itself. But as soon as the wind started up, it stopped, leaving me there alone, just a girl holding a basket of eggs, with a head full of messy hair.

It had rained the night before, so the dirt patches had turned into a fun game. By this time my little brothers were outside and running, causing havoc; my mom says all little boys do. The mud clung to their clothes, with sticks protruding from their hair. Mother will be mad, but you can never stay mad at these two, and so they wriggle their way out of trouble every time. I rounded them up, after a quick game of tag, and got them back into the house to get cleaned up. But when I entered the front door, I wasn't greeted by singing or the smell of spices as I had been earlier. Instead it was quiet, my mother stooped over the cooking pot looking so tired.

"Mother, what's wrong?"

She shook her head and looked at me with eyes full of unknown sadness, an emotion I never saw on her face. "Oh sweetheart, you're a mess. Go get cleaned up before your father sees you."

I started to walk away when she almost whispered, "And my little one, don't forget we are having company." The sadness once again crept into her eyes, almost apologetically.

My feet padded past my father's office. I tried to skip over the creaky board and press myself up against the walls so that he wouldn't see me. But, like a hawk, he spotted me and called me in.

"What's a daughter of mine doing running around in the mud?" His eyes beamed into mine.

I had to look away, feeling as if I had done something very wrong. I picked a spot on the floor and spoke, "Mother asked me to go gather eggs and milk."

The pattern twisted and turned, new shapes formed before my eyes as my father's eyes bored into my head, his sweet sing song tune vanished, leaving a man I had only seen a few times before. "Foolish girl, out and about playing in the mud. That's no place for a woman. What will people think of you? Of us?" His look of disgust towards me made my stomach turn and the room spin.

What had I done wrong? I've come home looking much worse than this before.

"We are having a guest tonight. I wish you to wear your *hijab*, and make no fuss. Go get cleaned up at once." With that he turned in his chair, his penetrating gaze finally off me.

I sucked in a breath of air.

There it was. Black and dull. My parents make me wear the *hijab* whenever company is expected or when going out to do anything but chores. It scratched my skin and matted my hair. It suffocated me and reminded me of sadness, but I would never voice such things. It was tradition, it was religion, and it was culture; you cannot speak against all three, let alone one. Every time I placed it upon my head wrapping around my neck, tucking in any hairs trying to escape, I felt like I was hiding away, placing a barrier between myself and the real world. My thoughts were interrupted by a knocking at the door and my father calling out to me to join them.

I don't know what I was expecting, who I was expecting, but there stood a man who must have been in his early thirties. I had seen him before, talking to my father, amiably shaking hands. That was the only other time I saw the sadness in my mother's eyes like this morning. His eyes shifted toward me. I felt naked. Even under all these layers I felt completely vulnerable. My father ushered me to sit down, while the man's gaze never faltered from me.

Bustling around the kitchen, my mother fixed us tea and set to work finishing up dinner while my father and this strange man talked. His eyes kept finding me though. A hot sweat on my neck formed, trickling down my spine, causing a cold chill. I shuddered ever so slightly. All I could do was look at my plate. Fixate on the different colors that decorate the simple white dish. Thankfully I was excused after dinner, and proceeded to retreat to my bedroom, just wanting to be away from this man and his eyes. Only, I wasn't so lucky.

The soft patter of my mother's feet came to my door and paused, turned to go, and finally turned once more and opened the door. Her face was pale, her eyes hollow. Her voice quivered as she spoke, "Oh my little girl, how you have grown. Such a beautiful woman you are becoming." A single tear fell onto her cheek, cascading down to her lips. "Your father wished to tell you this, but I just couldn't let him tell you. It had to be me. He, we, have made a decision." She paused, her eyes trailing out of the window to the bright moon outside. Her eyes fixated, she continued, "We try to give you and your brothers a good life, but the house is in trouble…. That man tonight wished to help."

I was so confused. If he was here to help, why was she so upset, and what did it have to do with me?

As if reading my mind she spoke, "He has everything he wants in his life, money, a house, success, but he does not have a wife, nor an heir." My confusion turned to terror as I started to realize just what she was trying to say.

She must have seen the look on my face, for she continued to say, "He's a nice man, a decent man. Your father has talked to him and he has reassured us that you will be well taken care of." Her head turned from mine, her hand placed on mine. "I know you are young, but your father assured me other girls in the town around your age have been getting married, and are quite happy." She tried to smile to reassure me, but I could see that even she didn't believe this.

As soon as the news was out, the wedding was being planned. I hadn't seen him since that day he came to my house, and didn't for a few moons after, not until the evening of the wedding. The dress was beautiful, crystals reflecting, dancing off the lights. I had never worn, let alone seen anything so pretty before, but it didn't feel like mine. It reminded me of the *hijab*, for the material scratched my skin, the beads dug into the side, and the veil made it so I could barely see except for my feet in front of me. I couldn't move, yet all I wanted to do was escape. It was too late, though, for I heard the music starting, and my mother came to retrieve me. I saw him there at the end of the rows. His eyes were on me. It didn't matter that there was a room full of people looking at me, but him. Those eyes made my flesh burn and my pulse quicken. I didn't understand it. It frightened me, and since that was all that I knew, I took it for fear, instead of something entirely different and new, not known to me at this time.

We got through the ceremony, and his fingers reached for mine in the declaration of him being now my husband: the man I now "serve," as my dad said when kissing my cheek after the wedding. Such simple words that stung like a knife. It was like I was told I'm not even my own person anymore.

I only looked at him briefly throughout the ceremony, afraid of the feeling I got when his eyes locked into mine. After the wedding was no different until it was just him and me. No one told me anything about my role, what I was to do or even what to say. My mother was full of guilt for almost bartering me away to save the way of life she so desired, but I understood. She had two boys to look after, and could never go against my father's word. And it was not father's place to tell his daughter about such things.

Here I was, fourteen years of age, married off to this stranger much older than I, someone who knew what it meant to consummate the marriage and to show love. While I was frail and afraid of his eyes, let alone his touch. There was nowhere to run. There was only him. I looked out to the moon, now big, full, and glistening, feeling the sorrow my mother must have felt, not because of this man sitting next to me and my role but because I couldn't pick or even have a choice. What if I wanted to pick who I married like my mother had with my father?

These thoughts made me so frustrated, a hot tear snuck from my eye; I try to wipe it away quickly as so he wouldn't see but he sees everything. He came to my side, wiping the tear away with his hand, tilting my face up to his. I kept my eyes on the ground, counting the tiles beneath my feet. His voice rang out, deep but with a honey sweetness, "Will you look at me? Your husband?" he asked it like a question, never demanding like my father had done in the past. My mother had a choice.

I am curious of this man who stands next to me, the one that claimed me as his. My eyes darting from the ground to the window, finally to him, ever so slowly making their way into his own till they locked. His hand reached for mine, I have the urge to pull away but I don't.

"I know I am only a friend of your father's, to them I am just helping them out and will be the guy who will protect and care for their daughter. It wasn't until I saw you that night that I knew my plans were complete and that I wanted you to be my wife." His honesty struck me hard, jolted me from the inside out. Men didn't talk like this to me. My own father didn't even speak to me in this fashion. His eyes looked deep into me and I allowed myself to truly look back, surprised at what I saw. These brown eyes I was so afraid of weren't just brown, like my father's, but had speck of gold in them, matching his honey voice.

It was all so confusing. I wanted to go home to my warm bed, to step across that squeaky floor board, and to feel the warmth of the sun through the window on my face and to wake up to the sing song tunes of my mother and father. Yet here was this man, so different, so sweet from what I'd known. I broke down and cried, not knowing even why but the tears felt so good escaping.

His fingers caught every one, kissing them away.

"I love you, and one day I know you too will love me. It will take time, but I will make life good for you, and will always care for you as long as you do the same for me."

Ignoring the marital traditions, he took my hand and led me to bed, placing me gently beneath the covers, kissing my forehead ever so lightly.

"Sleep little one. We have a lifetime to fall in love, and you are too frightened to do anything else tonight. I want it to be your choice, when you're ready. I will tell everyone we fulfilled the arrangement to please them, but don't worry. We have all the time in the world to fulfill our duties, and I don't want you to be scared of me when we do so."

Shocked, I pulled the covers around me tighter, going over what he said in my head. We had all the time in the world. It's my choice. His arm pulled around me, and we drifted into sleep, a smile resting on my face, his cheek nestled into my hair.

The sun shone bright through the window, kissing my face sweetly as if to say, "Wake up, little one. It's your day." I felt his hand still wrapped around my waist, his hair matted to the pillow.

A small girlish giggle came from my lips, but I tried to quench it so as to not wake him up. I carefully slipped my feet out of bed, the touch of the cold floor on my feet. I walked to the window to open the pane for a breeze, and a floor board creaked under my foot and made me smile. The sun on my face, I looked into the room surrounding me, the beams of light bouncing off every surface turning the room into a crystal ball. At this moment in time, I knew everything was going to be ok. I snuck back into the warm bed, wrapping his arm back over me, turning to look at him. He opened his eyes groggily, smiling at the sight of me, his eyes glistening into mine; I couldn't help but smile back. My fingers found his and we explored the new realm of this marriage together. My choice.

From Figs to Apples
Kadie Brenes

Kayvan, my father, and Afarine, my mother, fell in love with each other and I (Dorri) was born, but they did not have other children. As time passed family members would passively ask when the new baby was expected. Then some of our family members began telling my mother it must be an evil eye curse and they began reciting prayers and giving her blue amulets in the form of an eye. That eventually created a problem because my dad did not want to marry another woman in order to have a son to carry on his name and legacy. Ultimately, they began speculating that the problem was not my mom but my dad.

My parents were glad that at least they had me and felt blessed. But they also knew that as a girl in our culture, I would not be able to inherit or care for the family business. So they began saving money as they planned to move our family to a place where I could. My father's brothers kept pushing him to marry someone else but my dad refused. Instead by the time I turned thirteen he decided that it was time to move.

The American embassy in Tehran granted my family our visa to come to the United States, but my father still had to acquire a special pass in order for my mother and I to leave Iran. My father wanted us to be in a place that had a big Iranian population in hope to maintain the Sofreye Aghd family business running.

My father decided that Kings Point in Long Island would be our destination because he had a cousin, Hassan, who lived there and our family would stay there until my parents could find our own place to live. At first we were all excited then the fear of the unknown settled in and sadness followed because we had no idea when we were going to see our family again.

We left Shiraz, the cultural capital of Iran, the home of Persepolis and the tombs of ancient kings like Cyrus the Great and Darius, also of Hafiz and Sa'di, aboard flights first to Istanbul and then to New York City. Our travel time was over seventeen hours but all of the different people and things we saw kept us from noticing the long hours that passed.

Being at Hassan's house was an eye opener for me. Hassan was married to Nazgol and had three children: two girls, Alelah, seventeen years old, Laleh, fifteen years old, and Sam, a boy of nine. Their lives were different from the way I thought every Iranian family lived. Nazgol wore makeup and yelled at Hassan for not doing handy work around the house. The girls talked for hours on the phone and never helped around the house, either, while Sam just whined and got whatever he wanted. Back home, this would not have been tolerated, period! But here, they didn't even seem to notice it was wrong.

My father helped Hassan wash the taxis as he improved his English, learned about the city and its boroughs and saved money for our own place. My mother was always cleaning and cooking for everybody in the house and I was sent to high school to begin ninth grade.

My parents decided that I should go without a *hijab* to school, and my mother reminisced that she once too went outside without a *hijab*. But ever since the Revolution she had to wear one, and that is why my parents decided that I should not have to unless, I one day decided to wear it on my own.

I felt lonely and lost as I walked to my new class and began my own journey. It was the first day of school when I began making decisions on my own. Luckily, I knew English because my parents knew that this day would come. I started to study and write in a way I never had before because I had to give my own opinion and thoughts without the restrictions or distinctions of gender.

My family moved out of Hassan's house to our own place in six months. My parents set up the living room to accommodate the family business and my mom was in charge of it because the demand was not as great as they thought it would be. Many of the Iranian families had embraced the new culture and the majority of the time would use our services for marriages and New Year's.

At this point my dad began driving a taxi and would travel to the city for the most of the day. My mother was slowly making her Sofreye Aghd business known among the Iranian community. I was now wearing jeans and making new friends. But all of my memories are tainted because two events changed the way I saw or perceived life forever.

The first one happened on September 11, 2001, when I was in school and all of the sudden I heard that one of the Twin Towers was coming down. I wasn't quite sure what they meant but then the teacher turned on the TV in my classroom, and I witnessed how the second tower fell. The speculations were many but when it all came out that Islamic terrorists had been responsible for the events, Muslims and South Asians became a target for retaliation on U.S. soil.

The second event was that my father was one of the many innocent victims of these hate crimes. He was driving his cab in lower Manhattan when two men requested his services. When he reached their destination, they brutally attacked him. My father was taken to Bellevue Hospital and my mother was contacted. He survived the attack but now he walks with a slight limp.

I was now terrified, angry and hurt. How could someone blame my father or an entire group of people for the atrocities that few had committed. Even in school, a few kids would call me a terrorist, among other insults. It took my dad approximately three months to get back to "normal." He had spent that time helping my mother with the family business specially because the business was picking up due to New Year's coming up.

During that time all I could think about was Iran and the smell of jasmine and magnolia, sitting in the garden drinking tea and eating little rolls of raw walnuts, barbari bread, herbs and feta cheese; listening to the older men reciting poetry in the evenings; Isfahan and beautiful mosques in the square and my mother's Canasta group.

My melancholy was noticed by my parents and one evening, as we were making arrangements for the upcoming New Year's festivities for the clients, my father mentioned that even though we were not going to have our traditional visits of family and friends but we would have a picnic on the thirteenth day as usual.

At the moment I yelled, "We should never have come here!"

But my dad faced me and put his hand on my shoulder to say: "I know you are hurt about what has happened to me and it is not right, but if we allow anger or hate to grow in our hearts, they have simply won. We came here so that you could do just that: express your opinion, wear what you like, marry who you want, get the job you want, and be who you want to be. What happened to me is unfortunate but I cannot let them change my heart. People all over the world mistreat others because they are poorer than them, fatter than them, because of their gender, their beliefs, their religion, their color, their clothes and many other reasons. So don't you become one of them and be the best you can be. Forgive!"

After our conversation, as I lay down in my room I cried and remembered everything that my mom and my dad had done, for a chance to be who they are without the restrictions of our culture, to embrace changes for the better or to bring them closer to their ideal life. I was glad that not their ego, money or tradition ruled their heads or hearts but their love for me and for each other. I, Dorri, was a love child, one with choices and loving parents.

New Year's came and it was profitable and unforgettable for our family. A new day had begun with the knowledge that our dreams could come true if we pursued them and did not give up!

Blog Girl
Francesca Caulder

I couldn't ignore the pull I felt toward the crowd when I looked down at it from my window. Legs curled under me with my chin resting on my knees, I knew that Saleem would never permit me to join in with the people and I sighed. Just a week ago the protests started on the streets. There had been a desperate malaise in the air before that, but now every morning when I take a breath of Egyptian morning air into my lungs, I can taste the electric hopeful energy on my tongue and feel it in my bones. In the fresh morning air I could also smell smoke from fires and gunpowder, and dread and fear would then fill my heart and get stuck in my throat. Saleem was down there and I hadn't seen him for two days now. He had said he would be home today.

Saleem was always a passionate person—it was one attribute that we shared. It seemed that it was the only thing I really knew about him for sure. In my two years of being married to him, I didn't know my husband very well. The day of the announcement of our engagement was the first time I had met him. I was happy with my new life because he was handsome, and father told me I would never want for anything, that I was very lucky. Saleem had always been distant though, like a roommate, even though we shared a bed. He would leave early in the morning and come home late at night. I never knew exactly what my husband was up to but I assumed he worked very hard. When I went down to the market every week and I saw the poverty and suffering I knew that we had it much better than most because of our nice apartment and full stomachs every night. I didn't push with many questions because he never gave me a reason not to trust him.

Saleem always had many of his friends over almost every night to smoke the water pipe on the porch and talk politics. I read the newspapers that Saleem brought home with him so I was up to date on current events, but listening in on their conversations at night when I was thought to have left the room, that's where I got the real news. I walked as swiftly and quietly as a mouse and perched on the first step coming down from the second floor of our apartment. They talked of revolution, and their words were exhilarating. I felt their excitement and their fervor; it was infectious.

I was serving the men coffee a couple of nights before the protests started. Saleem talked about who was going to be where and when and that thousands were predicted to be there. I didn't react and walked back into the house and sat in my usual spot where I could hear them and not be seen. It sounded as if it was expected, to be dangerous, which made me nervous. That night I did something I'd never done before and that was touch Saleem's hand when he was getting ready for bed. I wasn't sure why I did it. Saleem made me feel safe and cared for. While I wasn't sure I loved my husband I was loyal to him. I cared for him and didn't want him to get hurt. He then did something he's never done before either. He took me in his arms and held me for a long time. He held me close to him and we were just breathing in unison. I felt his warmth and I didn't want to leave this safe place. It was in this moment that I felt the first spark of love.

"Don't go down to Tahrir Square tomorrow," he whispered.

"Why?" I asked.

He pulled away but didn't let go of me. He looked into my eyes. "I don't want you to get hurt."

He left in the morning before I woke up and I rolled over to his side of the bed and smelled his pillow. I never noticed how nice he smelled—it made me smile. Throughout the day I would periodically go outside on the porch and watch the gathering of people and all of the colors of flags waving and the chants of the people of Egypt. It brought me joy to feel so one with my people even though I was not on the streets with them. I had a smile on my face the rest of the day.

I was humming along with the radio while I was preparing our dinner when I first heard the loud sound of a gunshot that made me jump. Quickly I ran to the porch and saw the smoke and people running. It was a terrifying sight. I thought that the protests were going to be peaceful and nonviolent. I stared in shock and horror as I saw people running and screaming while loud noises and fire and bombs went off in the crowds. I heard gunshots and then more screaming and running. I didn't know what to do. I spent the rest of the night in the kitchen on the floor with my hands over my ears. I thought most of the time of Saleem. Where was he? Was he okay? Why wasn't he here? I then did the only thing I could think of to help and I started to pray. Please come back to me.

I don't know when I fell asleep. All I know is next thing I knew I was being woken up by Saleem. I knew it was him, but I could barely recognize him from all of the dust in his hair and all over his face and clothes. I reached up to touch his face, where I saw a cut on his cheekbone and my fingers came away with his blood on them. I panicked and quickly grabbed a towel and dampened it and held it up to his face. I looked into his eyes and was completely caught off guard by what I saw in them. It was if he was really looking at me for the first time. I couldn't look away, I was just so glad he was here. Then he did something that he hadn't done in a long time. He kissed me.

That morning I felt Saleem get out of bed because I was lying on his arm. I realized that he was going back down to the streets. The protests had paused overnight but I could still sense danger. I grabbed his arm and desperately said "Wait!" He looked back at me in shock. We stared at each other for a long time. He finally said, "I have to," and got up.

I followed him.

"Why? I'm scared for you. What happened yesterday? Who was fighting? Why was there fighting? What are you going to be doing?"

He turned back to me and said, "The police, Mubarak's men, they are afraid of change. They feel safe under his blackmail and threats."

I said, "Then why do you have to be there? How do I know you will be safe?"

Saleem put both hands on the counter and hung his head down. This sight startled me, because in front of me, he always stood so strong and proud.

"I am needed there. People are counting on me. I'm doing this for my people, for us, so we can have a better life. As for my safety," he exhaled. "I don't know." And then he shook his head.

"I'm scared for you," I told him.

He stood up and continued getting ready. He looked over at me and smiled. "Please don't, Hadiya."

He had such a nice smile.

"I'll be back tonight for dinner, I promise."

I felt a little more confident when he left.

I waited for him all day. I prepared a nice dinner for the two of us and waited. He didn't say when he was going to get back. It was getting late and as the sun disappeared over the silhouette of the buildings, and my anxiety was building. I looked out over Tahrir Square but saw only the normal activity. I went to sleep that night but didn't sleep well because I was afraid for Saleem and hoped that he would be next to me when I woke up.

"Hadiya! Hadiya! Wake up! Please! Now! Wake Up."

I was being violently shaken by my husband. I was so happy to see him that the fear and urgency in his voice was lost to me. It was only when he started packing our things that I felt his panic.

"What? What happened?" I asked.

"Please, I'll explain everything when we are safe, but right now we aren't, so I need your help. We have five minutes to pack everything important. They're coming for us and I don't know when we can come back." Saleem was packing important documents in a suitcase along with some clothes.

I had never seen him like this and had never been more afraid.

"Who's coming for us?" I asked.

He didn't stop moving and didn't look at me.

"The Security Police."

I just stood there for a second, paralyzed.

"Please Hadiya! I need your help. We need to leave now!"

My mind didn't make the decision to start moving but next thing I knew I grabbed a suitcase for myself and started packing everything I thought necessary. As we ran out of the bedroom we were greeted by men that I had recognized as the friends who had been over before many times. They ushered us down the stairs and Saleem took my hand and helped me into a waiting car, where another man was waiting for us. We pulled out into the streets before Saleem even got his door closed and started driving faster than I had ever gone before.

I didn't know I was crying until Saleem squeezed my hand and I came back into reality and I wiped my eyes with the other. I looked at his face and then at the other men in the car with me. They weren't talking to each other but their eyes were darting all around them like they were prey waiting for a predator's strike. I couldn't help but do the same even though I had no idea what to look for.

We drove through the city and stopped in between two buildings where more men were waiting for us. The door was opened and Saleem took my hand again and rushed me through an open door and up some stairs. The building smelled musty and was very dark.

Saleem opened a door, which revealed a tiny room full of men, women and children. When we walked in, the room went silent. Almost instantly the room filled with praises and applause from both the men and the women. Saleem was grabbed and hugged and cheered and I was pulled over toward the women who all talked to me at once, introducing themselves and saying things like, "You're the wife of Saleem!" "He's such a great man." "He is so brave!" "You must be so proud." "Wow, it's amazing to meet you."

My mind was going a mile a minute and all I could do was nod my head.

I sat down on the couch and got my bearings, and that was when I met Ghada. She was my age and I immediately felt comfort from her presence. I still couldn't speak but when she spoke of my husband and his leadership I believed her, even though I wasn't sure what she was talking about. My Saleem?

I finally started to listen to what she was saying and what people were doing around me. The men and women were all huddled around computers and maps and were all talking so fast. It looked like they were mobilizing a new protest and they were reaching people via a website called Facebook, which Ghada said many people had access to all around the world.

Ghada was one of the only ones who didn't look at me like I was stupid when I was asking questions. I used the computer many times in my life but it was really only for emailing with my family when I used it a couple of years ago. Apparently there was a whole virtual world that I didn't know much about. I wasn't naïve about technology, I just didn't have much use for it in my day-to-day life. I spent most of my free time reading books and cooking. Ghada told me that the new protest was to take place tomorrow and that the Security Police were taking action, this time to prevent it from happening before anyone could mobilize and that they had cut off internet usage in all of Egypt but the word was still getting out because we were smarter than the security police who underestimated our fire.

When I was alone with Saleem that night after all of the chaos died down, he filled me in on the details of the revolution and how sorry he was that he put me in danger. I assured him that I didn't want to be any other place than with him here, and he smiled at me again and kissed me. I pulled away and told him that I wanted to go out there with him. He looked at me fearfully and strongly advised me to stay here with the other wives and children, where it was safe. He wanted to know that I was safe so that he wouldn't be worrying about me too much, so he could concentrate on keeping himself safe.

I knew he was right.

That was the first night we said that we loved each other. There was so much about this man I didn't know and yet I knew my love for him now like the back of my hand.

As I watched him leave in the morning, it felt as though he took my heart with him. It was one of the hardest things I ever had to do. I could tell it was hard for him too, which made me feel better. Before he left he said that he might not make it back to me for a couple of days but not to worry about him until the weekend.

It was a long couple of days but I kept myself busy using the computer, researching and reading "blogs" and newspapers, but then disregarding the newspapers because I knew that the real news was straight from the people and not from corrupted journalists. I soon came to the realization that the rest of the world didn't know what I knew. I brought this concern up to Ghada.

"That's where the wives come in," she said with a smile.

I asked her what she meant by that, and she explained to me that most of the wives wrote their stories on the computer in blogs and Facebook, where people from around the world could see and share the real story of the revolution and not the one they see in the media. It was their way of helping their husbands fight. Ghada had a blog that I took to reading and so did some of the other women that I had met here.

I started reading some other women's blogs that I had never met before and found out the revolutions like the one going on in Egypt were happening all around the Middle East and North Africa. It was astonishing. I thought about Saleem and how proud I was to call this man my husband and I wanted him back here with me in that moment more than ever. I came to discover that this revolution was talked about and conceived right on our porch.

I waited for him for what seemed like forever. The day he was supposed to come back came and went, and I couldn't shake this feeling that something was terribly wrong. Ghada and the other wives tried to console my anxiety and keep me distracted. I would read more and more on the computer. I caught myself glancing up and seeing eyes on me that belonged to many of the other women and some of the children too.

One particular time I locked eyes with Yasmine from across the room. She quickly looked away as if embarrassed. I was about to open my mouth to say something when Ghada said, "They look up to you. We all do."

I didn't know what she was saying. "Look up to me? What did I do?" I asked. "You're Saleem's wife. You're an extension of him. We feel his strength through you. You're his support and therefore ours, too." Then she went back to reading.

I took that in for a minute. Saleem was always my protector, but it was only when our world was completely turned upside down where I could step outside and really see what a great man I had married. I was proud that I could be seen as his support and his strength. Where was he?

An hour later there was a timid knock on the door of the room Ghada and I were in. I looked up to see two men standing in the doorway. One I recognized as Ghada's husband but the other man I didn't know. They looked haggard and sad. Ghada's husband looked into my eyes and then looked away.

A bone-chilling dread filled my heart. I heard the words that they were saying, that Saleem was killed, but they didn't register in my brain. They said a man they believed to be an assassin sent by the Security Police caught him off guard, that they did everything they could to save him, but he was too gone. He didn't die in vain they said. He was a good man.

I heard the words but I didn't understand them, I didn't feel them; in fact, I didn't feel anything. I didn't feel Ghada hugging me and crying or all of the other people coming into the room with me and crying. I knew it was happening, but I was numb. I left them all and walked into Saleem and my bedroom. I sat down on the bed and hugged his pillow and smelled his lingering scent and begged for this all to be a dream and I drifted off into a deep slumber.

I woke up what felt like weeks later but what the sky told me was only the small hours of the morning. I felt like my body weighed a thousand pounds, my head hurt, and it felt like I had been hit with something. I needed to use the bathroom so I sluggishly got up and walked downstairs. I wasn't quiet; I didn't have it in me to care.

I used the bathroom and as I was walking back upstairs, a computer caught my eye. I don't know what came over me but I just knew there was something I needed to do. I needed the world to know everything. I opened a word document and started writing. It felt like I was writing for hours when emotion overtook me and I began crying, then sobbing, and then wailing as I wrote more and more and more but I couldn't take my fingers off the keyboard to wipe my tears.

I poured all of my sorrow and anger and love all in words and I kept going and going until my tears dried and the sun was coming up. When I stopped I found Ghada in the room with me, I didn't even hear her come in. She didn't say anything when I looked at her.

That night I created my own blog where I poured out my heart, where I told Saleem's and my story, where I wrote down all of the things that I wished I could have told him when he was here. During the next couple of weeks in that house, I wrote many posts about the current events happening in Egypt, as they unfolded in real time.

I felt close to Saleem as I wrote, it was the only place I could feel anymore, and it was cleansing to me. Many people from all over the world read what I had to say and I communicated with them. They are what got me through.

Now a year later to the day, I never once doubted my husband, and my love for him only grows stronger with every memory shared and every new life that we touch with our story. I still feel his presence when I take a breath of fresh air in the mornings, when I sit and have a cup of tea with Ghada, and when I found out that I was pregnant with our son, who I named Saleem after his father. He has his eyes. When he is old enough I will let him read what I wrote about his father.

My Journal: The Day Everything Changed
Anna Charland

Day 1:

I never thought I would do this; I never thought I could write about what happened. I've always been told that I am to respect my elders, that I shouldn't complain or tell on others, and above all I am to always respect mine and my family's honor. I never thought I would be talking about what happened, and if anyone ever finds this book, if they find out that I am writing and especially what I am writing about I will be shamed, or worse...

Day 2:

I hate reliving the experience, but then again, am I really reliving it if it never ends? It's my life and I have to live it like this, but for me, everyday is hell. I can't tell anyone; I can't talk to anyone. This book is all I have, and it really doesn't do anything for me. All it is is another secret that I have to keep inside.

Day 3:

I'm only sixteen years old, and every day I wonder what it would be like to be a normal sixteen-year-old girl. I dream about going to school, I dream about being a teenager, having friends, and going on sleepovers. I dream about looking for a husband, waiting to be asked for my hand. I dream about planning a wedding, or at least a wedding that I am proud of. I dream of everything, but mostly I dream of leaving. Unfortunately, they are only dreams, none of them will ever happen. I'll never be a normal girl again.

Day 4:

Sometimes I think about running away, about what it would be like to start over and never come back. I think I would be doing my parents and siblings a favor by disappearing. They pretend that they still love me, but I know they can't stand to look at me. I want to leave so badly, but then I remember that I'm sixteen, I have no money, I have no job, I have no one to help me, and there is no way out.

Day 5:

I am a disgrace to my family; I see the way they look at me. They treat me as if it is my fault, as if I am wrong. My own brother, Asim, slapped me and tried to kill me when he found out. Sometimes I wish he had just gone through with it. I attempted suicide one time after that--so at least I would have control over one last thing in my life, but it didn't work. I haven't tried since that night, but I've thought about it....

Day 6:
It happened again last night. I can't remember a night that it hasn't happened. When I feel his hands on me I want to be sick, I get this feeling in the pit of my stomach, and I can't control it. My entire body quivers, my throat clenches, and my heart pounds inside my chest. I close my eyes, but I can still see his face. I can feel him all over me, inside of me. Everything hurts, but I can't stop him, I never can.

Day 7:
I still remember the first time clear as day. I was only thirteen; actually it was my thirteenth birthday to be exact. My whole family was there for the big day. He was there too, but at the time he was my cousin, someone I trusted, someone my entire family trusted. I knew it was a mistake, but he insisted that we go for a walk alone and I agreed. He started walking towards a wooded area. I knew I should've turned around then, but my feet kept walking. We turned the corner, and he pushed me to the ground, I tried to get up, but he slapped me. I didn't know what was happening, I couldn't figure out why he was hitting me. The next thing I knew one hand was covering my mouth and the other was holding me down. He was on top of me and he was hurting me. I closed my eyes and tried not to cry.
When I finally made my way back to the party I was completely disheveled. My *hijab* was ripped, I had dirt on my arms and face, and my lip was starting to swell. My mother just looked at me and said I looked exhausted. She couldn't see the hurt in my eyes, the bruises between my thighs or the blood that I could feel dripping down my leg. She has no idea.

Day 8:
I don't know who saw what happened, or how they found out. I didn't scream when I was with him. I cried, but I didn't scream. I didn't even move. I don't know how they found out, but one morning I came downstairs and my mother was sitting at the table crying and my father was pacing around the kitchen. I asked them what happened and they just looked at me with disgust.
His expression broke my heart as he screamed. "How dare you Faria? How dare you? How dare you take away this family's honor?" I tried to tell them that it wasn't my fault, that I didn't want to, that he hit me and hurt me, but it didn't matter what I said, all that mattered was that I had destroyed my family's honor and I was going to have to pay for it.

Day 9:
My father went to him. He was given the choice to either go to jail or asking

for my hand in marriage. I didn't get a say in any of this. I know my father doesn't blame me for what he did to me. If given the option I know my father would have killed him. But then my father would go to jail, and I couldn't live with that. I know that my father told him to marry me to save me from going to jail, too. He knows they would've found some way to make this my fault. I know that in my father's heart I'm still his youngest daughter, I know he loves me, but sometimes I worry that he doesn't know how to love me anymore. I know he doesn't blame me, but he can't honor me either.

Day 10:

I was thirteen years old and the next thing I knew my wedding was being planned. I was a bride at thirteen—a bride to a man who had destroyed everything. I was told to marry him, I was told I had to build a life with him, a man whose face I couldn't stand to look at, a man who I despised with every inch of my body, a man who took everything from me. How could they expect me to marry him? They didn't care. It didn't matter anymore because I was his bride, and my body was now his.

Day 11:

There hasn't been a night that I haven't cried myself to sleep since the night of my wedding. It's been over three years and I still cry every night. It never gets better; I still feel the same sickness in my stomach every time it happens. I try to tell myself that by doing this I have protected my honor, that I haven't shamed my family, but everyone knows that isn't true. Everyone looks at me with their judging eyes.

Day 12:

When I found out I was pregnant I knew I couldn't have it, I knew that I didn't want it, but I had no choice. He found out soon after I did and once he did, I had no say in anything. He treated me well those nine months. He only hit me a few times; he made sure that I had plenty of food and rest. Now when I look at her I see her father. She's a spitting image of him and it kills me every time I look at her. I love her—I really do—but I hate how I got her. I hate that he is the father. I have to face it, even if I can manage to run away someday, through my daughter I will always be connected to him.

The Wave
Anne Clymer

Asra stared at the ceiling in her small dark bedroom. She couldn't be sure what time it was because she only had one window, which let in very little light, even at midday. It felt very early, though, because the street outside her home was quiet and very few birds were chirping. She knew, then, that at any moment her father would be knocking at her door to wake her for the day. For now, though, she could remain in the comfort of her warm bed, with her fluffed pillows and soft blankets, and close her eyes before the long day began. Just as quickly as she had woken, she drifted back into sleep and had a wonderful dream.

When the knock at her door came, she immediately forgot all that she had been dreaming.

"Asra, are you up?"

Asra sat up and wiped her eyes.

"Yes, father! I am awake now." She heard his footsteps grow faint as he walked down the hall and then down the stairs.

Asra stood and went to the high window across from her bed and pulled the curtain aside. A few rays of light fell in a small rectangle on the floor. With a sigh, she switched on her light instead.

In front of her mirror, she pulled off her nightgown and let it fall into a lump by her feet. She examined herself for a moment. Her small breasts—relatively new to her body—lay just above her ribs. She admired them and their shape and wondered if all breasts looked as nice as hers did. From the floor below she heard her mother's voice.

"Asra! Your father is ready to go. Please hurry!"

With that, Asra tore her eyes away from herself to dress. After pulling on her *abaya* and wrapping her hair and face in her *hijab*, she stopped to look in the mirror once more. *What a shame*, she thought, *no one would be able to even tell that I now have breasts.*

Once in the kitchen, Asra gulped down a cup of water before meeting her father at the door.

"Where's Faruq?" she asked.

"Your brother won't be joining us on our walk today," her father responded. "It will be just the two of us." He smiled.

Shafiq was a tall man with a big dark beard, whose face rested in a natural frown. He looked intimidating even to his closest peers. But he was a quiet and gentle man who liked to take long walks with his children each week to talk and catch up on their lives. It was important to him that he have a trusting and open relationship with his son and daughter, which was very different from the other fathers he knew, even his friends.

On this morning, the sun was out and it warmed the air. Shafiq and Asra walked together along the path that led to the water, as they always did.

"Why isn't Faruq with us? Is he sick?" Asra asked.

"No. I have good news for you, my daughter." Shafiq grinned.

"Oh? What is it?"

Shafiq cleared his throat as they came to the edge of the path. Before them was the sea that stretched out far into the horizon.

"Well," he said, "Do you remember Raja? My brother introduced him to us several months ago."

Asra thought for a moment. She did have a memory of a tall and lanky young man accompanying her uncle some time ago. He was kind, if she remembered correctly, and very shy. Asra nodded.

"Good!" Shafiq chuckled. "You liked him, yes?"

"I suppose."

Shafiq nodded while a silly grin stretched across his face. He stared out at the water for a moment before turning to continue down the path. Asra lingered behind. Her favorite part of their walks was when they stopped to watch the water. The waves moved up and down; the light hit the tops and bounced off.

What does it feel like to be a wave? she wondered.

"Asra! Come along," Shafiq shouted from several paces down the path.

Asra followed. Once she caught up, Shafiq had stopped again to look at the water.

"You know," he continued, "You're going to make a beautiful wife. Just like your mother."

Asra nodded. Her father always said things like this to her. She didn't mind, but knew she would one day have to tell him that she had no plans of marrying or being a wife. She was happy on her own now and couldn't imagine a life like her mother's. As much as she appreciated all that her mother did—the cooking and cleaning—and her gentleness, Asra did not envy her.

"You will have many sons and a loving husband. This is what I hope for you, Asra."

She nodded again. She did not want children, either. She wanted to live her life for herself and not be weighed down by anyone—especially a child that would need her for many, many years. *Surely my father will understand this in time.*

"That is why your mother and I have decided that you will marry Raja!" Shafiq turned to Asra, his eyes wide with delight. "Are you happy, my daughter?"

Asra could not move. She stared into the water, the rays of sunlight piercing her eyes. She did not squint. She became aware of the sun on her forehead and the small beads of sweat sitting on her nose. She tried to breathe in but felt her chest stop suddenly. Her heartbeat was in her ears. The water and world around her became dark at the edges. Her father's mouth moved but she did not hear the sound they made. Suddenly, darkness.

Asra awoke some time later in her bed again. She wondered, momentarily, if her father's good news had been some terrible nightmare and that the day was just beginning now. There was no rectangle of light on the floor from her small window, so it must be evening, she decided. Therefore, the day had already happened and it all must be true. Through the wall, the sound of hushed voices grew louder.

"Will you check on her soon, Aqilah?" Shafiq's voice asked.

"Yes, of course. Although I do think she should be checked by a doctor, don't you?" her mother's voice inquired.

"No, no. Asra will be just fine. It was happiness—or the heat—but that's all! I saw it on her face before her collapse. She was so flooded with joy by our news that she couldn't handle it." Shafiq laughed loudly. "It will be a very good story years from now, when Raja and Asra tell of their engagement to friends."

"Hmm," her mother said. "I suppose that could be the case."

"I think it's funny now," Faruq's voice chimed in.

Asra could just picture the glint in his eye and the sly smirk on his face that he always had any time he wanted to get a rise out of her or their parents.

"That's horrible, Faruq," her mother warned. "You shouldn't laugh at your sister's misfortune. I, for one, know all too well what she must be going through." There was a hint of sadness in her voice.

No she doesn't, Asra thought. *How could she?* Asra had always thought of her mother as an oxymoron: a happy, married woman. She was sure her mother was just as thrilled the day she and her father got engaged as she was each morning when she had to make him breakfast. That would never be Asra though. She would never bring Raja his plate of food any time of the day. He was kind, of course—and had nice eyes, the more she tried to remember him—but how does that entitle him to a life-long slave? She felt her heartbeat in her ears again but this time, she leapt out of bed on to her tip toes, as to not alert her family in the room next door.

Asra stepped lightly to her dresser to pull on her *abaya* and *hijab* again. She slipped her feet into her shoes and went over to the small bookshelf beside her bed. She took several of the thickest books she owned—her dictionary and encyclopedia, for example—and placed them beneath her only window. Once she had enough books stacked, she climbed atop them and slipped open her window. With all her strength, she hoisted herself up and was able to wiggle her way out onto the roof. From there, she could shimmy down a nearby tree.

On the ground, Asra ran as fast as she could out of sight from any of the windows in her home. Only when she reached the path she and her father had walked earlier that day did she slow down to catch her breath. *Everything looks quite different under the cover of darkness*, she thought, *especially me!* She giggled to herself, remembering that morning's examination of her budding body.

Several minutes later, Asra found herself at the edge of the water. Slowly, she slipped a foot out of one of her shoes. With precision, she lowered that foot until just the tip of her big toe touched the top of a wave. She yanked her foot back in surprise at how cold the water was, even after the sun had been heating it all day long. After a moment, she tried again, this time dunking the entire foot in. It was cold, but felt relieving as well, like all the heat from the long day just burst out of the pores in her skin. Soon, she was tempted to feel this on her calves as well. She stepped into the water, holding up her *abaya*.

Before she knew it, Asra was past her waist standing in the sea. But she wanted to feel the small waves that were crashing against her abdomen. With a quick glance all around, Asra decided she must be alone. Even if she wasn't, it was so dark no man could possibly make out her figure or face. She ran back out of the water and yanked off her cloak and the nightgown beneath; she unwrapped her *hijab*. Asra stood entirely naked, her dark hair just kissing the tops of her shoulders and reflecting the shimmers of starlight.

Asra walked cautiously back into the water. She got up to her waist again and was unsure of whether or not she should continue on. How far out was too far out? With that, she took a deep breath, plugged her nose, and dunked herself under the sea. A moment later she broke through the surface with a great splash. She laughed loudly, no longer worried someone might hear her. She splashed in the sea, she swam underwater and on the surface, she stood still to feel the rise and drop of the cool waves as they bumped her body.

After what seemed like hours of fun, Asra learned she could float on her back. She lay on the water, the whole front of her body exposed to the sky, for a long time. She was a wave that moved up and down, forward and back, but somehow stayed in the very same spot. She thought of large waves and very large waves and even tsunamis, and how many, many little waves could make great big ones like that.

The sun began to rise in the distance and Asra decided to sit at the edge of the water with her toes resting just close enough so waves would run up along the tips of them. As the sun rose higher and higher in the sky, the water she was drenched with dried. She didn't think it possible, but even with no clothes at all, it wasn't long before she felt hot. She was almost glad too, though, as the sun was touching bits of her it had never touched before. It caressed her curves with warm fingers and pressed against her small belly like an embrace. She closed her eyes and let herself melt into the warmth of a brand new day. The calm plip-plops of the little waves around filled her with joy.

She knew that soon the day would be starting for the rest of the world, too. Her mother would come rapping at her door, expecting her to get up. Her brother and father would be waiting for breakfast to be served. Somewhere, Raja would be waiting, too, expecting a wife. Life, like the waves, has many ups and downs, elations and disappointments, good news and bad.

At that moment, though, Asra buried her feet deeper into the sand. She wondered how she could ever pull that thick cloak over her body again, how she could ever go back to her tiny bedroom, with only that glimmer of a window to the world outside, waiting for a knock at the door.

Budur
Emily Coble

The whistle on the kettle was sounding as I heard a knock on the door. I switched off the burner and poured the hot water over the tealeaves. The knocking continued. I turned on the radio and made my way to the table by the window. The knocking turned into shouting.

"Budur, I know you're home. Please let me in." More knocking.

I sat there, sipping my tea and staring out the window.

"Budur, you can't just stay in there forever."

There was wrestling outside of the door and the sound of a lock reaching its climax with its helpmate. My stomach dropped; she found it. She came busting in with her handbag and gold hoop earrings. She glided over to me and put her hands on her hips.

"You're coming with me to the market. I can't stand the thought of you sitting in here all day wasting this beautiful sunlight." She turned into my bedroom and started shuffling through the clothes in my closet. She pulled out a peacock colored *hijab* and brought it over to me. "You need to wear something besides black for once. It's making me want to cry."

I took in a weighted breath and exhaled loudly. "I don't feel like going anywhere. Isn't there anyone else you can bother, Abra?"

"Please come," she said with a wide-eyed smile, "I'll buy you a cup of tea."

I stared at her and finally shook my head in agreement.

The streets were more crowded than I remembered them being. *How strange*, I thought, *I haven't been gone that long.*

Abra chatted with merchants as I lingered behind. After a while she took my hand and led me to a small café by the sea. The sun was high and the wind came and went with the waves. I stared down at my cup of tea as she spoke on about what she had been doing in university since the last time I saw her. The image of her brother flashed in my mind and her voice cut through the sadness.

"I'm sorry, I know this must be kind of hard for you to see me."

I turned my head and looked toward the sea.

"Not any harder than any other day since the accident."

"It's been months, Budur. No one would blame you for moving on. We all loved him. He was my brother! But you didn't die, Budur, you get to experience life!"

"I'm not ready yet, Abra."

Her typically cheerful expression had been replaced with one of concern. She pulled a cigarette out of her handbag and lit it with a match. "I have tickets to a gallery opening tonight and I would really love it if you would come with me.

It's going to be a lot of fun."

"I don't feel like having fun. I need to get back home." I threw some money on the table and got up.

As I passed by the waiter she shouted, "I'm not going to give up!"

I turned the key into the lock on my front door and made my way to the bedroom. I pulled the drawer open on my husband's dresser and began pulling out his linen shirts. I held each one to my face, as the tears that ran like engorged rivers soaked the garments.

"Why would you do this?!" I shouted to the sky. I had been so obedient and waited for a husband and we were happy. And then the accident. Not even a month after proving my honor, he was gone, taken from me.

I wept until the carpet on the bedroom floor was drenched with my sorrows and I had nothing left inside of me. Then it hit me. Abra was right. I was still alive and I couldn't keep wasting the time I had.

I slept on the floor that night, my mind clinging to my memories of Abdullah and the joy he had brought me.

I left the house the next morning and walked towards the beach. I sat with my toes in the water listening to the world going on around me: the sound of children squawking, lovers contemplating politics, and the waves crashing in rhythm. All day and all night I sat there, thinking of who I was going to be now without Abdullah.

I thought about Abra and how different she was from her brother. He was a man of the Quran and often argued with Abra about her decision to go to university instead of marrying one of his coworkers. He did as he was told; he never drank or smoked. Abra showed her shoulders and went to parties. She drank and smoked cigarettes. She was independent and courageous. How could they have come from the same family?

The sun kissed my face as I stood on the balcony. The phone began to ring and I slowly wandered back inside to answer it. "Hello?"

"Budur, it's me, Abra. I'm coming over."

Before I could get a word out she hung up. Half an hour later she was busting through the doorway. Her hair was pinned back and her lips were the color of a desert rose.

"My friend Jabir just directed a film and its premiere is tonight. Please come with me."

"I don't have anything to wear to that sort of thing, Abra."

"I thought you might say that so I brought something for you," she said, motioning to a garment bag she was holding in her hand. "I even brought you a matching *hijab*."

She handed me the bag and motioned to my bedroom. I appeased her and took the dress off the hanger. The maroon silk fell over my curves as I stared in the mirror. I wrapped the sequined *hijab* around my head and turned around to see the back. The neckline was modest but I tugged at the hemline hoping it would magically get longer. Abra came in and cupped her hands over my shoulders.

"You look beautiful!" She tugged on my hand and smudged lipstick on my lips.

Before I knew it, we were stuffed into a taxi and whisked off into the bustling city. The sun was setting as we stepped out of the cab and onto the sidewalk. Abra recognized a group of people and walked over to them. I quickly followed behind. Her friends were as gorgeous as she was. They chatted for a few moments before she said her goodbyes and we made our way into the theater.

"Do you want some wine?"

"I don't think so," I said. The growing crowd was making me anxious.

"Oh, come one, lighten up a little bit!" She said as she grabbed my hand and led me to the bar.

"Two *araks,* please," she said to the bartender.

"I thought you said wine!" I said quickly.

"I changed my mind," she chuckled, paying the bartender.

As we turned around, a tall, muscular man greeted Abra. "You made it!" he said as he embraced her.

"I told you I wouldn't miss it!" she said with a smile, "Jabir, this is Budur. Budur, this is the director of the film we will be seeing tonight, Jabir."

"It's nice to meet you," I said as I looked into his eyes. They were deep enough to get lost in.

"It's a pleasure to meet you," he said with a smile. "I have to go do the small talk thing but I hope to see you both after the film."

We found our seats and waited for the lights to dim. We tried to find Jabir after the film but the crowd was too large to find anyone. Abra called us a taxi and we took it to her apartment in West Beirut.

Her apartment was as modern as she was, with large paintings hanging on the tall white walls. She walked into her kitchen and opened a bottle of wine. She came back into the living room and handed me a glass.

"I was thinking it must be so lonely living in that house by yourself. I have an extra room here and I would really love it if you moved in."

"I don't know, Abra. That's a big change."

"Oh, don't be silly! It's less expensive than what you're paying now and you can keep me company. Will you at least think about it?"

"All right, I will think about it," I said as I sipped on my wine.

After finishing the bottle and giggling for a while, we both decided it was time for bed. She showed me to her spare room and closed the door as she left.

All I could think about was Jabir's eyes. How could they be so deep? I tried to remember what Abdullah's eyes looked like, but I had lost them. I couldn't find them anywhere in my mind. I had looked into them so often and now they were gone. I wondered what else had been lost in the past months.

The next morning Abra made us breakfast on the terrace. I looked out at the bustling streets and sipped my tea. "I think I want to move in."

"Yay!" she exclaimed. "This is going to be great!"

I moved in the following week. She took me to gorgeous parties filled with gorgeous people, but the only person I ever looked for was Jabir.

He was always there, talking about something fascinating to a group of twenty-somethings. He'd see me across the room and end his conversations. He'd stroll so slickly across to me, keeping me locked into those eyes. He made me laugh, harder than I thought I knew how to laugh.

He'd always get pulled away though; someone would come over and just have to introduce him to someone equally as fascinating as he was. I would always go home and think of his eyes. Imagining what I could find within them. I wanted to know their secrets. Weeks went on like this.

One night our conversation didn't get interrupted. I was waiting for it to happen, for someone to come break up whatever it was that we were doing . . . but they didn't.

I was listening to him ramble on about some film he was working on, getting distracted by his eyes, when all of a sudden it just came out of me. "Do you like tea?"

He stopped and looked at me.

"Do I like tea?" He chuckled. "Are you asking me if I want to have tea with you?

"I guess so. Yes, yes I am. Do you want to come back to my apartment for tea?" I don't know what came over me.

"Let's go!"

As we stepped into the elevator the silence was deafening. I felt my stomach turn into knots and my palms began to sweat. I turned the key in the lock and flipped the lights on. Abra was still at the party talking to some banker. I went into the kitchen and put the kettle on. I brought the teacups in. We sat in silence, sipping our tea for what seemed like an eternity.

Words were building up in my throat but I couldn't bring myself to say any of them. I looked up at him. His eyes were locked on mine; I fell into them. He raised a hand and slowly began slipping my *hijab* off of my hair. He leaned in and pulled my face to his and kissed me.

I froze in place.

He pulled away and my eyes shot to the floor.

Coughing, he stood up. "I—I'm sorry. That was out of line."

He rushed to the doorway but paused.

"I hope I can see you again." He opened the door and left.

The next day Abra and I got lunch at the café by the sea. As we were waiting for our meals I just couldn't hold it in anymore.

"Jabir came over for tea last night."

Her eyes lit up as she sipped her glass of white wine.

"Tea?"

"Yes, tea," I said with a smirk.

"So is that why you aren't wearing a *hijab* today?" She asked smirking back.

I brushed my hand over my hair, "No. I thought I would try something new today."

"Well, you look lovely."

A few days later the phone rang. Abra answered.

"Hello?"

Silence.

"Oh, hello! How have you been?"

Silence.

"Pleased to hear it. Yes, one moment." She leaned away from the receiver and toward the hallway, "Budur, phone is for you."

I walked over and took the phone from her.

"It's Jabir," she whispered as she walked away.

A smile crashed like a wave across my face. "Hello?"

"Budur, how are you?"

"Well, thank you. How are you?" I twirled the phone cord around my finger as I stared out the window.

"Are you free tomorrow night?"

"I believe so."

"I would like to take you somewhere."

"All right."

I had no idea what I was supposed to say to that. I didn't want to sound too eager.

"I will pick you up at eight." He hung up the phone.

Abra appeared around the doorway. "What did he want?"

"He wants to take me somewhere tomorrow," I said, smiling.

"He didn't say where?" She looked as excited as I felt.

"No…"

"Come with me right now! We are going shopping!"

I've never worn such a beautiful dress. It was the color of the sunset and Abra let me borrow her gorgeous turquoise earrings.

Jabir came exactly at eight o'clock. He looked so handsome in the city lights. He guided me through the streets on foot until we reached the Babel Theater. His friend was reading poetry with some other artists. We drank wine and wandered through the streets laughing. His spirit was infectious. I could've listened to him talk forever.

He took me out every week for months, and each time we had a bigger adventure. We began spending even more time together; I started cooking for him in his home. Every moment I spent with him I felt myself getting pulled farther into his eyes, I couldn't find my way out of them anymore.

We were sitting in his apartment one afternoon when he turned to me, "I want to marry you, Budur."

I didn't know what to say, I searched his eyes for the answer but found nothing. I closed my eyes and tried to pull an answer out of the darkness, "I would like that."

He pulled me to my feet and spun me around. When I came back to him his face had been replaced with Abdullah's.

I choked and Jabir pulled me into him.

I waited a couple of days to tell Abra about what Jabir had said to me. I didn't know how she would react. I finally worked up the courage on a breezy day at the café by the sea.

"Jabir wants to marry me," I said as I lit a cigarette.

She turned her head to face me. "What do you want?"

"You will always be my sister and friend, but I believe that I love him."

She smiled a wide smile and raised her glass, "I am nothing but happy for you, Budur!"

I'm Not a Star, I'm the Moon
Morgan Comolli

I am no longer awake or asleep; my existence is a secret tucked behind iron and stone. Another has decided my fate, but I no longer feel the agony drumming a beat on the icy walls of my heart. I no longer look towards the sun. I am full of inhabitants scaring the hard concrete blocks of my consciousness, warfare for remembrance. I am not Adira, daughter of Aasim. I am death row inmate # 23 and I am free.

My short story was woven in the Diaspora, amongst a herd of wild brothers and sisters. The last of seven children, my arrival was an exchange of life as my mother's flame was extinguished with my first breaths. I have never seen my father Aasim's eyes. Rather, he dodged my gaze, avoided my inquiries, and refused my embrace. I was born into exile, the shudders of their hearts nailed shut, boarded against the tempest Adira.

My education was the realization that I wouldn't get one. Instead, I learned to read off the scripture around the house piecing together the sporadic ink with the sweet melody of the kitchen radio. I was taught to keep the house by my sisters, whose piteous gaze and hushed giggles were the context of our relationship. My brothers tripped eagerly after my father, cubs to their king, licking up the bits of knowledge he lay in his wake and mimicking his mannerisms. Thus my existence was that of an old chair pushed aside until someone grew fatigued and required my services. Carbon copies of my father, my three brothers—after the age of six—fought continuously to avoid my gaze, as if my irises would scorch their skin and the Holy Quran forbids it.

As I grew into my body I was given a rough lesson on hygiene by my detached sisters and forced to cover my growing body from my long dark hair to my toes. Something about the growing tissue on my chest and bloody liquid between my legs advocated my veiling and I was confined to the *hijab*. I was forbidden to leave the wall of the house in fear my purity would be stolen. I didn't know how to steal someone's purity or where someone kept it-only that man targeted mine.

I asked my sisters where to find this purity in hopes I could give it to a man and be free once more, to which I received a high pitched laugh in my direction. For their own entertainment my sisters sent me on an expedition around the house looking for the purity under beds and in cupboards. Only when my father asked my sisters about my search was I told to stop. My new name by my sisters became Adira, the *jahila*.

From that day forward I became a prisoner of cloth and mortar.

After a time my courage grew along with my body and I began to take refuge with the moon and the stars, climbing the debris along the side of our house to escape to the roof on the hot summer nights.

My thoughts lost to their limitless shine, I told the stars my secrets and shared my questions with the wise moon. They were my comrades in this life, gobbling up my words and locking them away from the world. I often prayed to Allah to be reborn a star far from this world encased in the sky. Surely, people would look at me then. No one despises the stars for they are beauty and freedom forever out of reach.

During the chilled winter nights I would hide in the bowels of the house, tucking myself into a corner, wishing I could disappear into the wall as an unseen chip in the paint. I would dream of a different life amongst the people of the world. I would try to imagine what my mother would be like. I often wondered if she too would shut out my gaze. These questions came to me often until I grew out of all questions.

As I performed my daily chores around the house, my life moved on, a constant reel. I was left watching as my sisters and brothers grew, married, and left for work or education. Two of my brothers left for the West with praise and smiles from all in the village. My father boasted about their expenditures and smiled at their mention. I could hear the stretching of his beard as he joyously accepted husbands for my sisters, and I wondered if ever a caller would mention me.

Slowly, days leaked into years and I had scrubbed, washed, and swept until only my father remained. The phone stopped ringing and the dark silence of the house began to close in on me. I would search for movement in the shadows a small with tingle of hope that someone would materialize.

One day during the hot summer, my precious companion, an ancient FM/AM radio whose antenna long ago lost its clarity, grew tired of me and stopped singing.

My chest grew tight with an excited heart, as a strangled sob escaped my lips. The world grew blurry and my body began to sweat and shake as I grabbed my electronic friend between my callused hands and ran for the door. I burst into the summer sun, rings of light disorienting me as I stumbled into the street.

I didn't know this place, these people. I was walking through a wardrobe of faces and light that I couldn't comprehend. No one looked in my eyes or heard my heart as it pounded heavily in my chest.

I shouted, *"Hal beemkanek mosa'adati?"* *"Hal beemkanek mosa'adati?"* over and over again, shaking the radio above my exposed head.

I looked towards the sun, drying the tears and dirt to my cheeks as it judged my features. The blackness returned in my vision as the sun consumed my gaze, drinking in my soul. My limbs grew weak as I began to sink. Clutching my electronic friend I dropped to my barren knees on the hard dirt and was swallowed by the darkness.

I woke to the harsh grumbles of my father Aasim and eldest brother Dahi, a western medical doctor. The mixture of baritone was rushed as they argued about my wandering through the market place and losing consciousness over something called dead batteries. They scrutinized my virtue and intelligence, hatred leaking out of every syllable as they talked. I was an "*isra*," (difficult) according to my father.

The next moments changed me forever as my brother exploded through the doorway of my barred room, his eyes trained on the floor as he grabbed my soiled clothes and tore them piece by piece from my body.

My protesting arms and frightened screams were futile as my brother more than doubled my weight and threatened to break my limbs with his crushing grip. I was exposed and soaked with sweat as he pinned my barren body to the cruel floor and examined the flesh between my legs. I was declared "*naqia*," (pure) as my brother left me.

I no longer talked to the stars or reached for the moon. As the days trickled by I would move through the house, a corpse with no direction. I began to dream of sleep while awake, grasping my stitched clothes tight every time I heard the weight of movement in the house.

Sinking into my cold reverie, I was a Trojan horse of cheerlessness. My thoughts were all contained in the barbed arms of my rib cage, fracturing the infrastructure with every prisoner held behind. Beneath my flesh walls shook the suppressed emotions, spilling their black corrosive poison into my hollow limbs.

My thoughts became those of a tired slave emptied of life, and I examined the idea of lifelessness. I could make myself a star. How do you end your life? Maybe I could ask my sisters. Maybe my father would help me....

As my fourteenth birthday came and went without mention, my father's steps grew heavier as his intoxicated nights turned into days. The stench of urine and liquor flowed in waves from his room, escaping under the beaten door. I evaded him by walking with the stride of a ghost, working only when the poison had won over his consciousness.

One evening while scrubbing the remains of his feast, the hairs at the nape of my neck came to life. I spun to find my father's drunken eyes surveying my backside. Moving like an animal who has seen its predator, I ran.

His hand collapsed around my hair, ripping my body against his, and I was encircled in his hungry embrace. I could taste iron in my mouth as my heart beat against my head and I bite into my tongue.

My vision exploded into fireflies as I refused my lungs their air. My stomach lurched as pain tore through my body with every thrust and his stale breath danced on my neck.

Was this death? Was my father killing me?

Staring at my swollen and bruised body my father spoke to me for the last time. "Adira, no one will ever want you now."

Exhaling heavily he dropped a knife on the floor at my feet.

"You took your mother from me. Now it's time for you to join her."

With that he turned his brute gaze towards the door and shuffled away.

The strings in my chest shattered like glass, as my hand gripped the knife. A ravenous scream exploded from my ragged lungs. The blood poured down my arms, soaking between my toes, as my hand ripped the blade from his bare chest.

As my father collapsed at my feet I began to convulse with laughter, the joyous tears dotting my eyes. I felt the stars applauding my name and the blood in my heart pumped the mortar out of my soul.

My father's last breath vibrated through me as he looked into my eyes for the first and last time.

I'm not a star, I am the moon.

Spirit in the Sky
Stephen Conte

Qamar was born and raised in the Saudi Arabian Eastern Provinces' capital Dammam. Qamar was the youngest of four children. As a young girl she loved to play with her two older sisters and her eldest sibling and brother Isam.

As Qamar grew older she became recognized for her intelligence especially for her ability to memorize the Quran. This made Qamar's mother extremely proud of her achievements.

When Qamar turned thirteen she was taken aside at night by her mother and told that the meaning of her name was "full moon."

Qamar gazed up at the starry sky that night standing by her mother's side and saw that the moon above her was as full and as bright as she had never seen before. Qamar looked at her mother, tears forming in her eyes, and said, "Mother dearest, the love you have given me every day of my life was already enough, but the beauty of this full moon, and the beauty of my name which you have given me is truly a gift to remember forever."

Qamar's mother immediately began to cry. Once able to speak, she looked at Qamar and said, "I am so sorry Qamar, I must have you cut as your sisters have been, as I have been, as all women must be cut or face exile from the community."

Qamar did not understand why this had to happen. She had heard from her sisters what the process was like: the hot blade, the blood, the pain and healing afterwards. It all scared Qamar so very much.

Isam came to Qamar the day after her birthday and the talk with her mother. He said to her a few words hoping they would help to relieve her anxieties but to no avail.

Qamar looked to Isam and asked, why she must be cut, why must she shed blood as did her sisters? Isam only reconciled her with the words that his father put in his mouth for him to relay to her young confused mind.

Isam said, "It has been this way always, and it will always be this way forever. Women must be cut to retain the honor of the family."

Qamar went to bed that night without any intention of sleeping. All that crossed her mind was the thought that a stranger would touch between her legs and remove a piece of her forever. She had no desire for sleep, but she had a desire for rest, for solitude, for she at the moment felt nothing but restless uneasiness.

A few months passed from Qamar's thirteenth birthday. The time for the ceremonial practice was only days away. Qamar spoke with her friends about the news that she would be cut and her friends gave her mixed reactions. Most had already been cut, but at a time which left them no memory of the experience.

Only one of her friends would be open with her experience with the blade for it occurred to her in that year past.

Qamar had always considered herself more of a "Western" girl than a "Middle Eastern" girl for she was raised according to the American culture, and her parents immersed themselves and their home in American gadgets and furnishings.

Her room had a television, a desktop computer, a closet with blue jeans and shirts with American bands displayed on the front. Qamar even had a cassette player and a stash of recorded tapes with bands such as The Clash, The Beastie Boys, AC/DC, Grateful Dead, and even a couple Michael Jackson tapes which she had been given by her brother Isam when she turned ten. Qamar had seen enough American movies and heard enough American music and heard enough of American hookup culture to know that girls there were not cut.

Qamar said to her brother Isam, "Isam I know you are here to protect me as my brother, and father named you Isam, a self-made man and a protector. But if you are here to protect me, won't you tell me what you think and not what father has told you to tell me?"

Isam felt he needed to tell Qamar the truth for she deserved to hear it. Isam said to Qamar, "Some of my friends have married, some are happy and others not. The friends of mine with wives who are cut do not desire their husbands. They lack any love. They are not what my friends say they were looking for in marriage. My best friend Omar is married to a girl who is from Jordan. She is lucky enough to have been spared the cutting and tells Omar that when they make love it is a feeling unlike any other she has ever experienced.It brings them closer together, and when they fight, after, they make love and after forget any problems they had."

Qamar thought about what Isam told her and felt she would do whatever it would take to spare herself from the blade.

The very next day Qamar gathered everything she owned that could fit into her small backpack. She filled the backpack with canned foods, a loaf of bread, bottled water, a pack of matches, a blanket, a compass, and a map. She began to write a few words down onto a piece of paper that would be left as a goodbye note to her family, but the sadness Qamar felt caused her to cry and tear up all over the paper making the ink run illegible.

Qamar looked out her window at the world, which to her seemed so foreign. The very country she was born and raised in seemed to be the last place she should ever be. The night came and with it a bright moon.

Qamar looked out her window upon the glow of the bright full moon and knew then she had a chance to be free if she followed its glow. Quickly she grabbed her bag, wrote down a goodbye letter with a promise to return, and off she went into the night.

Qamar followed the moon into the distance, past the hills, past the moon, the stars, and found her place nestled in the back of the galaxy where she rested contently, her body pure, her soul at ease, and her mind at rest.

Smiles
Emily Cornwell

The blood caressed her skin. She felt the thick crimson liquid smoothly pooling in the crevices that her skin provided. Some of her wounds had scabbed over, but as she awoke, the crust began to break, allowing the yellow pus to mix with her red blood. As the two liquids swirled together, they created a beautifully haunting mosaic. Unable to look up at the crowd gathered before her, she kept her head down. The stiffness in her neck allowed her to fool the crowd into believing she was still unconscious.

Soon, she would have to look up toward her friends and family, toward her fate. Her town stood before her: her home, her friends, her family. Among them were her collected memories of her childhood. Together they held the time of her innocence. Now, her future lay at her bruised and naked feet. She had lied to herself for too long, believing that she could hold a presence among them. Raising her swollen head, she gained the strength to look into their eyes. Her gaze was met with cold eyes, empty hearts, and ignorant minds.

She would never know a future among her village. In some ways she had always known this fact, long before today. She had risked too much, hoping for a life that would never be hers. Simply wishing for freedom didn't mean it would come. There had only ever been one person that truly understood her pains and her longings to be free from the harsh reality of her life. She knew her fears would come from the abyss to visit the light of day. Today came too soon.

Her village had always maintained a low tolerance for those who were different. This was a place where one law ruled and tolerance was met with a sharp knife. You honored your family, completed your chores, and prayed five times a day. There was no laughter outside the home, where men would be able to hear; it would drive them mad with lust. If the men were to fall into a lustful state, any actions committed against the woman would be her fault, and she would be thankful to be put to death, rather than have to deal with the shame of her family. Only once had Muna witnessed a saving ceremony. She remembered that the day had been hot when her father passed her a stone. The rough edges of the stone could have cut her delicate hands. When she looked into her father's face, he had smiled at her. Muna never threw the stone; her weak arms wouldn't allow her to. She simply tossed the stone away and when her father looked down at her and noticed that the stone was gone, he had nodded his approval, thinking she had thrown the stone.

Only one person had understood Muna's dreams of freedom, passion, safety, and warmth. The memory brought a smile to her face as she closed her eyes and remembered her days long before this one. Long before the numb feelings would consume her body and soul. Long before hatred would be masked with the words of love. Long before death loomed in the stale air.

Salaam's image filled the space behind Muna's eyes. Salaam had been beautiful, an image of love captured and stored forever in a perfect vision. Her waist-length, curly brown hair had fallen in disarray around her shoulders as the wind played with it. The memory of running her fingers through Salaam's hair still brought Muna peace. She remembered looking into Salaam's deep hazel, almond-shaped eyes, slightly too large for a heart-shaped face. She had loved those eyes that were filled to the brim with intelligence. She wanted to lay sweet kisses over Salaam's long, pert nose and continue over her high cheekbones until she reached the sensitive flesh behind her ears.

Muna remembered the time that she and Salaam had met in the sandy streets as young children. Muna had been so awkward trying not to trip over her sister's longer skirt. Salaam had extended a small hand and helped Muna before she hit the ground. As they grew older they became inseparable friends. They would spend every spare moment talking in their secret spot where a bend in the river would shield them from prying eyes. Salaam had once told her that they were made for each other, molded by the choices they made. The cool, clear water would swirl around their feet, washing the filth of the village streets away.

Muna would glide her long, clean fingers into Salaam's and in those moments forget her worries. Salaam always had a way of comforting her by simply being. Using no words Salaam would sit beside her and hum, looking across the river to the other bank. The power of Salaam's music would wash through her body untwisting every muscle and ill thought from her mind and she would feel anew, reborn, and free for a few short moments. Muna welcomed the comforting memory of Salaam's smooth voice, forgetting for a moment the harsh words of hate and cruelty looming over the village.

She moved her head and gazed through the sweat-streaked hair that felt glued to her brow. Her gaze wandered over the enormous crowd. Everyone in the village had turned up to this spectacle. She caught the eye of the baker's boy and released the single tear she had been holding in. It fell down to her swollen lips and her tongue selfishly lashed out to catch it. Moving the moisture over her chapped lips stung, but she no longer cared about the physical pain. She would never be complete again, she thought to herself, not since the baker's boy had discovered her secret. That infamous day replayed over and over again in her mind. The heat began to grow more intense and the cuts she suffered began to burn, deeper than any pain she had every felt by her fathers' hands before. She knew these particular cuts would never heal.

The day she replayed in her mind had been a warm one. The sky was a clear blue, holding no clouds within it. She had felt like singing since coming back home from the river with Salaam. The day had been peaceful. She had walked through the empty kitchen humming and found her younger brother playing with his toy on the floor. She had scooped him up and had begun dancing while his young laughter filled the corners of the home. Her mother had appeared in the doorway with a solemn expression painted on her face. She rarely ever held her feelings at bay from Muna.

Her mother was a gentle, kind soul, which only served to enhance her beauty. She would always say her heart led her to endless happiness. Then she would look over to her husband and he would grant her a full smile. His eyes were always filled to the brim with love and longing as if he could never have enough time with her.

She came into the room and removed her son from Muna's arms. "Your father and I have something to tell you." The memory filled her with pain as she remembered the next events of that fateful day. Her mother had brought her to her father to announce that they had found a man for her. The man was wealthy and his family was well-honored in the village up the river. They wished her endless happiness.

Muna could do nothing but stare into the faces of the people she thought knew her. The faces began to change and then in an instant she sat before strangers. Feelings of sadness welled up inside her. She thought that she would be able to live her own life without the laws of her village crushing her dreams. The walls of her home began to contort into a prison around her. The air she had breathed her whole life suddenly felt heavy as it coated her lungs. She had to escape, to find Salaam. Only Salaam could make her feel better, alive and safe again. She ran from her home, from her parents' smiling faces to the river hoping Salaam would still be curled up on the bank.

The sand caught her feet at the last moment before she ran out of air and she tumbled down the hill toward the riverbed. When she awoke, she was cradled in Salaam's warm arms. She smiled up at Salaam, feeling safe and cherished. Salaam had brushed the sand from her face and hair. They had spoken before of leaving, of finding a fantastic place outside the rolling hills and confinement of their village laws. When Muna had brought up the idea of leaving, Salaam simply shook her head.

"We cannot run away. We must face our fears together, Muna. If we leave they will have won."

Salaam had run a delicate hand down Muna's back and comforted her as Muna retold the story about her parents' decision to wed her off to a wealthy man up the river.

She remembered that Salaam had ceased rubbing her back and leaned close to her. She remembered never moving away from Salaam. She remembered the way they kissed. She had always felt giddy and excited in the arms of Salaam. Her heart would swell with every embrace they shared. Salaam had kissed her long and passionately, revealing in that moment the true love they shared. Muna had kissed back, afraid that Salaam would end the kiss too soon. She longed for

Salaam, for everything her soul had to offer. As they began to move their hands over each other's bodies, a sound above them revealed that they were no longer alone. Muna looked up breaking the kiss with Salaam to find the baker's boy on the sand dune above them. She looked at Salaam and knew in that moment that their infinity had ended. "They will always win."

The boy had run and told his father. The news reached Muna's and Salaam's fathers, who were on the village council. The news had spread around the village in a matter of days and the whispers of impurity and evil engulfed both families. Muna had held Salaam for as long as she could before large hands separated their bodies. Darkness engulfed her and despair lingered on the edge of sanity.

The next time she saw Salaam was in the village square. She saw the mangled body of the girl she loved, bloodied and stripped nude for all to see. She had once cherished that body for hours, captivating the soul that lay within its now empty shell. Salaam's body would glow as she reached her height of pleasure or when they had talked about a long life together. Muna remembered everything about Salaam's body, every secret Salaam had promised only she would ever know. Secrets now laid bare before the village for all to discover.

She remembered Salaam's body, limp in the chains that held her. Her arms had been extended, pulled tight by the chains around her wrists. Her head had fallen forward and her delicate knees had almost reached the ground. The blood of her body caked the once-perfect skin.

Salaam's father had been in the crowd, his lips pulled tight over his gapped teeth. His arms crossed in defiance—what he had done was right. He was crying and Muna had hated him for it. His daughter didn't deserve his tears. She had wanted to charge him and tell him he had no right to cry over Salaam's death. As men had come forward in white robes to release the chains, Salaam's body had hit the ground, causing a cloud of dust to rise. Salaam's body had been taken from the raised platform and carried away. Muna had taken Salaam's place.

The shackles were warm now and stained with both their blood. The baker's boy had broken eye contact as he reached into the large woven basket being passed around by the same men in white robes. Where had they taken the body? Muna wondered. Her gaze moved from the men and baskets to her family, who stood not far from the platform. Their faces were masked. She noticed them all reaching into a similar basket. Her father handed her little brother a stone, just as he had with her, and smiled. She looked toward the sky into its blue abyss. The voice of the village chief caught her attention and she looked toward him. He stood tall on the platform to her right and looked out over the crowd. He spoke of evil and how it had infected two girls from the village. He rambled on about how it must be destroyed for the sake of saving his people. He talked, but Muna no longer found interest in his words. She began to hum a song that Salaam had once hummed on the bank of the river. She felt movement in her heart and knew that Salaam was waiting for her. Somewhere far from this place of hate, she waited. Muna hummed louder, drowning out the chief's voice. Her body was numb as the first stone hit. She continued to hum as the stones fell upon her. Then there was silence.

The villagers whisper that when they laid both girls bodies to rest they carried only smiles on their lips. The smiles symbolized their freedom and eternity of happiness in the life after life.

And the Sisters Wept
Rose Czech

Halima and Nuha were close sisters, raised sharing the same bedroom, and a bond that would not be broken. However, after the girls began to grow up, Nuha left their small rural Syrian village on the Euphrates, with the help of an uncle, to study in Aleppo. Nuha relished in the discovery of knowledge, plucking new ideas from the vines of the world to let them grow in her own mind and heart. Halima, her sister, was patient, kind, and loving in ways Nuha had difficulty understanding. The striking differences between the sisters forced their family to determine their separate fates: one of learning and one of marriage.

Nuha returned after her first year to find her lifelong friend and sister unhappily married, with a baby on the way. The year before, as their father lay dying, he had arranged the marriage as his last wish for Halima's life. The man he chose did little to appease Halima, and the children he gave her were the light of her life, rays of sunshine in a clouded world full of demands and routines that Halima had sought to master for their years of marriage out of her sheer sense of patience. Despite love for her family, Nuha did not see the honor in Halima's new life.

The next time Nuha returned home to see her sister and her mother, Ruqayya, Halima's first daughter was two and growing quickly. Along with another baby on the way, Halima's life revolved around duties to her husband and her child. Nuha's learning while away was affecting her; the life Halima had been granted was becoming difficult for Nuha to watch because she knew of the opportunity that had been denied her.

The sisters' mother had thus far not objected to Nuha's schooling by her husband's brother; however, her rejection of tradition was becoming more and more pronounced. As Nuha was preparing to leave again for her budding life in Aleppo as a young professional and student, her mother gave her an ultimatum: leave now, and never come back, for you will be no daughter of mine, or stay and marry the man my brother and I have chosen for you.

While Nuha loved her family and did not want to abandon Halima to her marriage without sisterly support, she could not make herself stay. The love of learning she had built, and the career as a scholar she was creating forced Nuha to leave her sister and the life she had once known behind.

The sisters separated for longer than they ever had, at the insistence of their mother, but Halima's daughter Ruqayya and, when she was born, her younger sister, Layla, heard stories of their brave aunt and her adventures. With the birth of her second daughter, Halima's life continued to grow darker still. Her husband's desire for a son overwhelmed his initial indifference towards Halima and made him wicked. While he only threatened to take another wife, Halima suffered without the support of her sister until four years later, when Nuha received a letter from a friend of Halima's in the village.

Halima had taken it upon herself to find someone to help her write to Nuha for help. In her letter, Nuha read about the ways Halima was suffering in her new life. The ways her husband was treating her and pressure from their mother was forcing Halima to consider Ruqayya's future, in particular, when her traditional cutting ceremony would happen. Nuha and Halima both remembered the terror that overcame them after their ceremonies, and had long talked about how they would treat their own daughters. Halima's letter asked Nuha to send her guidance in the face of pressure from her mother and mother-in-law.

Nuha's sudden rage at the idea of her nieces being subjected to what she had learned was un-Quranic and restricting to a woman's freedom—as well as potentially dangerous—overwhelmed and surprised her. While her denial of the family marked her as a traitor, she would forever be Halima's sister and she set out to defy her mother, return, and help to save her sister and her sister's daughters from a fate she hoped they would not be forced to regret.

Nuha returned to her village, no longer afraid of her frail mother who ignored her presence as if she were a mosquito. While she did respect the woman, she did not respect the ways she heeded her own ignorance. The needs of Halima drew Nuha back the way the needs of her other family members never would. She was happy to find that Ruqayya and Layla were curious, active girls who loved their mother very much. Ruqayya reminded Nuha of herself (engrossed in her own thoughts and adventures) while Layla was her mother at age four again, helping to tidy and clean already.

Halima shocked Nuha with a secret she had kept in her letter: she was once again pregnant, and this time the midwife Alya swore it would be a boy.

As Halima was due to give birth any day, Nuha decided she would stay to help her sister while giving her advice about Ruqayya and Layla's cutting. Halima lay resting as she and her sister discussed the options. While Halima remembered the pain and the horror at the cost of having her honor, pressure from the powers in her family were making her consider what the best choice for her daughters would be: standing up to the family for them, or making them belong and hold the honor of the family. Nuha considered this and knew how much her family truly meant to Halima. While Nuha knew that Halima only wanted to help the girls, she tried for hours to make her sister understand that cutting the girls could hurt more than help them, but with no success.

These conversations happened when the two sisters found themselves alone. As Halima came closer to birth, she knew she would have to make a decision soon afterwards. She confided in Nuha that if it was a boy, she planned to postpone her daughters' cutting a few more years. However, if the baby was yet another girl she felt the pressure from her husband and his family may grow too great.

Nuha knew that to save Ruqayya and Layla from the cruel fate that awaited them would be an act of fate itself and hoped beyond hope that they would be saved. Despite her sister's decisiveness, Nuha continued to whisper truths about the cutting to her sister. During one such conversation, Halima became upset, causing her water to break. The birth went smoothly, as had her preceding two childbirths, and the joy was astounding as Halima brought her first son, Burhan, into the world. Her husband warmed to her again in the coming days, and her son was the apple of her eye. The grandmothers rejoiced at their new grandson, his sisters grew to love him, and his aunt Nuha saw the glitter of her sister's eyes in his.

However, after a month of Burhan's life, the pressures on Halima about her daughters began to return. Alya the midwife came to check on Burhan one day, and by her side was Halima and Nuha's mother, as well as Halima's mother-in-law. As they entered the house, their intention was clear. Halima began to panic. Ruqayya's confusion grew as her mother started to cry. Alya had always made her feel better when she was sick, and helped Layla and Burhan into the world, so she trusted her. Nuha saw her sister's panic and began begging her to stop the women from taking Ruqayya into the next room to put her onto the table they had laid out.

The three women began and Nuha continued to talk to her sister, who silently cried as she watched her mother guide Ruqayya towards the table. Nuha started insisting that she put a stop to this. Beside her, Halima began to shake, watching as her daughter looked about confusedly. The grandmothers' prayers and the midwife's preparations overwhelmed the young girl and she began to cry for her mother. The tears of her daughter stirred something within Halima that all her sisters pleas had not. A feeble "momma" from the table forced her into action, and Halima broke through the prayers and words of the old women and begged them to stop—only seconds too late as her daughters scream pierced the suddenly still air. It was done, and the sisters wept.

The Escape
Rachael Dahler

He hit me again today. It wasn't so different from the other times that it's happened; the stinging in my cheek did not subside any faster or slower than previous blows. Even falling back—crashing to the floor, as my hand fell over my eyes, blocking my view from what was going to happen next—was not unusual. His foot connected, with force, into my stomach and my body instinctively curled into a ball to brace for the pain. Tears fell from my eyes, but I dared not cry out. It would only get worse if I protested in any way.

It came time for him to leave for work while I was still lying on the floor in pain, trying to think of what I had done to earn today's beating. At least, I thought, he hadn't forced himself into me—not today. It was then that I began to fear that he would return home later that night to finish what he had started.

The thought sickened me, even more than the blow to my stomach had. I could wait, on the ground, in the same position. It wouldn't have been the first time that my husband would arrive home to find me exactly where he had left me. That never once had stopped him from ripping apart my legs and pleasing himself, despite the excruciating pain it caused me. I could compose myself, get up, and start back on housework. Perhaps, if he came home to a well-cooked meal, he would save the worst of the beating for another day. I lay still, contemplating my choices, when I realized that I didn't want to go through with either of the options. I wanted to be done.

Once that thought became real in my head —once it turned into an idea rather than a fleeting hope, I was off of the ground faster than I had thought possible. Once the decision was made, I gave it as little thought as possible. I took no time collecting my things. I grabbed my *hijab* on my way out, only because I knew it would make my escape less noticed, and slipped it over my head. There was nothing else in this life that I needed to carry on with me into the next.

The next: a new start. This is what I was finally gifting myself. The terror of stepping over my home's threshold was quickly replaced by the realization that this place had never been home to me. I had no children to protect; my husband and I had not had the luck of conceiving, despite his incessant tries. I think that is where a lot of his anger came from, because I never could pinpoint what I was doing wrong to deserve the treatment he gave me.

It wasn't the first time I had considered leaving. I couldn't believe that there were many Arab women that hadn't considered doing so at least once. I thought back to my mother, who still lived an unhappy life at my father's side. I believe that she stayed for the goodness of her children and, for a moment, I thanked

Allah for not bestowing a family upon me. I was not sure I would have been able to leave my children behind, just as my mother was not, just as so many others in our place were not. Knowing that I would not be able to see my own family again was painful, but the promise of freedom was too good to pass up, so I bathed in the positive thoughts and expelled the rest from my mind.

The sun was falling, and the sky darkening. In my full cloak of black, my escape was disguised and went unnoticed. The problem that I faced once I reached the bustling streets was that I had no idea of where I could run. Instead of spending too much time considering the possibilities, though, my feet took off under me, carrying me away from the life that had turned into a nightmare.

I was out of the city before I even noticed it. I think tears were still streaming down my cheeks, but I couldn't be sure. All feeling had left my body. All I could feel was how close I was getting to my freedom, to happiness.

Soon, I came to some woods. My feet had carried me there, and I believed that there were bigger forces guiding me into a better life, so I did not let the difficulty of the steep terrain stop me. I climbed on, among the trees, continuing on my escape to a better life.

The woods were dark, and there were multiple occasions in which I tripped or got caught on a branch. The high heels on my feet, which I had not considered removing before fleeing from my husband's house, soon fell off—unable to handle the ground that was scattered with branches—and I was barefoot. The pain of my feet crushing unknown things was nothing compared to the pain I felt during my years in that marriage, so I did not stop. I did not even look at the wounds. I just kept moving, as far away from my old life as I could get.

The woods were rough; it was undeniable. Getting through the branches was not easy, especially since the sun had set and the moon only gave off a dull light. I looked up to the glowing orb in the sky, but made the mistake of doing so as I continued to walk. Just as I looked back to the dark woods, a low-hanging branch hit me in the face. In addition to scraping my eye, it also managed to pull off my veil.

I couldn't remember the last time my entire face had been exposed to the cool, night air. It was a feeling that I had to stop to take in. The air hitting my cheeks made me cry, again. There was no one around to tell me that I couldn't do what I was doing, which made the entire process more enjoyable. It was just me and the earth, and no one else.

Time eventually became meaningless. It stayed dark, so I knew I couldn't have been out there for longer than the night, but things started to move slowly and the trees around me all looked so familiar that I was sure I was going in circles. I began to worry that my escape wouldn't be as successful as I'd hoped it would be. Soon, my vision became blurry and I could not understand why.

I walked until I physically couldn't anymore. I collapsed against the ground of the woods. Twigs snapped under me as I landed. In the dark, I could not see my feet covered in blood. I could not feel the deep gash across my face dripping blood down my cheek. I had not realized how injured I was until my body was too weak to do anything about it. I could not get back up, so I lay, staring at the night sky. The pain of dying was still nothing compared to living the life I had been living. I was no longer trapped. I was free.

A'zam, A'idah, and the Road
Ann DelMoro

It was my wedding day but through the holes of my veil all that I saw was an ending. Later in the years of my marriage I would escape, though that seemed impossible at the time. It was my twentieth birthday, but that matter was ignored and topped by the lavish wedding I was to be a part of. My mother sat quietly while my hands were covered in wet, sweet-smelling henna. Surrounded by smiling sisters and family, I had never felt more trapped and alone. My veil was too warm on that hot summer day and I dreamt of a life without it. A life I often found myself dreaming of, one where I was educated, dressed in western clothing, and married to a man of my choosing. But for now, this day would tie me to a man much older than me, about whom I knew nothing. His name was Fadhl.

My father, Kadar, had told me that Fadhl had asked for my hand, and offered up gold and support for my father's farm in exchange. My father accepted; I would be the first of five daughters to be married and this excited him. Since I was the eldest daughter, my father was happy I was chosen, something he repeated very often.

In the kitchen, my mother often scolded me, saying, "A'idah, why did you take off your veil? Why don't you cook? Why do you always write?"

My mother was unaware of what I was truly writing. It was not common for girls to be educated, but I stole books from my neighbors when I had the chance and was learning a lot without having to go to school. My sisters thought I was weird. My younger sister by a year, Ghaada, was beautiful, and often got things around town without ever having to ask for them. Ghaada was always trying to read my stories over my shoulder, but she was too young to understand the love that I had been spilling into my notebook for the last two years.

I was on an outing with my mother when I first met A'zam, two years prior to my wedding. We were in the markets of al-'Aqabah, and as usual I aggravated my mother by wandering to the water and taking my veil off when no one was around. I sat at the water's edge watching how freely it flowed, wondering if I would ever be as free as the ripples of the water. As I sat and wrote and thought, a young man appeared next to me, which startled me. But when I looked to see who it was, A'zam smiled and I recognized him from my home neighborhood in Al Mudawwarah. Just the two of us stared deeply into the water; he sat close to me, and I did not move when he placed his hand on mine.

Men in my hometown had touched me before; they would rudely rub their bodies against me and hold me so I could not flee. This occurred enough that when I was older and understood what was going on, I began to be sick of the

68

warmth that radiated from their bodies. I would pinch them and they began to leave me alone. My father noticed that when I turned sixteen, men began to show no interest in me. He began to worry that I would not be chosen for marriage first, but instead, my beautiful younger sister, Ghaada, would be chosen. In his eyes this would mean he had failed, and Kadar did not fail. When I reached eighteen years old, I began to blossom, and this was when I met A'zam and learned that touch was not a bad thing, but something that should be enjoyed.

As A'zam held my hand by the water that day in al-'Aqabah, I knew that I was going to fall in love with him. Every day after that day at the market, he was all I thought about. We would meet up as often as we could, sneaking around town, stealing each other food and having picnics. A'zam would tell me the things he was learning at home and in school, and I would share with him my ideas about getting away from this culture I lived in. I wanted control over my life and A'zam agreed that I deserved nothing but freedom and power.

Two years went by in the blink of an eye but that day, I arose with plans to meet A'zam at a small cafe (not inside of course) so we could explore our land. But as I sat up in bed, my father, Kadar, walked into my room smiling wildly.

"A'idah," he said half yelling, half crying, "Fadhl from the center of town wants your hand!"

I was sick, my body felt weak, and when he came to hug me, I did not see my father any longer, but just the face of the man who would ruin my life forever. Kadar took me to the kitchen, sat down the rest of the family and told them what was to happen. Then Fadhl came into the kitchen, with offerings of gold bracelets for me, wearing a weak smile, and though he looked old, he was rather gentle in his features. I cried and left the room immediately.

Kadar sent Fadhl into my room to console me, telling him that this would happen plenty during the years of our marriage. Fadhl was not the devil I had pictured when Kadar told me of my marriage to him. Fadhl was kind. He did not touch me, he did not scold me for my fear; he just sat next to me and asked me to smile. I could not resist because it was something not many people asked, something that only A'zam had really ever asked me. But through my broken smile, tears streamed and did not stop for the year that followed until the day of my wedding.

I stand at my wedding, but I do not stand proudly. A'zam is in the back of the crowd. I see him and cannot bear to make eye contact. For once, my veil suits me, as it protects the spectators from seeing the bags under my eyes and the sleepless tears that stream uncontrollably from my eyes to my necklace. Fadhl tries his best to ignore them when he looks at me during our ceremony. My heart is breaking the closer we get to the end of the ceremony. With each word a slimy bug crawls through my stomach, biting at my insides, ripping me apart.

After the ceremony, after sitting through all of the hellos and congratulations, Fadhl and I are finally all alone. He holds me for the first time ever, and as he holds me, he tells me that he knew I was not happy. He asks of me one thing: he wants me to just be civil with him and allow our friendship to blossom. How can I say no to this man who had been nothing but nice to me?

For months following that conversation, Fadhl and I grow to be best friends. But nothing hurts more than the stares that I do not receive from A'zam every day. I miss the feeling of my legs giving out from under me that I got each time his eyes burned their holes in my body. His eyes and hands were able to cast spells on me that Fadhl could never understand.

After a year of being married to Fadhl, people began to question why I had not had a child. Fadhl would create stories about bad timing, and how my body was just not ready yet. But people began to speculate that Fadhl and I had not consummated our marriage. We did our best to ignore all of the talk around town. Fadhl grew a little angrier after these accusations though. He began to fight with me over little things and one day he went to the market and would not allow me to come along. He came home with a box and said I was never to look inside of it.

Finally one day, I grew so anxious about the little black box that I had to open it. Fadhl caught me just as I opened it and saw the shiny hand gun inside. I was hit for the first time ever by my husband that night, and I lost my trust in him forever.

I began to go to the market more and more frequently to escape the fear I had in my own home. Eventually, A'zam began to look at me in the market again. Our eyes would meet and his felt like daggers, hitting me right in my heart. Fadhl trusted me enough to allow me to go to the market alone, and one day, A'zam approached me. He grabbed my hand and begged me to go speak with him in a café up the road. We went there and he told me that he loved me still and that he wanted me. He had never married; there were offers but he turned them all down. He had created a home that fit the life he had wanted to have with me years ago. There were books and American-style furniture. Silently, I sat absorbing the things I had dreamt of him saying to me. A plot was created and I was going to be free in a day with the help of A'zam and the strength of our love for each other.

That night, I made a wonderful meal for my husband. I thanked him graciously for providing me with such a wonderful life for the last few years, and for taking his time in allowing me to love him. We consummated our marriage that night, which I used to my advantage to help get me to A'zam a little more safely. I folded his things and mine, and slowly walked out of the house.

About twenty miles down the road, I saw A'zam and began to walk faster, but when his eyes met mine, I saw the fear that lay within them. Halfway between Fadhl and A'zam I felt a sting in my back and heard A'zam yell. Watching as I fell asleep on the road between these two men, I saw that Fadhl had a gun and A'zam reached for me as Fadhl fired again. I lay with my lover, on this road in the middle, finally able to hold him, and as the feeling of A'zam's arms left mine, I looked beside me and he was there. Hovering above our bodies, we had finally found a way to escape this terrible life.

Women and Wives
Teal Denison

Hessa found herself, once again, facing the possibility of birthing yet another daughter for her husband. After the third, she was sure that this would be her chance to give him the son he truly desired. She was still waiting for him to come and wish her luck on giving birth to their next child. He had come to watch over the last three to see if she would give him a son, but all she could give him was daughter after daughter. Where was Gamal? Hessa worried slightly that he wasn't interested in whether she had a son or a daughter. Perhaps he had found another wife that would provide much more for him than she was able to. With this thought in her mind, Hessa began to panic. The nurses tried in vain to calm her, but the images in her mind were so vivid that she could not regulate her breathing.

She lay on a hard wooden cot in a small house near a murky brown river. The floor was uneven and permanently dirty. A man stood across from her demanding breakfast. It wasn't Gamal—this man was older and meaner. Hessa turned to find the kitchen and found only bars. Bars everywhere, growing tighter and tighter around her until she couldn't breathe at all. The man laughed at her and screamed her name mockingly over and over.

The nurses were yelling something at Hessa, but she couldn't understand them. Something about a baby, but why would she care about a baby? She struggled to decipher what they were saying, and suddenly it all came back into focus. Hessa, her baby, Gamal. Gamal. Where was Gamal? Wouldn't he be here by now?

Hessa saw Gamal standing over by the bed. She tried to walk toward him, but found herself frozen in place. She watched as another woman joined Gamal in their bedroom, in their bed. Hessa screamed for Gamal to hear her, but no words would come out of her mouth. The other woman smiled at Hessa. They seemed to be able to see each other. The other woman had not only stolen her husband, but her home, her body, and her voice as well. Gamal smiled. He looked happier than ever before.

Hessa awoke to cold water being splashed upon her face. A nurse stood before her, talking about her pregnancy. Hessa struggled to make sense of the words. She caught snippets as her brain struggled to stay in the present. Her baby...contractions...faster...ready...her baby. It was time for the baby? Hessa tried to explain that she couldn't have her baby yet. Not until Gamal arrived. His presence would ensure that she could have another baby. This baby had to be seen by her husband as soon as it was born. She had to give him a son. She had to stay his wife.

Hessa was holding on to her three daughters in the middle of a brutal wind storm.

The wind blew harder and faster as they struggled to stay together. Hessa's arms soon grew tired and sweaty as she worked to keep them around her girls. The wind blew harder still, and her oldest daughter slipped from her grip and was lost in the storm. Hessa screamed for her daughter, but there was no answer. As her second daughter fell from her arms, she knew it was futile to fight the wind. It was determined to tear them all apart, and it succeeded in the end. Hessa was left standing in the desert, screaming for her daughters to no avail.

This time when Hessa awoke, her mind was completely clear. She was able to understand the predicament she had placed herself and the nurses in. If she wasn't ready to push now, the baby would not make it. Hessa was now well-practiced in giving birth. As she pushed her baby into its new world, she hoped with all of her might for it to be a boy. If she could prove to Gamal that she could give him a son, then he wouldn't have to leave her for another woman. She wouldn't lose any of her daughters, and she would be well taken care of by Gamal in their beautiful home. The nurses wrapped up her baby, and turned and handed it to a man who had just walked in. Gamal. Hessa's eyes found his instantly, but his were looking at their new child.

"A boy! Well done, Hessa."

Relief washed over Hessa's entire body. She reached for her son, but Gamal held on to him fast. He didn't even seem to notice his wife.

"I shall name him Fakhir, after my father. A strong name for my strong son!"

Gamal chuckled to himself. He continued to admire his newborn son, while Hessa watched them both lovingly. She couldn't describe her relief at having fulfilled her duty as Gamal's wife. She closed her tired eyes.

Hessa found herself in a bedroom big enough to hold four people. As she slowly turned, she saw in each of the beds her own daughters. They were staring at her expectantly, waiting for some sort of instruction.

"Go get washed up and set the table for dinner."

The words came out of Hessa's mouth involuntarily, but the girls did as they were told. Hessa followed them out of the bedroom and came into a beautiful kitchen. She continued through other rooms, in search of something, someone. She finally realized who she was looking for: Gamal. She called his name a few times, but there was no response. When she called into the kitchen, the girls looked at her quizzically.

"Who's Gamal? Why are you calling his name?"

Hessa was confused. How could they not know their own father? As she explained, the girls looked even more confused than she felt. They didn't seem to know Gamal at all.

"Well, who is the head of the house? Who is the man?"

At this, the girls began to laugh.

Hessa eyed them angrily and they suppressed their giggles.

When she asked her youngest why there wasn't a man in the house, the girl had to take a moment to compose herself. 'There isn't a man in the house because we don't need a man. That's what you taught us, isn't it? A woman doesn't need a man to survive, and she can be happy without one. Men don't want to have women in their lives; they want to have wives. You have to choose which one you want to be."

Hessa awoke in the dark hospital room after her long sleep. She considered this past dream. Who did she want to be?

Just A Dream
Jeffrey Fredrickson

Lana could not take it anymore. For the past week she had been subject to harsh criticism of her near-perfect cleaning. Ever since her father had seen her talking with Bakr, the boy who lived a few houses down in the village, he had treated her harshly. Nothing she could do for the past week had pleased him. He even went so far as to threaten to marry her off to the next suitor instead of waiting for the man a woman of her looks and intellect deserved. She could not understand what was so wrong with talking to Bakr. They had an innocent relationship, purely based on growing up close to each other and being of the same age.

She just wanted it to stop. His verbal, and occasional physical abuse was becoming too much for her to handle. While cleaning dishes from the night's meal, she could hear her father and mother suddenly yelling, but she could not make out what they were saying. Nor did she really care to. The sooner she finished washing and drying the dishes, the faster she could be in her bed, alone with her dreams. Her father suddenly burst into the kitchen and slammed the door so hard Lana dropped a plate, which smashed onto the tile floor.

If this had happened a week ago, she might have gotten away with a verbal lashing, but her father was at his breaking point. He unleashed a nasty growl and grabbed Lana, dragging her from the kitchen into her room.

Once he set her down, he screamed, "Is there anything that you cannot manage to break or ruin?!"

He slammed her door shut and she could hear his footsteps slowly going down the hall back to the kitchen where she had broken a plate.

Lana burst into tears once she was sure her father was far enough away, saying to herself, "Why.... Why? What have I done to deserve this?"

On a usual night she would have gotten ready for bed before falling asleep, but she did not dare risk angering her father even more tonight. After cleaning herself up a bit, she was finally able to fall asleep amidst sobs over how her life had turned upside down in the past week. It seemed as though just as soon as she fell asleep, she was awoken by her mother to start the day's tasks. Lana washed up and changed into some fresh clothes before heading to see her mother.

Much to her surprise, she had visitors sitting in her living room across from her father. There was a dashing young man whom she recognized as Fakhir, who was two years older than she. Without giving it too much thought, mostly as not to seem rude and interrupt their meeting, she rushed off to her parent's bedroom.

"What are they talking about out there, mother?" Lana asked.

"Fakhir and his father have come to ask for you to marry him," she said.

She was taken aback by this. While she knew that she was a beautiful woman, she did not expect that someone of such prestige as Fakhir would seek to marry her. She quickly ran over to the key hole and stuck her eye up against it to try and see what they were doing. Unable to get a good view, she was forced to wait with her mother a while longer until the agreement had been made. It seemed like years went by while she waited for her father to come into the room. The anticipation was killing her and she wondered what was going to happen.

Finally she heard the door creak open, and she jumped off the bed, frantic to find out what her father had to say. He led her out to the living room, where Fakhir and his father were still sitting.

"Lana, this is Fakhir, whom you are set to marry in two weeks' time. We all agree that it might be best to let you get a chance to know each other better, so you have the afternoon off. I expect you back before sundown though," her father said.

She was ecstatic but equally nervous. She had never really talked with him much before, but she knew that he was a good man with decent intentions. They set off towards the village market so they could grab a bite to eat together. They spent what seemed like hours wandering the streets trying to learn as much as possible about each other. Fakhir was an only child, just like Lana, and they shared a passionate love for soccer. Lana had been prohibited from playing for quite a few years now, but this never stifled her love for the game as a child.

While they were near the outskirts of the city, Fakhir asked, "Would you like to take a walk to that tree on top of the hill? I hear it has a great view of the farm fields."

Lana screamed, "Of course!" a bit too loud, and they shared a laugh.

Lana could not believe what had transpired these last few days. She went from being the brunt of her father's anger for socializing with a shady neighbor, to being treated like a royal princess, set to marry this gorgeous, charming young man of her dreams.

They made their way out right below the tree and sat down, holding hands. Lana noticed that the sun was getting close to the horizon, and she could imagine her father pacing about saying, "Lana, Lana.... Lana, Lana...." She was in pure bliss, though, and this was just a fleeting thought. They sat there slowly cuddling up, just gazing into the horizon, talking about what kind of family they wanted, and what the house would be like. They thought of names for their children, and decided that two boys and two girls were the perfect number for their family.

Increasingly, Lana could not help but shake this voice in her head that was slowly growing louder—her father saying, "Lana, Lana..." repeatedly. She tried shaking it off and concentrating more on what Fakhir was telling her about his dream career.

All of a sudden, she was back in her bed at home and her father had burst into her room, screaming "LANA, WAKE UP!!!!"

She was frightened and confused. What had happened with Fakhir? Why was her father so mad at her? Was she still supposed to get married? Once her father knew she was awake, he left her room but kept the door open.

Lana realized that she had been sleeping, and that this entire escapade with Fakhir was just another dream she had had, a ray of hope that some day things could turn around for her.

What Men Do
Abel German

On the morning of his seventh birthday, Najm asked his mother, Zaira, about his name.

"Najm means star," she said, "And you were our light in the darkness."

"Why was it dark?" he asked.

His mother smiled sadly and looked towards the kitchen. Najm could hear one of his many older sisters doing dishes. Zaira began to speak, then shook her head and turned back to him. "It doesn't matter anymore."

Najm watched his mother as she collected herself. "Did I make you sad?"

"No, little one, it's nothing you did."

Later that evening, the whole family sat around the dinner table. Najm was seated at the head of the table to celebrate.

His father, Hassan, stood up. "Today is the seventh year of Najm's life. He is a blessing upon our family." He reached down to Najm and clapped a hand on his shoulder, "You will carry on the family name proudly." His father sat down, and his sisters cast their eyes to the floor. Najm looked at his mother, smiling wanly at her husband.

His father said, "Now, let's eat. Thank your mother and sisters for this meal."

"Thank you."

Najm's sisters served steaming plates of delicious food, paying special attention to Najm and his father. Just as they sat down, someone knocked on the door. Hassan excused himself and went to answer the door, and Zaira herded the sisters into the back room, leaving their steaming plates of food still on the table.

The door opened, and Najm could hear his father talking with one of his friends, "Hassan! I hear it is your son's seventh birthday."

"It's true, it's true. With every passing year, I can feel the years of misfortune sloughing off my shoulders."

"I always told you that if you were persistent and devout, Allah would one day bless you. He'll be around to protect your daughters when you grow old. Can I see this little man?"

Hassan and his friend came into the dining room. Hassan's eyes were perhaps a little wetter than usual.

His friend came up to Najm, taking his hand in his own. "Do you understand your duty?"

Najm shook his head.

"Your mother and sisters need you to protect them. Whatever happens, that you must remember."

"Why would they need me to protect them? I'm small."

"But you are a man, and that is what men do."

"What do women do?"

"They help to make you."

Zaira, wearing the *hijab*, stepped into the dining room. "Husband, the food will get cold if we don't eat soon."

Hassan frowned, "I'm afraid my wife has become too sentimental from the festivities. She does make a point though. I will see you soon, friend."

His friend nodded, then made his way out the front door.

"Woman, why did you interrupt my friend?"

"My daughters are getting hungry. We spent all day cooking this food, so I'd like to partake before it gets cold."

"The food doesn't go anywhere! Have you no shame?"

Najm watched his parents fight. He thought about the words of his father's friends. He saw his sisters washing dishes, his mother's sad, empty smile, and himself. He watched as his father threatened to beat his mother.

"Father, wait!" Najm rushed out of his chair, and stood between his parents.

"Najm," his mother said, "what are you doing?"

"I'm protecting you, mother. That's what men do."

"You're too young to understand that I'm protecting our family," Hassan said, picking up Najm and moving him. The night proceeded as many others had.

Beyond the Harem Walls
Jenna Giguere

Dear Aisha,

I saw you over the walls of the harem.

I knew I shouldn't be peeking over, but the thought of not being allowed to see made me want a glimpse even more. Looking over the wall I saw the long oblong pools, connected to one another with the clear, crystal dripping of water from each turquoise landscape pool to the next. Many stone benches that encompassed the pools, along with large slender columns that supported the grandiose shape of the harem's courtyard.

That is where I saw you.

You looked so pure and alive, shamelessly lounging, naked. You seemed relaxed as another woman sat and combed your hair.

Your hair.

Oh, how I was mystified by such a thing. Dark, long, and tousled. Hair that was as black as night but shining as though the moon was full and round. I couldn't tear my eyes away if I tried.

The other women in the courtyard danced, laughed, ran in and out of the magnificent pools, while you…you sat, so poised. I heard one of the women yell your name "Aisha."

Aisha. What a beautiful name.

Dear Aisha,

I peeked over the walls again.

I wanted to see you again before I let you know how I feel. Oh, what a sight I saw! The colorful walls of the courtyard with their designs made me feel as though I was inside those walls with you.

You were lying on such an extraordinary rug. A wealthy sheikh or some sort of prince must have bought it. The bright but earthy colors of the rug made your olive skin glisten in the sunlight.

While you relaxed in the courtyard, I could see the other women bathing in the outdoor baths in the corner.

You, Aisha, are not like these other women.

How can I be so intrigued by you when we have never met?

How can I, a man, feel so strongly for a woman who is not my wife?

How I wish you would leave the harem to meet me!

Oh, Aisha! I know I should not be in the presence of the harem but you are too enticing. You remind me of a flower, patiently waiting to be picked by the right hands.

How I wish to be those hands, to nourish you, and to keep you elegant, as you are.

Dear Aisha,

Have you ever been in love?

My brothers followed me early today when I came to admire your beauty over the walls of the harem. I was so embarrassed when I discovered that they were spying on me. My oldest brother, Ali, threatened to tell my mother. Ali tells me that men are not supposed to show their affection to women. I think he watches my father too intently.

But, what if he is right?

What if men are not supposed to love?

What an absurd thought, as I am a man who loves you.

There was shame in my eyes as I lowered myself from the walls of the harem, for I was not able to get a glimpse of your face.

Shame, in letting my brothers find out about you and the other women.

Will I ever be able to see you alone again?

My brothers encompass thoughts of lust for women behind those walls. I am sure they will return and discover your beauty.

Aisha, how can I compete with Ali? He is much older and wiser. He is intent on getting what he wants.

How can I compete?

Dearest Aisha,

I can no longer bear this burden of not seeing you, your sharp features and mesmerizing figure.

Each time I try to retreat to the familiar walls of the harem, I am followed by the snarls of my brothers. They have found my secret and will not stop raving over the women that encompass the harem.

Ali has mentioned you.

He talks about the gorgeous Arabian woman with the long hair; so poised, so mature. He lusts for you, and it disgusts me.

Aisha, I cannot forget you. Why am I, a man, so infatuated with you? I feel that I cannot go on another day listening to my brothers indulge in my secret.

I must run away.

For you, I will give up my whole world,

The poised harem girl.

Dear Onlooker,

I have noticed you peeking over the walls of the Harem quite generously. I wonder if you noticed me…

The harem is no place for a woman like me.

You probably feel joy as you watch my sisters step out of the glistening oblong pools, laughing and dancing around the fountains, squirting long pigments of turquoise water up over the bright colored painted stone of the courtyard walls.

You probably wonder why I am silent and alone as the other women flourish.

The harem is no place for a girl like me.

I could be like the other women if these walls did not encompass me from the world.

How badly I wish I could hop down from the walls and run as you do each time you leave.

Why have you not you come back, onlooker?

You are probably bored with me by now.

Oh, how I wish I could run away with you,

Adventurous village boy.

Becoming Myself
Nicole Handel

I am all and I am nothing. I am sure of so much of myself and unsure of even more. If you met me, you would like me. You would know, undoubtedly, that I am a woman of faith, a woman of obedience, and a woman of confidence. I am not those things. I am not anything.

I walk up the stony pathway to the small, unassuming structure that looks like a home. If you weren't a client, you would think that normal people with normal lives live here, and that nothing of any significance has been said beyond the wooden doors. There is, after all, no sign in front saying that this is a medical office, of sorts. I guess that this is to protect me, and others like me. People don't like you much if they know you're not a real person, a whole person, a together person.

I sit in a chair that feels like it is swallowing me with the hunger of a thousand wolves. I fixate on the sinking, because it matches the sinking of my stomach as I wait for the woman to finish jotting down what I presume are judgments of me. Judgments always, from everywhere. I perceive judgment, anyway. But then my head does some thinking and decides that maybe I'm just imagining the judgments. Maybe they are just me—mine—and not owned by other people.

The woman I talk to each week does not know me. How could she know me? I don't know me, either. I tell her about myself, or what I think is myself, and I tell her about those who determine what my "self" is. Sometimes she says, "Fayruz, what about *you*? How do *you* feel about yourself?"

I tell her that I feel trapped by my head. My head is like a hurricane and it is wild, full of particles and chaos and it uproots things and throws them somewhere else. But hurricanes can't be stopped. You have to let them happen and hope you survive. My head cannot be controlled, and that is why I write.

She asks me to write about who I am and what or who I think owns me, controls me. I tell her that I can't.

She says, "Fayruz, try. Write a poem if it helps. Find your own clarity."

I nod, but decide for myself that I am incapable of sorting through the bodies and words and lips that define this entity which I call *me*. The concept of self is so foreign to me but so absolutely engrained and within, too. I am entirely imprisoned and ensnared and engrossed by the idea of contemplating myself, but I am cast away by this thinking; it throws me back into the sea and tells me that I will get nowhere with it. And, I do get nowhere.

I think of myself as a heroine, sometimes, but I despise the idea of feminism and self-righteousness. And why would I be a heroine? I have done nothing and am nobody. But there is a part of me that I sometimes glimpse in the mirror that shines like gold. I think about her, and I think about how whole she is and actualized and realized she is, and I envy her. This woman never blinks and never hesitates and never answers. She only asks, and I am on the answering end, left drowning. And answers are weakness. Questions are power, but I cannot ask them. Only she asks them, and she is greater for it. Sometimes I think that she is my ideal self, and if only I could convince the Prophet to rip out my soul and replace it with hers, perhaps I would feel like a person, a complete person.

She wears no ring, and therefore she is not trapped, not held, not forced into a dreadful, incarcerated routine of self-sacrifice to another body that stabs at hers with the same panting, same force, same conquest of a primal hunt.

She wears no head covering, and therefore she is not enshrouded, not shameful, not bathed in the shadow of everything that she is expected and wished to be.

She wears no makeup, and therefore she is not sculpted and molded and designed, like a toy, by an existence that demands she be both chaste and chased.

I am daydreaming again.

I feel my long, rough hair brush against my cheek, an indicator that I am tilting my head in contemplation. I straighten up. There are hundreds of voices in the room, some yelling, some abashedly whispering, afraid to be heard , some artificially confident.... I, too, am one of the voices in the room, but I cannot tell which... She is looking at me. Her brown eyes match mine. Her oval face matches mine. I don't see her anymore and I don't see or feel me anymore.

I am in the room and it is silent. There are books along the walls that I never noticed before. Books that I have read. Every one of them. My chair faces an empty chair that looks as though it, too, could swallow you with the hunger of a thousand wolves. There is a knock at the door. I do not know whether to answer it or not. I am only a guest here.

A moment goes by. The knock continues. It is like a ticking clock, pressuring me and prodding me and urging me, growing more insistent and indicating more and more passing time. It drives me to near madness within moments.

I rise. I take short, cautious steps to the door.

I wait; maybe it has stopped and I may sit in peace. But then it begins again. I open the door a crack, and a woman, adorned with a *hijab*, in business attire, addresses me with hesitation. "*Sayeda...* Are you ready for Mr. Faysal?" I stare blankly, not even attempting to form words. This is not my place, not my conversation. I am only a guest here.

I am prompted again with, "Dr. Fayruz... your next client is here to see you."

I wrote.

Dream catcher,
dream snatcher,
you cannot hold my hope.

What am I,
but the Arab spirit;
a thickening rope?
You should not have
thought
that your rawhide
could make me hide;
I will stretch for my
starsights,
far and few,
into a new
horizon.
With more pride than a
lion,
I will be iron-
strong and native.
You may wait by my bedside,
like the Fridays to come
and Sundays past,
but I will still be the sun
of day's youth--
neither meek nor mild;
I am no longer a child.

I am the wise fox
which you cannot trick;
your loving household's
bricks;
the mosque at which I
prayed,
the anxious ship at bay.
Like an omen,
like a jinx,
I despised you like the kinks
of my desert-bred hair.
Somehow, you were there
to deliver the war cries
in my Razia Sultana eyes.
Like a spiny,
sinewy spider,
remain hanging by your
web

above my bed.
I have revealed
the dictatorial masses
whose limbs I believe to be
thieves.

Daydreams Stay Dreams
Georgina Harmer

Hasuna was always looking out the white-framed window of her small, suffocating room. She had a beautiful view of her neighbor's lush green garden that she hoped she could have one day when she had a home of her own. She would gaze out for hours, daydreaming about leaving her country for America so she could fall in love with the most amazing, genuine American man, who would love her for her personality and treat her like a queen. She would cook him breakfast, by choice. She would wash his clothes for him, by choice. She would give him back massages at night, by choice. She would wear the prettiest dresses for him and go on walks with him in the park like people do in the movies, by choice of course. Hasuna was currently dreaming about going to a restaurant by herself in America, on a bright sunny day, with no one giving her dirty looks, free to order whatever delicious food she desired. Maybe she would order pizza with a tremendous amount of toppings on it, or maybe she would get some gooey melt-in-your-mouth chocolate cake, or maybe—

"*Hasuna,* come down here immediately."

Hasuna's daydreaming came to a quick stop. She was already at the door heading to the kitchen to respond to her father's call. Before she entered the room she quickly straightened herself up, making sure her skin was covered and everything was in the right place and presentable for her father. He would get mad if she didn't look perfect at all times of the day. He was always worried about someone coming to the door to ask for her hand and then her not looking her best for her future husband. He was a strict father, but wanted the best for his daughter.

"Yes, Father?" Hasuna responded, as she walked into the kitchen.

"Dear Hasuna, do you remember Bashir from the doctor's office?" The excitement in her father's eyes was making her nervous.

"Yes, I do," Hasuna replied uneasily.

"Well, he has asked me for your hand in marriage, and I have said yes. You will go upstairs and put on your best dress. He is coming over for dinner tonight."

Hasuna felt like her heart just fell out of her chest. She felt an uncontrollable wave of rage go through her body as if it was taking her over. At the same time she just wanted to cry, for the words she wanted to say to her father wouldn't come out. Hot tears started rolling down Hasuna's face. She turned her back to her father and ran back into her room, fumbling to lock the door behind her. She sat on her bed shaking, her head in her hands, rocking back and forth. She was only fifteen. She had so many hopes and dreams, and the worst thing that could have happened to her just had.

"Hasuna, please open the door," her father said from the hallway. "This is a good thing. He is successful and will take care of you."

"I don't want to be taken care of. I can take care of myself," insisted Hasuna through tears.

"I am not trying to harm you, dear Hasuna. I am trying to help you. I will give you a couple of hours to collect yourself. Then you will meet us downstairs for dinner."

Hasuna didn't respond. Instead, she grabbed her suitcase and started rapidly packing all of her belongings. Once she was done packing, she carefully opened her window, making sure not to make any kind of noise that would draw her father's attention to her. As she climbed out her window and walked down the path towards the main road she stopped. Hasuna took one last look at the beautiful garden that she had gazed at through her window for fifteen years. She grew sad for a moment, knowing that she wouldn't be seeing that garden again for a very long time. However, she knew she would be seeing an even more beautiful garden every day where she was going—America. She wasn't sure how she was going to get there, but Hasuna was determined.

As Hasuna walked down the main road, she contemplated where she would start once she got to America. She knew she had to find work straight away—she planned to work somewhere simple and then work her way up. After all, in America there wouldn't be men judging her if she went into a workplace and asked for work. Where Hasuna was from, men would ridicule and stare at her in judgment if she were to ask such a thing. They would tell her that she should be working for her husband or parents and helping out the family; what women were expected to do in her community. Hasuna hated the way she was treated in this community; she was fed up with the stares and judgment. She was fed up with being told what to do and she was even more fed up that she would obey and listen to them! Why had she always followed their directions all of her life? It's not like it paid off and she got something out of it.

Hasuna suddenly became angry while thinking about this concept. She started walking faster and breathing harder. She was so enraged, she felt so trapped, and she was set on breaking out. As Hasuna looked around to see which road she should take next she heard a faint screaming coming from behind her. As she turned around, she froze. It was her father in their car hanging out the window screaming for her to come back, and he was getting close. Hasuna snapped herself out of shock and turned again to try and outrun her father's car. She couldn't go back with him. She would not allow him to force her to marry someone she did not love.

"Hasuna! Hasuna! Stop running immediately. You halt this instant. You must obey me!" her father belted at her. He sounded terrifying, and she was terrified, but not of him. She knew he was only trying to help, but he did not understand her. Hasuna longed for adventure, for excitement and her own choices. What her father was doing was Hasuna's worst nightmare coming true.

Hasuna knew he was getting closer because his voice kept getting louder and louder. Every time she would hear him come closer she would try to run just a little bit harder. With sweat dripping down her face, Hasuna tried to throw off her father by making a quick left. Little did she know, there was a ditch right after the corner of the left turn. Hasuna tripped into it, scraping up her knees and her arms in the process. She felt her heartbeat throughout her whole body. It was so loud, beating in her ears. She saw her father's car turn in front of the ditch, blocking her off so she couldn't try to run away again. She could see his mouth yelling and his arms flailing in the air but she couldn't hear anything he was saying, or anything at all. It was silent, a weird calm sort of silence that she couldn't understand. It reminded her of one of her daydreams for some strange reason, maybe because the silence was so peaceful. She allowed her father to pull her out of the ditch and walk her to his car. He made sure to lock the doors once she was inside. The entire way back to their house Hasuna's father scolded her, but Hasuna had nothing to say. She wasn't even scared anymore; the only thing she felt was defeat.

Hasuna walked to her closet after her shower. She wanted to pick a long-sleeved dress to cover up the scrapes she had on her arms and legs. She made sure to pick the best long dress she had for dinner. Along with the dress, she put on her best makeup and jewelry. Her father couldn't possibly get mad at her now, but that wasn't why she was dressing up. She was dressing up to impress a man who had her hand in marriage. She was dressing up for someone who would take good care of her and support her. Someone who would "respect" her. She was dressing up for nothing.

Stagnant Water
Sam Howard

Are you there, Child?

It has been two days since I last felt you move. It was thirty weeks ago that your father, Samir, planted you inside me, an act I am no stranger to. You will be the fourth child in three-and-a-half years that I have provided for my husband.

Samir will keep trying until he has received a son. When he had seen that his first child was a girl, he acted pleased, pleased to have a child. It was with the second and third girls that I sensed his impatience.

For his sake, I hope you are a boy, but this hope gives me no strength. Instead it weakens me. If you are a boy, then you will never see the pain that is experienced by women. You will be born blind to the injustices suffered by women. Your blindness will not allow you to see the fire that burns in my eyes, a fire that will soon engulf your sisters.

If you are a boy, then I will watch as you adopt your father's traits. Your youthful innocence will quickly be polluted with your perceived birthrights. It won't be long until "my right" becomes an everyday part of your vocabulary. If it is Allah's will that you are a boy, then I will challenge you to overcome the mountain of entitlement, to cast aside your male pretentiousness and to open your eyes. For if you do this, then you will have made me truly proud to be your mother.

Can you hear me, Child?

Is it wrong of me to hope you are a girl? I know the challenges you will face, both in the home and outside. As a girl you will have to wear masks. You will have to cage your emotions, and if you don't then you will be made to feel depreciated. But don't let anyone misprize you. All the suffering you experience will only make you stronger. If you have done any wrongs in this life, then let only Allah judge you in the next. It is no man's place to decide how you must live, for each man and woman is equal in the eyes of Allah and the real judgment will take place in front of him. Too many people forget this.

If you are a girl, I will do my best to guide you. I will help to make you strong, but strength must come from within. I will not allow you to be like the girls who accept their fate to be a vessel for man, the ones you see surrounded by idols. When the day comes that you are married, your father will want to surround you with these same idols that encompassed me on our wedding day. If on that day you see these objects for what they really are I will be happy. And if you can manage to undermine the societal oppression that women face, whether that be conspicuous or discrete so that women may one day feel free, whether that be in your life or your children's, then I will truly be proud to be your mother.

Are you there, Child?

What will Samir do if you are a girl? Will he take up another wife? If that happens, at least my body can rest from the stress that constantly carrying a child causes. I could then focus on steering you and your sisters, so you may work for a better future, and he could then focus on his new wife. This would give me a sense of freedom, but there are many other locks on the door that stands between me and true freedom. I can sense that he has lost any confidence in my ability to produce a son for him, but if it is God's will that I am to give birth only to daughters then it has to be for a purpose. Am I destined to bear child again, or will you be the last?

Are you there, little one?

Hijabs
Paige Humphrey

She woke up every morning and donned her *hijab*s, the first as she made breakfast for her family—her rough husband and their two boys. She always wished she could have a daughter, but knew she was better off without one, better off because she never wished her hardships on her own children. She loved her boys but, like her older brother and husband, they grew up into hard men. She felt that her life was lived in a black and white picture, that there were no gray areas where rules didn't apply—and no colors where freedom could flourish.

Just before she left her house she looked at her husband's photo, put on her second *hijab*, and entered the world, leaving herself behind, taking on her assumed and expected identity. Nothing else took precedent over this, just as she was never taken seriously by anyone. It was lightly raining today and she saw a rainbow in the distance. She disliked them because they always appeared when something undesirable and massive was happening in her life.

She remembered the rainbow on the day she was cut, and how she was grateful to have her older sister to tell her it was all going to be all right.

She remembered the rainbow on the day of her marriage. She saw it appear as she woke in the morning and had almost laughed, knowing that of course, that day something would try to break her. On her wedding night her dowry and purity were valued more by her father than her happiness. Her groom was young and kind, but she still sought independence over needing this man to make her parents proud. After her purity was confirmed, the color on the sheet was held high for all attending the reception, and cheers echoed in her ears as she took in what had just happened, fast and forced.

Then there was a time when there were no rainbows—the births of both of her sons and the peace in the time after. Her husband wanted another son though, and she felt that it was her duty to provide that to him, a duty that she was unable to fulfill.

She remembered the rainbow on the day she found her baby to be miscarried better than any other she had seen up to that point in her life. That rainbow was big and beautiful. That rainbow, although it brought bad news, was the most beautiful thing she saw for a while. She became disinterested in sex with her husband after the miscarriage. Her heart shrank every day like a rotting fruit, turning darker and darker, becoming smaller and smaller; she lost hope like water in her hands. They were distant in the close quarters of their home—she longed to leave this life behind.

Rainbows appeared behind her eyelids as she slept. She saw the colors when she cleaned her home and dishes. She saw them before she felt the tears on the days her husband scolded her for her mistakes and shortcomings. She was grateful that he went elsewhere for sex and didn't take any physical aggression out on her. Even though her scars were unseen, they were still there carrying her pain.

She started writing once she was aware of his actions: "What luck: love is a fantasy and disappointment is a destiny."

She always dreamed of falling in love when she was a girl, of living in a beautiful home that she took pride in caring for, but her home and husband felt like a prison and warden on her soul, because around them she could never truly be herself, she was never comfortable, and absolutely never felt loved.

As her husband grew older and needed her to care for him she did so and took no pleasure in it. He was a grumpy old man who was completely unbearable to be in the presence of. She dreamt of just picking up and leaving most days, and was haunted by the usual colorful images when her eyes closed each night.

On this day though, as she was headed to the pharmacy to get his prescription, the rainbow she saw was ominous, holding a secret in its colors. She thought that this rainbow was different, and she thought that maybe this one held a special meaning. She retrieved the prescription for her husband and began on her walk home to him. She could still see the rainbow. She hoped for freedom one day.

As she entered back into her home she noticed how quiet it was. It was odd for her to enter her home without hearing her husband address her upon her entry. Her curiosity piqued and she went to see him. He was in their bedroom, but did not appear to be breathing. She slowly approached his body and lightly began speaking his name until she was almost shouting. He was dead though.

The rainbow peeked through the window.

The tears surprised her. They were not tears of sadness or joy; neither were they tears of relief. They were tears of regret. She wished her whole life away and especially wished that she had the strength to carry on and live a life without him.

She has written many stories about women such as herself, but instead of ending in heartbreak and despair, they end in happiness and freedom. She lets her dreams live in her stories and they make her happy. She removes her *hijab*s when she writes, peeling off each layer to reveal her true self in the worlds she creates. In her latest story, the heroine defies society and refuses to be cut, refuses marriage, and becomes a painter. As a painter, this woman uses all the colors, making little rainbows hidden in the sky and big ones that form faces and crowds of smiling faces.

In her writing, rainbows are beautiful. They are paintings from her own soul, where the coloration comes directly from her womanhood and being.

This story of the painter is so close to her, but she no longer dreams or wishes she had the strength to share it. She is determined too. So today when she puts on her *hijab*s to leave, she won't come back. She only brings her words with her to take out and show the world, and when she does so she will be stripping herself of the *hijab* and its endless limitations to advance to a life lived without restriction and full of color.

Forbidden Pleasure
Sonja Janjic

I rush to my room, shut the door quietly, and gingerly put on a black skirt and shove cloth down my underpants. Curling into a ball, I hug my cramping stomach and embrace my tender breasts. I think of what my future may hold; I know it could be bright as long as I stay pure and do what women before me have done. I long to be a loving mother and wife, but am I prepared for love in place of my feeling for pleasure?

"Man up," I tell myself. Opening a chest at the foot of my bed and grabbing Azhaar, I pull her to my face and take a long, deep breath in through my nose, bringing back old memories of my long lost friend. In hopes of going to a lovely place, I close my eyes, squeezing them shut tighter and tighter, but I cannot escape the pain and fear.

Woken by shrieks of terror and pain, I rub my eyes and quickly sit up, then slide out of bed and stand at my door with ears peeled and eyes wide. The shrieks continue as I stumble out of the room. Creeping down the stairs, clenching my doll Azhaar, I fear for what I will see. In the pitch dark I hug the wall and tremble walking through the hallway. After seeing a light from a closed door, I approach and peek through the lock hole.

My sister Saadat lay with her legs spread, thrashing and weepily pleading. I recognize my mother and grandmother, Teeta, but the other two people I cannot make out. The other woman was standing at the foot of the bed holding gauze and tending to my sisters delicate wounds. She pulls what was once white cloth off my sister and I gasp at what I see. The woman then sprinkles something black over her tender wound, but I can't make out what it was. I nearly burst through the door, but know that will not be in the best interest for anyone. My mother is holding her hand and my grandmother kissing her forehead and whispering into her ear. As I begin to cry, I turn, gripping Azhaar tighter than before, and head for my bed. Sleeping little to not at all that night, I lay awake thinking of my poor sister's experience.

Saadat didn't come out of her room for seven whole days after that night. Momma would often bring her soup with lentils, hummus, and veggies, cookies, or some sort of treat, and a nice cup of tea. Even my innocent self could tell Momma was spoiling her in hope of forgiveness. She told me to stay away, to let her rest because she was sick.

I stayed away from my mother those days—I was angry at her, but still unsure why. Even with my anger, I obeyed her the first day. But on the second, I had to talk to my sister.

I opened Saadat's door and walked in with Azhaar in my hand.

"Saadat, a-are you okay?" I whispered. "Please tell me you're okay."

Nothing came out of her mouth. I simply stood there staring. She turned her back to me facing the opposite wall. I wanted so badly for her to talk to me, to tell me what had happened. I must have stood there for thirty minutes, but not a peep.

"I love you, sister!" I murmured, then whispered, "Here—have Azhaar. Cuddle with her until you feel better."

She looked at me with amazement, knowing Azhaar was never out of my sight and when I would lose her, there was always a frantic search by Teeta, Saadat, and myself until she was safely in my arms again. Without a word, I turned and left.

I heard her whimper as I left and all I wanted to do was crawl in bed with her and hug her, but I know this is not what she wanted and I feared I might hurt her.

The following day, I returned.

"Saadat, please talk to me! What happened? Why are you so sad?"

"You are much too young, my sister. Just leave me to weep in peace."

Feeling as if the pain inflicted on my sister was living inside of me, I silently turned and left her. I did not return the following day, although I passed by her door several times throughout the day. Each time, I stopped for a few minutes and listened for any noises she would make. My poor sister consumed my thoughts for those days—the vision of all the blood and of my sister whipping from side to side played over and over in my head.

The fifth day she didn't get out of bed, I tiptoed in and simply said, "I saw all of the blood, sister. I saw and heard that night."

She turned and looked at me. I could not figure out her expression for the life of me. Was it anger, shame, or fear? I really did not know, but the sadness in her eyes was definite. Before she even made a word, I continued to ramble.

"Why? Why were momma and Teeta there with you? Who were those other women? Please, I beg of you!" I whimpered as tears filled my eyes. "Talk to me. I am living your pain. I need to understand."

"Ghasna, you are much too young to understand as even I do not fully understand. Momma hurt me out of love. I am a woman now and in order to get married a little blood is what must be done—that's what Teeta told me. You have lots of time, at least five to seven years before this pain is inflicted on you. My sister, do not touch the forbidden place and you will not know what you have lost," she said as she tried to hold back the tears welling in her eyes.

I sat and listened to every word she said without interrupting once, even though I had more questions than before. I tried to ignore the tears she so clearly wished for me not to see, but the vulnerability of my sister was something I could not deny and will never forget.

She went to hand me Azhaar back, but I muttered, "I won't be needing her anymore. Please cuddle with her until your wounds heal and then we will find a place to put her."

I caress myself as tears well. I fear this is one of the last times I will feel pleasure.

"Ghasna," I hear my mother call. "Come here now!"

Perhaps I should have taken Saadat's advice all those years ago.

Godless
Sebastian Karch

The first man of the night was blunt. He began undoing his belt before the door was shut and he had dropped the money on the table.

"Get on the bed, and do not look at me," he mumbled through his rough beard. "A woman so far from God will not taint me with her lecherous looks. And keep your face away from my shirt. I don't want your paints to show up when my wife cleans it."

He sat on the edge of the bed and removed his pants. His shoes stayed on, she noticed. Clearly he wanted to be in and out, and she didn't mind. His attitude was toxic, and did not bode well for the rest of her night.

"As you wish. I'll just look away." The prostitute complied. She lay on the bed, raised her dress, spread her legs, and turned her head to the side. Within minutes, he was up and out the door. While his attitude had a poor effect on the mood, perhaps his urgency would be an indicator of many clients for the evening. This could mean some new bracelets.

The next was a handsome young man with a short and neatly-trimmed beard. He closed the door and walked to her with a charming smile.

"Hello, young queen of the night," he greeted her alluringly. "You are looking enchanting tonight."

She giggled and responded with a downcast look. "And what brings such a handsome, young charmer to my room?"

The womanizer chuckled and revealed his intentions, which mirrored those of many others. "Well, I seek nothing but some companionship for a few moments of your time. As I understand, you tend to help men pass the time quite well."

As she sat on the corner of the bed, she put on a perplexed look and moved her finger to her chin, as if confused. "Well, what ever could we do about that?" she asked. After a very brief pause, a twinkle in her eye accompanied the mischievous, cat-like smirk that invaded her face. "Why don't you come closer and we can think of something together?"

With that as an invitation, the well-groomed man took off his coat and took her in his arms. This one took his time and was more sensual, but the same selfishness that showed in the urgent man was evident in this ladykiller. After an hour of turning and moaning, he was done. This one, too, dropped the money on the table and left without a word.

Hmm, I wonder where all his charm went once he got what he wanted, she thought to herself. Perhaps he also wanted to leave a woman absent from the sight of God. *Maybe it's contagious,* she mused, finding the situation funny. No matter. His exchange of pleasantries and extra tip paid for all she could be happy for and more. Tonight would certainly be eventful.

Her third visitor was an unlikely one, but it was not the first time she had to deal with his kind. The long-bearded holy man came in briskly and with a purpose in his step.

"Siren, you need to stop your filthy business at once!" said the lecturer. "You, who lures in the men of this city with your immodesty and unfaithfulness. Such ways are blasphemous and you taint the city with your vileness!"

Her face darkened and her expression grew serious. "Tell me something, you who persecutes me as the evil in this city," she said defensively. "Before you walked into my room, did you talk with any of those crowding outside? Many have not even seen my likeness, yet you accuse me of seducing them somehow."

"Your sinful actions are known in this area. They entice those who have faith but are lacking in will power. You push these otherwise good men to join your sin and destroy their lives. Do not deny this!" he exclaimed.

"Those men outside the door came of their own volition," the temptress refuted. "Instead of naming me evil and wasting your time, you should give them your sermon. Convince them to walk on the path of God and join you in pestering someone else." She shooed him away with a flap of her hand.

"Succubus, you will not convince me with your lies and lack of faith. Give up your tainted life of lust and live according to His laws! They will surely lead to your ruin, as well as all of your victims."

With his speech over, he quickly exited as if a demon was on his heels. It wasn't long after the door slammed shut that it was opened again by a hungry customer.

The sermonizer's holy aura clearly was not strong, for it hardly put a dent in her clientele for the rest of the evening. There seemed to be a large amount of good men who were weak-willed, according to him. The night's earnings were plentiful and the woman of the night enjoyed the fruits of her labor at a nearby den. Sitting alone with a bottle of wine, she would not seem like a sinful witch to anyone looking her way. She did not seem to be filled with regret, passing up on the life of manufacturing children, one after another.

She smiled and paid the bartender for her drink and exchanged a few familiar words. She left the bar content that night, and she was certainly not absent the next.

Ten Toes
Caroline Ladd

I step in the shower with the water on hot. The water is hitting my face, warm steam surrounding the stone wall, surrounding me, closing in on me. The steam is as thick as I imagine clouds to be. A thickness that almost seems to be a solid structure, but when I reach my hand out to touch it, I realize that it is just a dreamt idea. The steam is how I see my life: thick and cloudy, and yet when I try to take a hold of it, it all disappears, as if it never existed in the first place. The stone in the shower is cold, ugly, and has no real texture or importance, just like myself, I suppose. As I stand in the shower, I notice my toes, ten little toes that have supported me, day in and day out, ten little toes that I recognize, that are important to me, that are beautiful, the way that I should be able to see myself. But it isn't my ten toes that dictate the way that I feel about myself but the dozens of pairs of ten toes that have convinced me of my dishonor.

As I stand in the shower, previous hours in the day start to come back to me. I was strapped to my bed, a place that is supposed to be comfortable to me, and yet felt so foreign. My hands were tied with yarn, an itchy and cutting sensation. My feet were tied down with a softer material, something of silk, which was a soft but a year piercing sensation. A man's weight was weighing down on me, forcing me into discomfort. I was never given a choice to say yes or no, but I guess that is just the way that I live now. I don't know what he was doing to me, and I don't care to recognize it either; all I remember is ten toes, ten toes that were so foreign to me. Even after those ten toes finished whatever they were doing to me, I saw them move quickly around my room, never pointing towards me or looking to see if I was okay, even after I had just gone through such a struggle. I looked at the ground and at those toes, toes that were ugly, hairy, and oddly shaped. Toes that looked cold and dark and rather lifeless. Who were these ten toes and to whom did they belong? Because as far as I could remember these ten toes looked foreign to me.

I am told that these ten toes support a man who is my husband, a word that I don't like to use because of its loving connotations. I can't convince myself to look him in the eyes or even look at him as a person. I can't look at someone that has killed who I thought I was. I can't look at a person who day after day continues to take advantage of me in ways that I cannot even fully understand.

I hate these toes, but I have to ask of them a favor. I ask, "Can you untie my hands and my feet so that my ten toes can roam free?"

My question elicits no answer, and these ten foreign toes walk away from me. Sometimes I wonder if my voice even makes a noise or if these foreign toes just simply ignore me?

I lay there, limp and lifeless, questioning my every move. I drift into a deep sleep, then awake and decide to step into the shower. The shower is a place that I know, something that is comfortable and no longer foreign.

I turned on the faucet as hot as it could go. Maybe I could burn away the sins that have been forced upon me. As I stood in the shower, I felt myself staring at my ten toes. These ten toes no longer looked beautiful and vivacious. They looked dull, dirty, and lifeless, with a resemblance to the foreign toes I had seen around. As I soaped up my body, I could not get a good lather. The water was burning, so hot that my skin turned to a pink color, like the roses that I remember seeing, smelling, as a young, innocent child.

Not that this was truly that long ago. No matter how much water or the temperature of it, I still cannot manage to get a good lather. I let the soap wash away, and I decide that I will try again. I take the bar of soap and hold it in my hand with a firm grasp. I hold it under the water and let the hot water wash away its surface, hoping that the underneath will be even more beautiful. I take the bar of soap and rub it all over my body, washing away my sins and my misfortune. Again, I cannot manage to get a thick enough lather. Once more, I hold the bar of soap under the scorching hot faucet, and let the water burn through its outer layer. Maybe this time, the soap will be strong enough to get the dirt and scum away from my skin. As I rub the soap up and down my body, I cannot escape the dirty, dingy, and old feeling. I continue to rub the soap all over my body, scrubbing and scrubbing to rid myself of the unclean feeling. I stand under the faucet, looking up at the sky and let the water pour over me, washing away the soap, washing away all that I had done. After minutes of letting the water brush over my entire body, I shut the water off.

I step out of the shower and dry off, but still I have an unclean feeling. My toes are dark, dull, and lifeless. These aren't the toes that I had always remembered looking at when I played outside as a young girl. It seems like just a few years have passed, and yet my toes look foreign to me. I used to play in the dirt, the mud, and the hot pavement. And yet when I used to play, my toes looked cleaner, more vivacious.

Maybe it wasn't the toes that I was seeing differently but myself as a whole. I am now fifteen years old and am finally making my family proud. It is an honor to be married so young, and yet I feel more dead than ever. My toes are a part of me that always looked young and full of life. If my toes have fallen dead, then I am not so sure what that says about myself. As I come to this realization, I am thinking back to my day. When I asked those foreign toes to untie me, was I asking him to set me free? Had I actually said it or was it merely a dream? I cannot imagine speaking to those toes, especially in such a condescending way.

Sometimes I just wish that I could stand in the shower and let the water wash away my tears and also my fears. Sometimes I just wish that someone could untie me and let me free. Maybe one day I will find my way to freedom.

For now, staring at my toes, my pink little toes that after a shower still look young and delicate, makes me feel free. They resemble the way that I see myself in my dreams: small and fearless. For now I will continue to think of myself as my toes, for I cannot stand to see myself in the mirror. My life has become something that I had never imagined, something where I can't look myself in the mirror and respect who I am. I want to love myself, so for now I will love my ten little toes, my ten little toes that represent who I am and who I want to be: young and free.

Window Girls
Shea Leading

I have watched all the girls I know leave. When we were little, we'd play out in front of our houses while our mothers watched and talked. As we got older, they began to disappear, and they never came back whole. When they returned, they carried mirrors over their eyes, and hunched their shoulders like their mothers. They shuffled their feet when they used to run, while their fathers and brothers marched.

I didn't have any brothers to march with, but my friend Abra and I would look at these girls at school, and while we walked home. We knew they'd seen Amatullah. Amatullah wasn't her real name, but my mother and all the other women in the neighborhood never called her anything else, and they said the name as if opening a bird cage, always afraid something might escape. She had thin, rough hands, and they reminded me of talons.

Abra and I wondered when we would have to go see Amatullah. While I hoped that day would never come, Abra spoke of it in a hushed voice, like the other women. I don't think Abra had ever been to Amatullah's home, like I had. She'd never been there when someone left, never heard the women putting the mirrors in your eyes.

When my cousin Badi'ah left, I had to wait outside the house while she went in with Amatullah and my grandmother and my aunts, and even my mother. She cried so loud, I thought someone surely must come. Someone must have thought something was wrong. But no one came.

That night, I dreamt that it was dark, and I was lying down. All the girls who had left were standing around me, staring at me with their blank eyes. They had bruises on their arms, and their legs were bound in black rope. As they stood, a wail started to pick up, swirling through their hair and lifting it up. It got louder and louder, wavering like the crying wind, and it felt like my ears might shatter before I realized that I was the one screaming.

I recognized each girl, and began calling to them by name, begging one of them to look me in the eyes.

Fawz. Iman. Najat. Qamar. Daliyah.

Sana. Abla. Kifah. Zuha.

Maysam. Intisar. Badi'ah. Abra.

Abra! No! Abra hadn't left. I shouted Abra's name the hardest, but her eyes never looked into mine, only somewhere through my body. I wanted to grab her, to shake the mirrors out of her eyes and knock her shoulders back into place, but my arms and ankles were pinned by hands that as I watched, grew into my grandmother, and my aunts. Their grip was like stone. I struggled, still screaming, gritting my teeth.

As I thrashed, I watched the rope around the girls begin to glow, like embers in a dying fire. They burned, brighter and brighter, eventually bursting into flame. I started crying, throwing my shoulders forward, trying to break my limbs free. Directly in front of me, I saw the light of the fire glint off of something metal. Amatullah stepped out of the shadows. She was holding a knife.

I woke up when my mother slapped me across the face. I was only eleven, and her strong arms gripped my face tight between her hands.

"Shahd," she whispered, "you must stop screaming." She held my gaze, shifting her focus between each of my eyes until she was sure I was back in my body, that I knew where I was and had left the room full of fire. She picked up a bowl and pulled a cold washcloth from it, setting it against my forehead. I realized I was sweating, and the white nightgown I wore clung to my neck and my back. I closed my eyes and let my mother continue to wipe the washcloth against my hot skin and I breathed deeply. As she wiped, I rubbed the spots on my wrists, unable to get the feeling of stone hands clutching my skin out of my mind.

After a few moments, my mother got up and retrieved a hairbrush, and came back to my bed. She lay down with me, brushed my hair, and sang to me. Her voice carried ocean waves, and softened the ringing in my ears and the heat in my face. I fell asleep feeling her heartbeat against my back.

When I woke up in the morning, my mother was already in the kitchen making tea. I got ready for school and ate my breakfast of flatbread and goat cheese in silence. Across from me at our small kitchen table, she had placed a cup of coffee where my father used to sit every morning. I watched my mother's long, dark hair swing behind her as she drifted through the kitchen, humming a song I didn't know. Sometimes, I stopped breathing trying to hear her feet touch the floor.

* * * * * * * * * * * *

Three weeks later, Abra wasn't in school and we didn't walk home together. I watched the girls who had left ambling home and I missed walking with Abra at my side, comforted by her easy smile. She was always thinking about what it would be like, after.

Maybe she was sick. Maybe she'd come down with something and was actually home in bed, resting. Maybe there was some chance my friend would come back. I decided to ask my mother when I got home from school. But when I approached my house, I saw my grandmother and two of my aunts were visiting.

I entered the house quietly. My grandmother and my aunts' voices sounded sharp. They bounced off the walls like banging pots, and I froze, hoping no one had heard me come in.

"What are you doing, Rafidah? You're only making this harder for Shahd." My grandmother shushed my aunts' murmurs of agreement. I could hear her frown, imagine her hands reaching out to my mother. "You have a responsibility to that girl, to all of us."

"She's my daughter," my mother said, her voice small but strong. No hint of pleading as she sipped at the coffee she'd made in honor of our guests.

"And she's *our* niece. You're ruining her chance for a future. Just because *you* don't want to find a husband and get married, doesn't mean you need to ruin *her* hopes for a husband!" My lip twitched. That was Rabab. I'd learned she'd never liked my father, and after he died, she'd done everything she could to remarry my mother. Who was she to talk about ruining my life?

"I *was* married, and this is not your choice." My mother's voice broke. She never talked about my father, only poured him his coffee and refused the proposals Rabab threw at her like seed at birds.

"I've allowed you to make your own decisions since Ubaid passed, but you've had three years and you're not going to do this. This doesn't just affect you," my grandmother said, nearly hissing her last words. The room went silent, but I could hear the *swish* of one of the women shifting. Probably Takiyah, who always seemed to fidget with her chador, pulling it closer to her body and around her stomach, heavy with her third son. My mother could always count on her judgmental glare for bearing only a single daughter.

I didn't want to hear any more of my future being planned. I started to back away, ready to close the door and announce that I was home. When my grandmother finally spoke again, her voice was final.

"I'll call Amatullah tomorrow. We need to move this along." Suddenly, my ankles were weighted with stone. I felt my legs bound and burning. A scream built in my lungs.

"Ah, no, Mother. It's fine." She paused and sighed heavily. "I'll do it." I could hear my mother stand and begin clearing the glasses from the table. The other women all practically sang their pleasure at her choice, clinging to their coffee though my mother appeared to be done with their visit.

I closed the door behind me, making sure it was heard, and made my way into the kitchen. I greeted my grandmother and my aunts warmly, before excusing myself to my room. I never asked about Abra.

And my mother never called Amatullah.

* * * * * * * * * * * *

Every time my grandmother has looked at me since, I have worried she's seen windows in my eyes instead of mirrors, and that she would know. Know that I hadn't been cut. That there was still something inside me that yearned to scream, rather than burn in silence.

My mother told me to lie about it. Say that I'd seen another woman, not Amatullah, when we went away a few weeks after my grandmother and my aunts cornered her into making the decision they wanted.

"I'm sorry, Shahd. I had to tell them I would do it," my mother said. "It's going to be hard, but I can't…" She spent that whole evening crying into my hair and thinking about my father. She never said that's what she was thinking about but I knew. She stopped setting out a cup of coffee for him at breakfast a few days later, and I forgot to hold my breath to listen for her footfalls.

When I finally saw Abra again, I knew she wasn't lying. She shuffled home with all the other girls now, girls missing the puzzle piece to their womanhood, while I walked stiff-kneed and hoped the secret I carried never showed. After that, I practiced bowing my shoulders and shifting my gaze, but I was never able to make my eyes lie the way my mother could. Six years of practice, and I've never been able to lie the way she could.

Once, when I was out with my mother, I passed a girl. I had stopped to glance in a bookstore window as she hurried out of it, arms full of the spoils she'd purchased. We crashed right into each other, sending her books to the ground. I apologized profusely, knowing I'd been lost in my thoughts instead of paying attention.

I bent to help gather them back into her arms. She must have been going to college, as she was carrying mostly large, heavy hardcovers. As we each picked up the last of the books, I moved to hand them to her and our eyes met.

Windows. Windows, straight into golden brown seas, pools of honey, and laughter lines. For a moment, one of her dark eyebrows raised, and I swear a corner of her mouth twitched into a memory of a smile. She gulped it down, almost as quickly as I saw it, and she shifted her eyes back to her books, hunched her shoulders and thanked me. As she walked past, she grazed her shoulder against mine.

I couldn't help smiling at the ground as I hurried to rejoin my mother.

The Yellow Bird
Katy Maier

Lina loved being outside. When school got out she would play in the street with the other children on her block, kicking a soccer ball back and forth under the bright yellow sun. She would see the older girls on her block walk by in their dresses and head scarves, as Lina wore the sneakers and shorts that used to belong to her older sister. The older girls admired the children's games because they were no longer allowed to play. About to turn twelve years old, Lina never considered the day she would have to be like the older girls. Despite the dry and hot summers, she loved the feeling of sunlight on her bare skin; it brightened her spirit and made her feel alive.

At the end of the day Lina would come home to find her mother preparing dinner in their hot kitchen. The large meals her mother prepared were for Lina's father, a man that she rarely interacted with; he only came home to eat his meals and sleep. Some weeks he wouldn't come home at all. Other weeks he would spend three days sleeping. Lina's mother did not have an education and therefore could not work. When he came home for dinner it was the same routine every time—her mother and father fighting about money. However, this time on Lina's twelfth birthday, the fight was a little different.

"You spent your whole week's pay again!?" She heard her mother yell.

"You know how much I am struggling right now! If I don't use this money, I will get sick and I will not be able to work."

"But how will we eat? You have a wife and a daughter to feed. You support your drug habit more than your family!"

"Lina is a young woman now; she is starting to develop a body. We can marry her off. I know many wealthy men who will take her."

"She is our youngest daughter and you already married off her two older sisters to pay your debts. What will happen when we are in this situation again and you have no more daughters to give away?"

Lina covered her ears. She did not want to hear any more of this conversation; she did not want to face her fate that her father laid out for her. *Why do I have to be punished for my father's addiction? Why must my father take advantage of the fact that I am a female and treat me like a piece of property, auctioning me off to support his habit?* These thoughts raced through Lina's head as she looked out her bedroom window, watching the sun slowly disappear below the distant horizon.

The next day, Lina put on her sneakers and shorts, preparing to play outside with the other children. But before she could step out the door, her mother stopped her.

"You are becoming a woman, Lina. You can no longer play outside with the boys and wear dirty shorts. You must learn to be a modest woman," her mother said to her as she gave Lina a long black dress to put on.

"But I do not want to wear this! It will cover my whole body. I want to feel the sun on my skin!"

"I am sorry Lina, but you are to get married soon. No man will marry an exposed girl. Please clean yourself up and put this on Lina. You must prepare for a guest we are having over for dinner."

When the guest arrived that night, Lina felt her heart sink. He was a large, older man, about thirty years old—and Lina was his bride to be. She cried and begged her parents not to sell her away to this repulsive man named Sayid, but despite her crying, her wedding day eventually came.

The wedding took place in a courtyard at Sayid's extravagant home on a hot and dry summer day. With her long gown and *hijab* on, Lina looked up at the blinding sun, longing for the warmth on her skin and knowing that she'd never feel it again. The butterflies in her stomach were of disgust and nervousness. Her eyes became blurry, filling with tears, and as a single tear rolled down her face, something out of the corner of her eye caught her attention. It was a small figure darting around the courtyard. Finally it stopped right in front of Lina's eyes on the branch of a tree. It was a small yellow bird that calmly sat in the tree, observing the commotion going on around it. The bright yellow color of the animal intrigued her; it reminded her of the sun. The bird turned its head and locked eyes with Lina, then immediately flew away into the hot sky. Lina had never seen a yellow bird before; she wondered where it came from and where it was going.

A few weeks passed and the days grew longer and darker as Lina stayed trapped inside her husband's house. She was no longer allowed to attend school because her new responsibilities included cleaning, cooking, and doing whatever Sayid ordered. Every night when Sayid came home, he scolded Lina for forgetting to clean a spot of dirt, or not putting enough spice in his meal—every time was a different reason. At the end of the night when they went to bed, she resisted his advances which often lead to her being hit and having to endure forceful sex. *When will this end? My body aches and my stomach is hungry,* Lina thought to herself.

One night, while Lina lay awake in bed, in pain from her husband's abuse while he slept tight, she heard a high-pitched sound outside the bedroom window. Slowly and quietly she walked up to the window and gazed outside. The full moon in the sky that night illuminated a yellow bird. *It's the bird! I cannot believe it came back!* Smiling through the glass, Lina sat and watched the bird until it flew away. This bird was free, free to go wherever it pleased, free to be independent. So why did it often make an appearance at such a suppressed household? It flew in the sky above the city, never feeling the constraint of the people in it. It was capable of leaving the city and traveling to new places without consequences. Lina admired the bird and its freedom.

Lina woke up in the morning and started her same routine of chores. Sayid left the house for work and an hour later Lina left as well despite his orders not to. She walked downtown to the hospital that one of her older sisters worked at. With her sister's assistance she walked up to the roof of the tall building. On top of the building she could see her whole city around her and beyond that. Beyond the city were mountains and deserts, places she had never been. These unknown territories were her independence and freedom, yet she knew she could never reach them. She wanted to be like the bird and fly to wherever she wished. Lina unveiled herself atop the roof of the building. The sun beating down her body made her feel warm and happy, a happiness that she knew she could never feel again. She wanted to feel pain and sadness no more; she wanted this one ounce of happiness to last forever. She looked over the city, imagining how it would feel to fly with the sun and wind gliding across her body. Lina stepped to the edge of the building and imagined herself flying away as she closed her eyes and jumped.

The Guitar
Brian Monahan

I always wanted to play the guitar, even though the leaders of Saudi Arabia deemed it a sin to play Western music. I had a friend who had learned to play the guitar and was a part of a metal band, and he tried to show me how to play the instrument a couple of times. He's gone now, though; he was forced to leave Saudi Arabia with his band after a gig went wrong, and the police arrested the band.

After that, I was determined to get my own guitar and learn how to play. If I could join a band, that would have been even cooler, but first I had to learn the instrument. Actually, first I had to find someplace that sold instruments. Then I would have to figure out how to hide it from my parents.

So one afternoon, I walked to a shop in my hometown of Khobar, off in a more discreet area of the city. I had been to this shop once before, with my friend who played guitar. This was a bootleg store which sold a lot of items that are not allowed in Khobar or Saudi Arabia as a whole. My friend bought a couple of metal albums that day, and I noticed that the shop owner sold a couple of guitars. Though I didn't buy anything that day, I felt that I would be back someday soon.

I walked into the shop that afternoon, and my ears were greeted with the sound of heavy metal playing from a CD player on the counter. The singer was shouting lyrics behind two thunderous electric guitars, a thumping bass guitar, and some of the fastest drumming I have ever heard. I walked up to the counter and asked the shop owner, "Excuse me sir, but who are these guys?"

"This is Slayer, kid," the shop owner replied, and he molded his fingers into what I learned was something called the devil's horns. "These guys are the shit. In my long time of collecting Western music, I have never heard anything as awesome as Slayer, but if you take a look around here, sonny, you might find something even better."

"I was actually hoping to buy a guitar," I said to the shop owner, and I pointed to the guitar behind his head. It was a sleek black guitar with the body crafted into a V. The shop owner turned around and looked at the guitar, and then looked back at me.

"Have you ever played guitar?"

"I had a friend teach me how to hold one and use a pick."

"But you don't know any chords?" The shop owner was amused by my assertion.

"No, but I figure I can just play the guitar and get good."

The shop owner laughed and put his hand on my shoulder. "Listen, sonny, if you want to get good at playing the guitar, let me show you a few things."

The shop owner took the guitar down from the hooks holding it to the wall. He took the Slayer CD out of the CD player, and he put in a different disc: *Master of Puppets* by Metallica. The shop owner skipped a couple of tracks ahead, and when he found the one he wanted, he pressed play. For the next six minutes, I listened to the shop owner play along with the band, playing most of the notes perfectly. When the song ended, I clapped and the shop owner bowed his head in appreciation.

"That was amazing," I said to him as the next song played.

The shop owner put the guitar back on the wall. "Thank you. I was taught how to play guitar during my travels in America, which is why I started this shop up. This collection of music is from my travels as well. I recommend you try and travel if you can, since the music interests you. It's the one unfortunate law of the land here—pop culture must be Arabic in a way."

"Can you teach my how to play the guitar?" I asked him.

"I can teach you a little bit to get you started, and if you feel like you've learned enough, I will sell you the guitar and a few CDs so you can play along and learn more."

"Thank you."

For the next two hours, the shop owner—who I learned was named Firas—showed me the basics of the guitar. He taught me some of the basic chords for most songs, as well as fingering positions for other popular chords in metal songs. He taught me about strumming with the pick and how to strum the strings really fast, as well as how to palm mute the strings for some songs. Finally, he showed me some other little techniques like tapping and trilling to help me get started. I was a quick study, getting all of these things down pretty easily, and by the end of the two hours, I was beginning to play the beginning of Slayer's "South of Heaven."

"I am impressed, I truly am," Firas said to me. "I shall give you a discount on the guitar, and I shall let you take a couple of CDs for free. Make me proud, sonny."

I thanked Firas for the guitar, and I browsed through the store until I picked up Metallica's *Master of Puppets*, Slayer's *Seasons in the Abyss,* and Iron Maiden's *The Number of the Beast*. When I was done, I thanked Firas one last time and I made my way home. Luckily mother and father were not around, so I was able to sneak the guitar and music into my room and play on the guitar for a while until they arrived home.

For the next few weeks, I would only listen to my music and play the guitar while no one was home. I was afraid of how my mother and father would react to the guitar. My father, Mohammed, was an old religious man who took Islam to the heart. He was an *imam*, and while he loved me very much, he always made sure that I was following the Quran perfectly. My mother, on the other hand, was not as strict, but she followed my father and obeyed his wishes. While Mohammed allowed my mother, Alima, to work and be a little more Western, she was expected to be a mother and wife first and foremost. Her duties to my father made it harder for me to play the guitar and get better, since she was home most of the day. Whenever she went out for any reason, I would get the instrument out from under my bed.

For practice, I would take the guitar out and just play around with it for a bit. I would see how fast I could strum the guitar, and I would try to figure out what chords sounded good and what chords did not. After that little warm up, I would bust out the CD player and my bootlegs, and I would get to work learning these songs. I started out easy, trying to learn "Welcome Home (Sanitarium)" by Metallica, and I was steadily getting better. After a couple of days, I could play through the introduction and I had learned the first solo, and was starting on the first verse. At the same time, I didn't want to learn only one song at a time, so I worked on "The Prisoner" by Iron Maiden, which I found was really fun to play. After a few weeks, I had learned most of both of those songs, as well as a couple of others. I had yet to start working on learning Slayer songs because those two guitarists sounded a lot faster.

One day, I forgot that my sister Salma was still home when I took out the guitar and started playing. She came into my room to see what I was doing, and when I saw her standing there at my doorway, I froze. Salma looked like your average Saudi sixteen-year-old, cloaked from head to toe in dark-colored clothing. The only part of her skin which was visible was her face, and she still had a small bruise on it from where Father had hit her a couple of days ago for forgetting to veil herself when she and Mother went shopping. My sister and I were close when we were children, but as we grew up, and our gender differences got in the way, she looked at me with contempt, and I understood why. Mother and Father loved me and would do anything for me, while Salma was rejected most of the time since she was a girl. I felt sorry for her, and I tried to help her whenever I could.

"What are you doing?" Salma asked me. "Do mother and father know you have that thing?"

"No, Salma, they don't," I continued to play with the guitar.

"Hakim, they will forbid you to play this thing if they see you."

"Probably, but that's why I won't let them see it."

I continued to play the guitar, popping in a CD while Salma continued to stand there and watch. She saw me playing along with my music, and I could see that she was impressed by my skill.

"How long have you had this thing?" she asked after a while.

"'This thing' is called a guitar, and I've had it for a couple of weeks now," I replied. "I only play it when no one is home, so that Mother and Father don't take it away. I know how they would feel seeing me play this. But Salma, you must understand, this is the one thing right now that gives me pleasure in life here. Music has become my everything."

Salma nodded her head and continued listening to me play. After a little bit, she asked, "Hakim, can you teach me how to play?"

"I guess I could, but not today, Mother and Father could be home soon, and knowing father, he would be disgusted to see me teach you this."

"Oh, I know he'd hate it, but I don't care what he thinks anymore," Salma said, and the anger in her words made me recoil.

"Salma, those are words of blasphemy."

"Then tell Father, Hakim."

She walked over to me and sat down on my bed. She kissed me on the cheek and continued, "Little brother, you don't understand the pain and suffering I live through every day. You are a man—you have everything. I am a growing woman who is steadily losing everything. Learning guitar will give me pleasure like it has to you. And if Mother and Father find out, I'll face the consequences like I do with everything else."

For the next couple of days, whenever both Salma and I were home alone, I would teach her how to play the guitar. Like Firas before me, I taught her basic chords, how to hold the pick and strum the guitar, and some other little things. She was a fast learner, and after a couple of days she had already begun learning how to play "The Thing That Should Not Be" by Metallica.

However, one day we lost track of time, and we didn't hear our father walk in the house. He walked up to my room, and when he opened the door, he saw Salma with the guitar in hand and me watching her.

"Salma, what in the name of Allah are you doing?" Mohammed shouted at her.

"Playing the guitar," she replied happily, and she continued to play. Mohammed walked into the room and grabbed the guitar from her.

"And where did you get this devil's instrument?" he continued to shout.

"It's mine, Father," I spoke up, hoping to deflect some of his anger on to me and help Salma.

Our father turned to me and said, "Hakim, you should know better than to use the devil's tools, and teaching them to Salma? Son, I am disappointed in you." Our father walked over to me and slapped me. He then walked back over to Salma and punched her in the stomach. My sister doubled over in pain.

"And you, you should learn your place." Father walked out of the room, leaving the guitar at the door.

I walked over to Salma, expecting to console her, but she was not crying. Instead, she had a look of anger in her eyes.

"That was it. Hakim, I'm running away, and I am never coming back."

"Salma, don't. You'll never make it anywhere you go."

"Anything is better than being here. I will try to get to America. Hopefully things will be better there. I will sneak out tonight."

I took the guitar from the door and gave it to her. "Sell this for money. I can get another one, and I want to help you."

"Thank you little brother." Salma gave me a kiss on the cheek, and we hugged one last time. That night, I heard the front door open and close, and I knew that Salma was gone forever.

When my father came home that day and saw that I was not playing the guitar, he asked me, "What happened to your infernal instrument?"

"Salma ran away and took it with her. They're gone," I still had my head in my hands, and a few tears remained on my face.

"Good. Praise Allah that I don't have to listen to that devil's tool ever again," he replied to me, and he left my room.

Angels
Haleigh Morgan

Growing up as a child were my happy days, filled with simplicity and joy. I often would play with my neighbor, Atif, dancing and laughing in the summer heat until we could hear our mother's yells for us to come for supper. We would pretend we were the greatest detectives of Cairo, investigating and exploring anything we could, many times getting into trouble.

One cloudy afternoon, we stumbled into something larger than we could comprehend. We had always seen young girls go into a small home covered in vines and overgrown plants. I remember looking at the girls entering, their faces white with fear. Atif and I had heard screaming coming from that home, so we went to investigate the house. We crawled through the dry grass and peeked through an opening in the window. I used Atif as a stool to peek through the window. The room was covered in Quranic verses, but when my eyes wandered more, all I saw was red, and I fainted. I was woken by Atif who helped me to my feet and we walked back home without saying a word.

I was home early for dinner that night. I got scolded by my mother for not touching my food, but the sight of the knife sent a pain through my body that I could not bear. I had to do all of the dishes as punishment that night, but I still did not touch the knives.

When it was time for bed, I quietly removed myself from my sheet and slipped into the darkness of my home, tiptoeing past my parents' room, where they were sound asleep. I went outside, hopping through the grass to Atif's house and tapped on the window that belonged to him. I told him I needed to leave, and we disappeared into the night to an abandoned shed that we had once investigated.

Once we arrived, we sat inside on buckets and old crates. I felt my heartbeat grow faster and faster. "Atif, I need to tell you why I fell when I saw that little girl through the window. The room with the Quranic verses, and angels of purity stood around the young girl in dark robes." I told him about the river of red that ran through the dark room, and the angels with knives that cut away sins. I told him the loud screams were the sins leaving the little girl, leaving her pure and untouched for a man to marry her someday.

When we went back home, I said a prayer before I fell asleep. I said a prayer that the angels wouldn't come to purify me, and prayed they would let me remain whole.

Salimah
Julia Nittler

The sun breaks the darkness reaching over the horizon. Roosters coax it further out with their crows. As the sun rises further up in the sky it casts its rays across the land. Its golden reach makes diamonds out of dew.

Salimah discreetly slips back under her covers and closes her eyes. She tries to slow her breathing. She tries to seem as if she has been in a deep dreaming sleep for the whole night. For she knows that her mother will be in shortly to wake her up. She must not know.

Her mother enters the room with little regard to her sleeping. She yells from the doorway, "Wake up Salimah! You lazy girls would sleep all day if I let you."

She proceeds to pull open the drapes and removes the warm shroud of covers blanketing Salimah's body. Salimah has little choice but to sit up and swing her feet over the edge of the bed. It is only then that her mother retreats from her room, shouting on her way out, "Today is a big day! Hurry up and get dressed, you do not want to be late!"

Why is her mother always in a hurry? Why must she always push her around like this? Why today of all days?

Salilmah meanders over to the bureau where her clothes have already been laid out. Not just any clothes, but her wedding dress. The floor length mirror on her wall waylays her progress. Like a rabbit caught in a trap, she is stuck. Her gaze fixes on the eyes in the mirror. These are the same eyes she sees every day, yet today there is something different about them.

She steps back and takes in the whole mirror. Her naked body stands before her. Her olive skin is glistening with perspiration, but other than that she is still the same girl. Her supple breasts, buttock, and raven black hair sit the same way they always have. She has seen everything in that mirror the same as it is today a million times before. Yet her eyes are different.

They are not swollen from crying or droopy from not getting enough sleep. There is a hint of knowledge in them that has not been there before. A secret is hidden within them. A secret held deep within those eyes and the eyes of one other. Other than that the change in her is undetectable.

She hears her female relatives stirring in the kitchen. She rushes to get dressed. They must not know.

When she finishes dressing herself, the mirror catches her again. Still she is the same, only now she is wearing a pretty dress. Her aunts, cousins, sisters, and mother all come rushing into the room like a sandstorm—unwanted, loud, irritating, and destructive. One of her aunts yells, "Salimah where is your makeup?

We must make you look good for your husband."

Her mother has already found the makeup and is pushing her way to the front of the crowd. She hastily pushes it into her sister's hands so that she can help Salimah, and leaves the room to search for something else. She returns with a box that is nicely wrapped. With a single tear she shoves it into Salimah's lap and says, "Your father and I bought you a present. Go ahead and open it! We never thought this day would come."

Salimah averts her gaze to roll her eyes so she does not seem ungrateful. She then proceeds to open the present. She finds a plethora of jewelry inside. She looks at her mother and says, "You shouldn't have. This is too much. I can not accept this."

Her mother looks at her and says, "Don't be silly! Every woman needs to look pleasing for her husband on her wedding night, and men do not like plain women. We just want you to be happy."

Salimah reluctantly embraces her mother and thanks her. The gift is not one that she deserves, but she takes it anyway. After all, everything she is doing is for her family and not for herself. She loves them more than anything, but she hates the rut of tradition that they are stuck in. They will sit there and rot while the world around them changes. They want her to be happy, yet they do not know what happy means.

Her parents had always had a cordial marriage. No one was used or abused. But there was no love. Sure they made three beautiful daughters, and a son. Salimah could only assume that they were together for the business of it and not the pleasure of it. They never kissed or hugged in front of anyone. What happened in their bedroom was noiseless and passionless. Salimah had wanted something different. She had had something different.

Her wedding comes and goes, and the wedding night goes about without a hitch. She bleeds on the sheets, and her father displays them like a victory flag up and down the streets of her town. She is married.

As she leaves her wedding bed, with her sleeping husband lying in the sheets, she closes herself in the bathroom. There is a mirror there much like the one in her childhood bedroom. She stands naked before it. The eyes are there again. Only this time nothing in the mirror is familiar to her. Her skin no longer glows, her breasts sag, and she looks as if she was a piece of leather lying in the desert sun. Her eyes are empty. She has nothing left.

How has she changed so quickly? What did he do to her?

She no longer feels passion. There is no lust. She is stuck in the same rut that her parents are in. She left all notions of escaping that rut when she married her husband and not the boy that she had snuck out of her room to see each night. She will never know what it feels like to have him inside of her and not her husband. She will never know what it is like to have him kiss her in places that an unfamiliar man should not kiss a woman. She feels ugly.

That morning the sun does not break the darkness by peaking over the horizon. The roosters' crows sound like wailing women and the dew no longer sits like diamonds on the land.

Salimah steps into the bath. With warm water and soap she is determined to scrub away this feeling. She scrubs until her skin is raw and the soap and water stings. That is when her head becomes heavy and she holds it in her hands, sobbing. She sobs not because she was no longer a virgin, but because she is stuck in the same rut that her parents are in. She has become everything that she had not wanted to become. She sits there and sobs because her love for her parents and their traditions overcame her love for the only man she had ever loved and would ever love until the day that she dies. And so she cries.

Against Their Will
Eric Pacelli

It was rare to ever see them apart. After school, they would meet up and play until they were called for dinner, and then they would part ways, promising to see each other again the next day. They spent every afternoon running around, playing games, neither of them ever running out of energy. He looked forward to this every day and spent his time in school imagining what they might play later that day. This went on for years, every day laughing and running around until it was time for them to go back home.

But one day, she wasn't there to meet him after school. He waited around all afternoon, hoping that she was running late and would be there soon, but she never showed up. Finally he had to admit that she wasn't going to be there, and so he walked home alone, on the verge of tears. When he arrived, his mother could tell that he was upset and asked him what was wrong. He explained how she had never shown up to play after school, and his mother realized what had happened. She explained that they were nine years old now, and that her father would have stopped allowing them to play together. He was confused; why would how old they were affect if they could play together? But his mother refused to explain any further, so he ran to his room and cried until he finally fell asleep.

Years later, the two of them were still very close and spent a lot of time together, even though they no longer played together the way that they once had. He now understood the reasons behind her father forbidding them to play together, but every day, he wondered why there was such horrible discrimination towards women. No matter how hard he tried, he couldn't comprehend how other people saw women as inferior to men, or why they needed to stay covered up while in public. To him, it seemed unfair that she was forced away from the things she enjoyed, simply because other people didn't find it acceptable. But try as he might, he was never able to convince her father to change his mind, and he thought that it would be useless to try to reform society; he was still young and would be ignored. Still, he hoped that one day things would change and be the way that they should be.

It was the day of his wedding, but he wasn't happy like he should have been. He cared for his bride-to-be, but all he really wanted was to be marrying her, the girl he had known for years and spent all that time with long ago. But she was already married to another man, one whom her parents found suitable for her, without even asking what she had wanted. They had talked since her wedding, and she despised her life with the other man and wished that she could leave him. But if she did, she would be seen as dishonorable, and so she was forced to stay with somebody she did not love, instead of being with him, as they both wished they could be. Instead, they had to be miserable in the lives that were set out for them, with few options available for them to take in an attempt to make themselves happy.

As he prepared for his wedding, he made a resolution to himself that he would spend the rest of his life doing whatever he could to end the horrible discrimination that had been the cause of the unhappiness that both he and the woman he loved were unfairly forced to deal with.

Author
Nicholas Pearson

For as long as she could remember, her family had always been traveling through that desert. Her mother, her father, her brother, and, of course, herself. They always had enough food, they always had enough water, and the camel atop which her father and brother rode never seemed to tire. Over time, she herself had even developed an impressive resilience to the stubborn weight and cling of the sand. Because she always walked, she had to. Through the long days, she and her mother always walked while her father and brother rode in comfort. But when she was small she never had to walk. Her mother would carry her on her back, wrapped in cloth, the gentle bobbing of her footsteps often soothing her to sleep.

Looking back, she realized how much of the world she missed by being asleep. And how strong her mother had been. It couldn't have been easy. But now she walked alongside her mother, sharing the load. As harsh as the journey could be, she quite enjoyed walking. It was liberating. That physical contact with the world and the verification of her own presence in it. It was a confirmation of a world that she could explore and behold. But drinking in all of that beauty and life felt almost to be in vain as her account would never be remembered in her own words.

Everything the family saw, everything they experienced, was committed to the scrolls, their personal scrolls. One scroll for each of the four of them. And responsible for maintaining all four was her father and her father alone. Her brother had not yet learned to do so on his own, and as women, she and her mother were not considered fit to keep the script. As a child, it had made little difference to her. But as she grew older, with the world becoming more and more complex and intriguing, her curiosity grew with her. And with the passing of the first oasis, her curiosity began to spill over.

A crisp draft cut through the warm desert air and kissed her face; vibrant green, unlike any hue she had ever seen, swallowed her vision, and the gentle churn of running water tickled her ears. Captivated and inspired, she asked her father for her scroll, proclaiming a desire to write for herself. Her father was surprised at this, but regarded her request with little seriousness, maintaining that she lacked the capacity. He tried to brush her off, but she persisted. Instead of punishing her, he decided to humor her. After handing her a quill, an inkwell, and finally her scroll, with a smug grin on his face, he motioned for her to begin. Almost overcome with joy, she wasted no time in scratching excitedly into the parchment's surface.

Immediately, she realized that something was wrong. Her words would not appear. She dipped the quill into the inkwell again and thrust it back onto the page, but still nothing. She dipped it yet again, and again there was nothing. With greater deliberation, she immersed the quill a fourth time then held it up close to her eyes for inspection. There was something wrong with the ink. Before she could assess any further, her father reclaimed the scroll and snatched the utensils from her grasp, ridiculing her for her foolishness. They packed up and went on their way, leaving the oasis behind. Puzzled and defeated, she had no choice but to yield.

More oases began to punctuate their trek with increasing regularity and spectacle, each was larger and lusher than the last. Months passed, tumbling then years, and the weight of her stolen authorship was becoming unbearable. To see so many things, think so many thoughts, and feel so many sensations and to then be denied a voice with which to share those wonderful things was suffocating. The very last that she could withstand came the day the suitor arrived. It was early morning, the sun had not yet totally escaped the pull of the horizon. Her father was quite pleased with the young man, won over by the skilled composition of his script, and he proceeded to offer his daughter's hand in marriage, her scroll with it.

Never mind that she had just met the young man and had no interest in marrying him—she would be damned before she let another dictate her script before she held that authority for herself. She requested another chance to prove her ability. Her father teased, reminding her of her past failure, but she vehemently insisted. Sensitive to the judgments of the young suitor, her father denied her absolutely. But fairly amused at the idea, the suitor persuaded him otherwise. Her father handed her a quill, an inkwell, and finally the scroll. He and the suitor grinned smug grins as she began.

Unwavering in her conviction, she dipped the quill and began. Eyes shut in concentration, she let the quill dance and flick across the parchment. Upon opening her eyes, a great dread fell over her as she saw that its surface remained empty, save for a mess of black crumbs. She couldn't believe it. Why? Why again? She lifted the quill and ran her finger across its blackened tip. Dry. The same as before. Then she looked to the inkwell fixing her gaze for a long moment. Her father advanced to take it from her, but she was faster and swept it up first. The inkwell was dry. It was dry now and it had been dry years ago. She looked to her father, a glint of anger in her eyes, as he peered arrogantly right back at her. Her mother hung her head in quiet sadness and the suitor's smug grin had yet to leave his face.

Abandoning her grip, she let the inkwell fall onto the desert floor. Within her, swells of curiosity and longing had transformed into broken waves of fury and determination. She would have her scroll.

Without another moment of hesitation, she raised the quill into the air and plunged it deep into the palm of her hand. Together, her father and the suitor wore faces of shock and disgust. Warm blood pulsed from the wound, dripping and pattering into the sand at her feet. She removed the quill, soaked it to the core, and realized her thoughts in vibrant red script on the surface of the scroll:

"*I saw the sun rise*"

A smile on her face, she looked to her mother who smiled more radiantly as had ever been seen. She held the script high and spoke. "This story is mine. I and I alone will tell it and I will sooner die than have it taken from me."

All were silent.

Hope
John Pettit

It is now time to escape. As the sky fades to black, I return to my room. There is nowhere to go, no one to talk to. The flame in the corner of the room flickers and casts an eerie shadow of someone who used to resemble me. I crawl back into my bed, hoping that the covers would provide some comfort and warmth, which is nonexistent ever since the day that I left home, my home. I cling on to every second that I am here, because for these few seconds, I can dream.

That is…until he shows back up. The door slams, and my heart sinks. I am but a lonely prisoner trapped in a world in which I don't belong. I am but a mere possession which is caged, clothed, and fed. There is no connection between me and Abosali.

He calls my name. "Qailah!" He shouts, but I don't respond.

I pretend to be asleep, eyes forced shut as I try to escape into another world. Escape to a world where I do not feel his cold hands against my body. I am still asleep. The very thought of him next to me sends chills throughout my body; I become numb. Tonight I escape through the darkness as the candle is snuffed. Into my dreams I fade, for the morning is yet another day under his rule.

As I slip out of consciousness, I began to regress to a time full of light and happiness. It was only yesterday when I was young and in love. I did not yet speak to this man and yet I trusted him. He was to be my husband. The setting was beautiful, the sky was like a somber ember burning in the distance. My family and friends all gathered around as I awaited the ceremony. I was adorned with spectacular gold pieces, so much that at times it was hard to move. I was just…. happy, but I didn't know why. Maybe it was the atmosphere. I had no fear of the future, I only had hope. As I walked towards my soon to be husband, I caught a glimmer in his eye.

This must be what love is, I thought to myself. My father was next to my husband, smiling and proud. The sheikh was the one who was going to read the words of the prophet. He spoke about how Muhammad honored his wives, how a husband should honor a woman, and how women should their husband. Abosali and my father both accept the words of the sheikh, and we are now married as husband and wife.

That night was something I will never forget. My family rejoicing, there was dancing and soft drinks for the guests. But we left before the party was over, and as we left the party and returned home I saw something. Those eyes, there was something else hidden behind them that I did not see earlier that day. This is where the dream ends, and my nightmare begins.

Every day I wake up to find that my dream is just a far distant memory. I still am trapped, spending most of my day in silent protest of the situation that I have found myself in. I wish so badly to go back to the time when smiling took no effort. When my day was filled with light and exuberance, when I was alive. Day by day I push forth, allowing for our marriage to deteriorate. I wish there was something that I could do. Something to make us close once again. I understand that I may not be able to leave this situation, but I believe that there is a great man somewhere deep inside my husband. Somewhere there is the man with the eyes that I saw on my wedding day. I just need to find a way to talk to him, to let him know that I want this to work. I want to be able to share with him my thoughts and feelings, I want to be able to open myself up and let him in. I know that it is not likely that I can escape, but what I can do is make the most of the situation I am in.

I wait quietly at the table for him to return home. I am nervous, shaking, and unsure if this is something that I was prepared for, or that he was prepared for. But I know for sure that this is something that has to be done, for both of us. As I hear the creak of the door, I freeze, and everything becomes tense. I have prepared the whole day, practicing what I'm going to say, but in an instant I go blank.

Standing in the doorway is Abosali. As he towers above me, "As-salaam alaykum (Peace be upon you)," he says.

I am about to bow my head as I have for countless days and months before, but something rises deep within me, and I begin to speak. It is my turn, my chance to let him know how I really feel. "Please sit down, Abosali, I need to talk to you."

Confused and concerned, he stays where he is.

I urge him to sit. "Min fadlak (please), ana bahibak (I love you)."

Surprised and confused he sits down. I express to him my concern that I am a mere object to him, a possession. That every day since we have been married he has been more focused on my body than on what I have to say. I tell him how I want to be close to him, but it is hard to live with someone that I see as a stranger. I remind him of that wonderful day, our wedding, that night when I stood in front of him and my father, that I saw something within him, I saw a man with a kind heart and soul.

"I was so innocent then, and I believe you were too, Abosali," I exclaim. "Let's be children again and become closer as husband and wife, embracing each other's idea's and dreams and supporting each other. Let us stop the silence and begin to talk, we can make this work, Abosali." I promise him that, as we begin to connect intellectually, the more we will connect and attract physically.

I sit quietly as he sits there silent and frozen. I believe he is processing the harsh reality of what I had told him. I am scared, but hopeful that he will understand, that he will not take my words the wrong way.

Out of the silence, in pain he whispers, "Ana bahibek jiddan (I love you very much)," as a tear rolls down his cheek. I smile, and come closer to him.

At that very moment time stops as we hold each other. I feel as if I was dreaming.

"Ishta'tillak (I missed you)," I whisper. In this moment I have hope, that one day my words would become a reality. This night we do not try to say much more, for our eyes tell our story. One thing is for sure, I see this night the man that was there on my wedding night. I can see it and this time I can also feel it. He does not try and make any advances to me that night; instead, he holds my hand softly as we slowly drift off to sleep. My eyes dance around the room and the candle in the corner of the room flickers. I am excited, hopeful. Come tomorrow I will know for sure, whether I will wake up to my dream come true, or if I will fade back into my nightmare.

Mixed Realities
Chelsea Raftery

The fire blazed on, never dying down enough for me to breathe. The walls cave in on me, crushing me, making me small. Past the fire I see eyes watching me, not helping. One set of eyes is helpless. The rest were blank and dark, watching. I cry for help, but not even I can hear the scream trying to escape my tiny little mouth.

Every time I close my eyes, I see a light. I picture what it would be like if my life was different. When I close my eyes, I can feel the wind in my hair. When I close my eyes, I can feel the sunlight on my skin and it feels inviting. My skin is cool. I sing my favorite song; the beautiful sound radiating through the air. I feel the desire that I always long for. He looks at me like I am the most beautiful woman on this earth. I can feel how much he loves me just by looking into his eyes.

But that is all just a dream. There is no desire. There is no wind in my hair. He does not look at me like I am the only thing that matters to him. I am invisible. I am invisible until it's time for him to control me. He tells me he loves me, but his actions tell me differently.

I was given to a man whom my father had chosen for me. I pleaded with him not to abandon me and give me to this strange, older man. I was only twelve at the time, my breasts just beginning to develop. I was still trying to understand why I needed to be covered from head to toe.

When I was younger, my mother would tell me stories about what life would be like once I got older, like it was a fairytale. "One day, when you are mature, you are going to marry a handsome man. You will bear him children, giving him the son he always wanted. He will take care of you."

At the time it sounded nice, but now it doesn't. This is more like a prison. I love my children, but they came from an arrangement that I did not agree to. I tried to fall in love with my husband but now the only time we speak is when he tells me when he wants me to sleep with him or he yells at me when I don't make his dinner the right way. He treats the boys special, leaving the girls to help me with the housework. That was how it was growing up in my house, but there is something wrong here.

I want to break the traditions. I am afraid that if I say something he will hit me. I want to feel again, like when I was little and didn't have any responsibilities. Everything changed when I was told I needed to dress more modestly. The *hijab* is something that has been passed down through generations of both sides of my family, but *why do I feel like it is weighing me down? Why do I feel like it is separating me from the world in which I was placed?* These are thoughts that I keep to myself. My voice is one that should never be heard. My mother would shush me every time I had a question about the things that I was required to do. My laughter was stolen from me. My curiosity abducted. My smile stitched away.

I want to know what it feels like to be happy. I want to feel pleasure and do what makes me feel good. I feel numb and lifeless. *What happened to me? How did I become like this? How could my mother, of all people, allow this to happen?* She knows my pain. I have seen her go through similar experiences as I am right now. I know she loves me and she is doing what is expected of her.

I learned to try and make myself live through the pain by learning to empower myself. I am too used to agreeing to all of the bad treatment that is thrust upon me. My brother used to tell me that I could do and be whatever I wanted. He was the only one who wanted me to be something other than a wife. He told me about getting an education for girls and that it is possible, but when I brought it up to my father, he shut me down right away. He says that men don't like educated women. They talk back and I would never get married if he allowed me to go.

The fire blazed on, never dying down enough for me to breathe. The walls cave in on me, crushing me, making me small. Past the fire I see eyes watching me, not helping. One set of eyes was helpless. The rest were blank and dark, watching. I cry for help, but not even I can hear the scream trying to escape my tiny little mouth. This wasn't a dream. This is my reality.

Transformation
Jocelyn Sargent

Behind that sweet exterior lies a pit of darkness. Darkness full of monsters, demons who possess him. They're like a nightmare he can't wake up from, even with open eyes. He struggles to fight the monsters, but they often win.

Days full of stress or frustration lead to no sunlight, just darkness. I try to calm them, but there's no use. The shock across my face silences my attempts at breaking silence. The monsters never cease to surprise me with their iciness. Could that really be my husband in there? That monster is not the man I married—he would never strike me.

The way things started out, other Arab women would always look at me green with envy. The happiness of our marriage was so real I could taste it, and I've never had anything sweeter. When I first met him, there was no love, as he was not my first choice. Love grew like a tree from its roots as I got to know him. There was this almost immediate bond that formed once I began to notice the gentle manner of this once stranger. He spoke to me with manners that I had never seen from other Arab men; it felt like what I imagine respect feels like.

I had been brought up knowing to cook and clean, and performed these duties without even thinking about them, though I had a lot to learn in the cooking department. The first meal I cooked for him, I had gotten carried away cleaning while it was on the stove and it burnt. Fear instantly overwhelmed me and I lost all control. What kind of wife can't cook a proper meal for her husband?! My sobbing was interrupted before I could even think of a plan as to what to do next by an embrace of his arms. It was startling at first, but then the comfort I felt in his arms seemed as natural as breathing.

I was brought up hearing horror stories of new marriages and there was even a point in time where my shock stopped. I no longer thought it unusual for women to get beaten and consistently raped by their husbands, as that is the norm, and you should always be a perfect wife—clean, cook and produce as many baby boys as you can. This fear of men developed over time, and the thought that there could be a man out there to change that was bewildering. The beginning of our marriage is where I found happiness. Maybe I was just a fool for thinking that it could last.

I often find myself spacing out and thinking to myself how foolish it was to think that I could have a different life than all other Arab women, as if I was better than all the others. It didn't take long for my husband to show his inner demons. You can only pretend to be happy for so long before that shiny exterior starts to crack. The first time he hit me it was like an explosion and I could feel it throughout my body. The awe I had burned like fire, and for a minute I could feel the hell that he was in. I said goodbye to my own demon, which had given me false hope and said hello to his dark side. He had only hit me once that time

The first hit was followed by flowers and sincerity. It wasn't like an Arab man to ask for forgiveness, but he was so good at it. When I re-envisioned it later in my daydreams, he would always bring me a big, fresh bouquet of flowers and get on his knees and beg for my forgiveness. It never quite went like this, but his words of sweet, sweet poetry always made me forgive him.

After he first hit me, there was a long stage of happiness where he spent his time being kind, as I could tell he still felt remorse. I think of these periods as what the Americans would call the 'Honeymoon Stage,' as it was like a dream, where everything went the way it should be. It's like we were just playing house, and it would never end.

Dark emotions built up and there was no way to get rid of them. I could see his inner self becoming darker and knew of dark times ahead, but chose to ignore them, as ignorance is bliss. Once again, I had messed up while cooking dinner, and this time was not the same. I was shaken more than I ever thought humanly possible. There was no way I could pretend that this didn't happen. He couldn't even deal with how far he took it this time and left the house immediately. I didn't see him for two days. They were the longest days of my life. I was so sore the next day that I could barely do my chores. The only thing that gave me the strength to do them was the fear of getting beaten again. I don't know if my body could take any further pain.

My life after that consisted of me walking on eggshells, trying not to do anything wrong so I wouldn't get another smacking. Just thinking about getting rocked that hard again made my body ache. I couldn't believe he was capable of such consistent behavior. How does one man change into a completely different man? It was almost like I was cheating on my husband with another man. I didn't even know how to behave around him. The silence within the house was almost as heartbreaking as the idea that I used to love this man. I just wanted him to know that I understood he had monsters within him, and I could help him deal with them. I love him and I want to help him move on from those monsters. I thought, *Let me feel some of your pain for you. Let me help scare the monsters away. Just let me love you, entirely. I want the old marriage back, and the man that came with it. A typical Arab marriage is not what I want; I do not know how women put up with this. Eggshells break easily, and monsters are not as easy to scare away.*

My life is full of what ifs and paranoia. What if I burn this next meal? What if I don't finish my chores? What if I just say the wrong word? What has my life come to? How hard is he going to hit me? A new way of life has come out of my marriage, and I am now also green with envy of my past self. Each day is unclear and full of fear. Maybe one day I will find enough ignorance to mistake it for happiness.

Yearning For a New Life
Wesley Silver

Once upon a time, in a small city just west of Baghdad, Iraq, there was a young woman named Mawiyah who attended a girls-only Arabic school. It was here that she began her education with the help of her parents, who had finally given in to her nagging about taking classes like the other normal girls. However, since school wasn't something Mawiyah's parents had a strong interest in her pursuing, they limited her to taking only certain classes, such as ones involving the Qur'an or other traditional subjects. Mawiyah was nonetheless excited to even be attending school, and so she put her full heart into whatever it was that she would be allowed to learn.

As her classes went on, Mawiyah soon began to make a few friends. However, the relationships she had been making weren't very sincere, and the conversations she usually participated in were aimed more towards school than any personal interest. Mawiyah was told by her parents repetitively to not let anybody get too close to her, and this caused her to remain focused on her studies. But there was one day though that changed this, and actually, it happened to be on the first class of her second semester.

The students were beginning their new courses, and that meant that the rosters would be changing. Mawiyah was overwhelmed by the number of new faces surrounding her, and almost felt as shy as she had on her very first day. Things began like they did on any other day in the school year, and the students' names were all called for attendance. While the teacher was reading off the names though, something different happened that nobody in the room was expecting. A girl named Asmah who happened to be sitting next to Mawiyah had her name called, and in response she decided to say "present." Mawiyah and many other girls looked over immediately in shock, because they knew that it was not right for a woman to answer like that. The teacher asked to talk with her out of the classroom, and the girls all watched through the window as she reprimanded Asmah for her wrong doing. The teacher then walked back in followed by Asmah, who made a funny face behind her back, and proceeded to wink at Mawiyah as she sat back down in her seat. The rest of the class was silent and didn't react to her gesture, but Mawiyah gave a quick smile and thought until lunch about why she decided to wink at her.

As everybody sat down in the cafeteria to eat, Mawiyah was looking closely for a spot next to Asmah. Soon, the two found each other face to face, with sandwiches in their hands.

Then, Mawiyah thought closely about how to ask a question about the incident earlier, and finally leaned over the table to say, "How come you answered to your name like that?"

In response Asmah told her, "Because that's what I wanted to do."

This puzzled Mawiyah because her entire life she had been told do things according to what other people wanted, and never even thought to try and do anything her own way. It was in this moment that Mawiyah started to think differently, and she liked it. The thought of being able to do whatever you want filled her with imagination, and her mind started wandering until she eventually said back to Asmah, "So what else have you wanted to do?"

Right away that line opened up the door to a conversation that Mawiyah had never had with anyone before. It was full of new ideas, and stories that astounded her. She kept asking Asmah questions that would fill the lunch period with discussion until the bell rang for class again.

This quickly became the cycle in both of the girls' daily routines, and soon Mawiyah admitted to Asmah that she loved talking with her about everything and anything because she wasn't allowed to at home. Asmah had responded to this by saying that she wasn't allowed to either, but that she used to be able to. This made Mawiyah wonder why the girl had once been allowed to, but not anymore. And so she convinced Asmah to explain the story to her. As the words began to flow from Asmah's mouth, Mawiyah discovered the truths of her friend's past.

First, she told Mawiyah that she actually grew up in Beirut, Lebanon, and was in school there for almost ten years before she moved to Iraq. She explains how there were no uniforms, and she didn't have to wear a veil. It was a much more westernized school, and the ideas presented to her in class were much more open-minded, rather than the traditional classes she was forced to take now. Basically, she revealed that who she's living with aren't actually her parents and instead they are her grandparents. This was because, when she was fifteen, her parents were murdered while she was at school one day, and the only relatives left to take care of her were her grandparents who were very traditional, strict, and enforced the veil.

At first living with her grandparents was very difficult, but she was at an age where she had no other choice but to obey their demands. So, after a while of struggling with her thoughts and rebuttals to her grandparents' new teachings, she finally gave up trying to express them. Instead the thoughts would battle inside her mind, and often times she would lie awake at night, tossing and turning from the anxiety running through her body. Sometimes it wasn't until just before sunrise that she would cease this suffering. Luckily for her though, the sun meant it was time for her morning routine, and in an instant she would hop out of bed in excitement for her time away from home. Asmah continued, she felt trapped in her new living situation, and she hasn't been able to express herself like she had when originally living in Beirut.

This sparked a new light bulb in Mawiyah's head, and she thought to herself,

How can we both be free to express ourselves again?

An immediate answer didn't come into her mind, and so the thought headed to the back of her brain to be brought up at a later time. Things continued in school like normal, with the girls daily lunch conversations, until one talk in which Mawiyah said to Asmah, "What if we were able to get away from our parents more often, and be free to talk to each other without the confinement of school?"

This was a very interesting idea for Asmah, because it was something that she wished for all the time. In response she said, "Then we would finally be doing things our own way."

That really resonated in Mawiyah's mind, and after returning home from class that day she asked her father if she could have a friend from school come over to the house that coming weekend. Her father was surprisingly willing to let her have the friend over. As the final days of the week passed, Mawiyah grew anxious from waiting.

Once the final bell rang on that Friday afternoon the girls sprang up out of their seats and immediately ran for the door. The walk from school wasn't long, and the girls' houses were just ten minutes apart. This marked the first play date for the girls, which soon became a regular thing. However, as the two began to hang out more and more, the school semester was passing by, and so the girls started thinking of plans for the summer. Their weekly after school hangouts turned into a time to devise a plan for the most fun summer possible, with no restrictions from either of their parents.

One late afternoon though, when Asmah had left for home after one of their play dates, that day Mawiyah decided it would be a good idea to let her parents know about what she and her friend had been thinking about. But, when Mawiyah started to explain how she wanted to buy a bike, and venture out from the house, she was quickly told to stop thinking these unrealistic thoughts, and that there would be serious repercussions if she continued with the ridiculous ideas. It was not lady like for a woman to be riding a bike at this point, and so the thought of having Mawiyah cruising around the dirty roads disgusted her traditional parents.

At that moment Mawiyah became upset as her father asked her, "Where did you even get these unacceptable ideas? Was it from that friend you have been having over so often lately?"

This made Mawiyah feel very uncomfortable, and she began sobbing and ran back towards her room without answering.

While she was on her way, though, her father yelled after her, "You will not see that girl again, do you understand me, Mawiyah!?"

After a restless night, Mawiyah woke up the next morning for school. She walked into the kitchen where her parents were both sitting and talking to each other. They looked up at her and immediately told her to fix them some tea and toast. Mawiyah obeyed them as she always had. Other than that,, the morning continued like usual. As soon as Mawiyah was done serving her parents, she rushed out the door for school.

Once classes were over for the morning, Mawiyah sat down at a table next to Asmah, except today things seemed different. The conversation didn't start out like normal. Instead Mawiyah right away told Asmah of how imprisoned she was feeling lately, especially after another morning answering of to her parents beck and call.

Oddly enough, Asmah responded by saying, "Don't worry, Mawiyah, I have a plan," which startled Mawiyah, who then became extremely interested in knowing what she had in store for the two girls. So, she started to explain, and explain she did for the rest of the lunch period, and she had Mawiyah's full attention the entire time.

After the bell rang again, Mawiyah could not sit still in class, and her legs bounced with excitement from what Asmah had told her that day. The girls had chatted about summer again, but this time the plans were full of freedom. However, for their summer to become a reality they would need money, and the decision was soon made to start selling friendship bracelets, and taking any other small jobs in order to save money. This would all help add up to hopefully be enough for the bikes they had discussed buying, which were going to be their main form of transportation for the summer. So, as the semester continued the girls were getting closer to summer, and their piggy banks were getting heavier and heavier.

Next, Asmah and Mawiyah decided during lunch one day that they had enough money to buy the bike, and they would have to go early one day before school started to pick them up. Mawiyah was a bit nervous about this plan, though, because she had never snuck out before without telling her parents where she was going.

The morning came when the girls had decided to meet up, and Mawiyah was slowly creeping towards the door to outside. It was barely light out, but just enough for Mawiyah to see a shadow that wasn't hers forming on the floor next to her. Quickly she turned around.

Her father stood there asking, "Where are you going so early, when you haven't even prepared us a morning meal?"

Mawiyah responded in a way she had never before, saying, "I don't care, I have to be at school early."

Her father was left in shock. She rushed outside before he could say anything else, but knew she was going to be punished for this later on when she returned home.

Mawiyah made it to the bike vendor, where Asmah was patiently waiting, and the two girls spilled out all of their savings in exchange for a couple mediocre bikes. Finally holding the two-wheeled machines in their hands felt like a dream come true, and the girls knew this was just the start of their fantasy to come. The girls rode the bikes to school that morning, and stashed them in a secret spot until they could get them again after classes were done that day.

When Mawiyah got back home her father was waiting, and so was her punishment. She became very upset as she realized that her family wanted her to essentially be a slave and never leave their side; and they only wanted her to be educated in the Arab school so that she could be intelligent enough to serve and act properly for them and bring honor and respect to the family. This solidified Mawiyah's yearning to fulfill her plans for the summer.

As the last week of school was now in session, she and Asmah finalized their vision. They decided that they would take their bikes and leave Iraq in search of a better, less restricted, and more meaningful life. Through their lunch discussions, they realized the truth behind each other's lives, and finally figured out how to be the change they wanted to see. The plan was to head west back towards Beirut, where Asmah had originally grown up.

With the destination determined, they decided to meet up between their homes, after midnight during the first full moon after summer had begun. They would proceed on their bikes from there to the first village on the journey west, and continue to stop in many other places along the way. While in each region, the girls were planning on talking to as many people as they could in order to open their minds, and discover and reveal problems or situations that would add to their knowledge of freedom, justice, and equality. These conversations would then turn into a single short story for each of the places they stopped—the goal was to compile an entire book of short stories by the time they reached their final destination in Lebanon.

The night came where the girls were to sneak out. Everything went according to plan. And so, as the full moon lit their trail the girls ventured off to start gathering the stories which unbeknownst to them would later turn into a compilation that would influence generations to come.

To Cut or Not to Cut
Kelsea Smith

I was ten years old when it happened to me. The horrific image is stuck in my head and I am reminded of it every day. The screams, the knife, the pain, it all haunts me in my dreams. This is what Female Genital Mutilation is like. It happens to many young girls on a daily basis and it needs to stop. I am now twenty-seven years old and I still have flashbacks to the day my mother put me through hell and back.

I remember that day just as clearly as if it were yesterday. I remember asking my mom why she would do such a thing to me. The look in her eyes held guilt, but she had no choice. It's what society wanted and she wanted the best for me. She wanted me to be like every other girl my age: pure. She didn't want me to struggle, trying to find a man who would marry me if I weren't cut; instead, she wanted them to chase after me.

I now have three kids of my own, two of them girls, and I struggle every day with the decision whether to have them cut or not. I told myself I would never put my kids through it because it needs to end. There is nothing good that comes from having them cut. If anything, it just makes them ill. I want that to change, to be the mother who doesn't have her children cut, but it is so hard to go against society and what my own family thinks. What is best for my daughters is an ongoing question I ask myself daily. With the decision coming near, I feel the pressure to have them cut, but my heart tells me otherwise.

My oldest daughter Basilah comes to me with fear in the nights before the midwife comes to our village. She is well aware of what is going on and fears for herself. She has heard girls at school talk about how they were cut, and there are very few who mention they are not. She tells me over and over she doesn't want to be cut or go through that pain. She just wants to be a normal little girl who gets to play outdoors.

It breaks my heart to hear this from my little girl and know that she is aware of what might happen to her. How could I put her through this as my own mother did to me? I know how much I resented my mother for it and how I blamed her for putting me through hell, how could I possibly have my daughter feel this way towards me?

Today is the day when the midwife is coming to perform the cuts. I have decided that I am not going to allow Basilah to be cut. It took a lot of willpower for me to make this decision, but I think it is the right one. This has kept me up at night, re-thinking her pleas to me at night before she went to bed. All I want is for my daughter to be happy and healthy and not to put her through being cut; I just can't do it. I think that by doing so, I will help to empower other mothers to do the same. This will be the test, though, of whether I had made the right decision. I have one other daughter, Najiyah, who is far too young to be cut now and if all goes well with the decision not to cut my oldest, I will stick to my decision for my second daughter as well.

There are a few other mothers in our village who have chosen not to have their daughters cut. While they told their girls to hide, I let Basilah sit freely and make it apparent that she will not be cut. Why should she have to hide because we believe something other than what society does?

As I see girls go into the room one by one, I wonder if I made the right choice. I am fully aware of the repercussions I will face but is my daughter? I tell her not to look over towards the hut where the cutting was taking place but I can tell she was curious. She can see numerous friends being taken into the hut, and you can hear the agony in the screams coming from the little girls. This is the point when I realized I have made the right choice. Mothers carrying their daughters out of the hut because they can't walk or do anything after being cut brings nothing but sadness to my eyes. I tell myself that I can handle being harassed by the other people in our village, but I wouldn't be able to look my daughter in the eye after I had her cut.

The next day at school, the girls know that my Basilah hasn't been cut. Some are jealous, while others question her morals. It's hard for me to see my daughter go through this, but I know she is strong and she stands up for herself. She knows that we did what was best for her. There are only six other girls who haven't been cut in her school. When she is asked if she wishes she were cut, she replies no. My daughter is happy with the way her body is and will accept what her future brings. The other girls who weren't cut stick by her side and tell her things will get easier.

When my family finds out I made the decision to not have Basilah cut they are furious with me, especially my mother and sister. My sister had both her daughters cut and she strongly believes that I should have done the same. Whenever I leave the room, I can hear my mother scolding her granddaughter for not going through with the procedure. How can your own blood scold and harass you like that? If anything, take your anger out on me since I was the one who made the ultimate decision. Day after day, week after week, my mother and sister still ask Basilah if she has been cut yet. Her answer remains the same: no. She has yet to be cut and never will be as far as I am concerned.

Years pass by and Basilah still gets asked if she has been cut and her answer is still no. She sticks up for herself and explains why she wasn't cut. I have found that more and more mothers have been protecting their daughters and not allowing them to get this horrible thing done. Basilah has grown into a young woman now and has been married off to a man. At first she didn't tell him she hadn't been cut because she didn't feel like it was a big deal. Later on she revealed it to him and he was shocked. To my surprise he didn't immediately divorce her like any other man would have, considering she wasn't "pure" and would have pleasure. This man was very sympathetic and understanding towards her decision and I feel like there needs to be more out there in our village like him. He truly loves her for who she is and not for whether she has been cut.

The time has come for me to make the decision for Najiyah. It has been lingering over my head for weeks now and I feel I know the right decision. How would I explain to her that she was going to get cut when her older sister wasn't? My oldest daughter made out fine not being cut, so why should I make my youngest? These questions run through my head day and night.

When I tell her she isn't going to be cut the following day, she thanks me but is scared. She is scared for her future and what everyone will think of her. She has a totally different personality than Basilah and I fear she may not handle the pressure as well. I reassure her that everything will work out but she has her doubts. She tells me that Grammy and Auntie will be mean to her and not like her anymore if she doesn't get cut.

I fear this comes from her witnessing what her sister went through. As much fear as she has now of being bullied and looked down on, it can't be any worse than going through that horrific pain of a knife to your vagina. I don't think she understands what exactly would happen to her or what the pain would feel like. I always fear for my children's lives day after day because you never know what could happen to them in a blink of an eye.

My family is still upset with me over not getting Basilah cut, and now I face them again for the same issue with my youngest. I don't think they will ever understand why I made the decision I did, but I stand by it. I don't see anything wrong with it at all. My thoughts are that the younger generations are starting to see things differently and not cut their children.

I hope that because I chose not to cut my daughters, more mothers will realize that it is okay and actually better for them not to be. Both Basilah and Najiyah are living happy and healthy lives now and are out on their own. Unfortunately, Najiyah has yet to find a husband but I am hopeful she will soon. I don't regret my decisions to not get them cut one bit and if I had to make the decision again, I would do the same thing. Female genital mutilation is wrong in so many ways, and I even see that as an Arab woman. I feel it needs to stop and by keeping it from happening to my children, my hope is they won't do it to theirs, which will, hopefully, stop this horrible trend.

The Pig
Mary Still

It crept across my cheek. A dull warmth, slowly mulling and growing until it was silent no longer. It chased across my nose, clawed its way into my eyes, and tore its way down, down so deep. To my hands, to my toes, to an abyss that sunk beneath my ribs. It was excruciating, for the warmth now engulfed me in heat. On my tongue, there on the tip of my tongue, fire burned. I wanted to scream out, but my lungs had filled with smoke, black smoke that was layering upon the night's darkness and covering the stars. The flesh contorted and coiled. Bubbles trapped upon the surface blackened. The heart no longer pumped, but in the fire's heat it boiled and raced. A knife through the heart could not stop the blood.

"Du'a." My mother gripped a hold on my shoulder, pulling me back from the flames. "You could have lit yourself on fire. Get away from that."

Her pulling had repositioned my veil, tilting it and unlatching a section causing it to fall away. Nadia would have fixed it immediately, positioned it perfectly back, covering herself away. I didn't move. I didn't care too. My eyes stayed fixed on the fire and the carcass at the center of the flame.

"Allah *yesumeh* (poison) him, habibty, the pig." My mother mumbled.

I turned a partial eye towards her. Did she feel it? That heat, the smoke's pressure building within, and that burning. Did her tongue scream out inside her? Did it scream as it burned? Did she too hold her lips closed to silence its shouts and cries? Did she too feel the burning of the silence?

She was staring off, not looking at the flame like me, but at my younger brother. Her lips were parted. Her month was opened into a smile. Her teeth and eyes glowed a soft orange reflecting the flames in front of us. So close, but not seeing it, closing her eyes to it.

The courtyard was a vision of celebration. Cousins and uncles were circled around the bonfire in the center. My brothers had hoisted my youngest brother above them, chanting cheers of praise and love.

"The Savior."

"The Restorer."

"The Pig-Slayer."

Only a small year older than fifteen, his face was covered with the signs of his youth. His chin held the ragged attempts at a beard, and his smile was one of innocent excitement but his face conveyed his anxiety to please our father. He had done his duty though, and he most certainly had. His hand was wrapped tightly around the hilt of a metal kitchen knife, the one that had slid in and out of the flesh. I stared at his jade eyes. They were the same color of all siblings in our family. Had he used those eyes to watch the knife pierce the skin? Had those hands that had hugged me just this morning felt the heart stop beating beneath them?

I felt my breathing tighten, the smoke pulled into my lungs once more, and my tongue once again felt the weight of a burning coal upon it. Should he be stained with blood? Some remnant of the act. The knife glistened with the fire's light as flames danced on the shiny metal. His other hand held tightly to a white cloth, which did have blood on it. The maroon and brown streaked across the contrasting bright white.

My father had placed that cloth atop his cane and raised it high above him. He had walked our village's streets and proudly displayed it. Tonight it was my brother's turn to hold it above him, and to reap in the honor it held. Tomorrow it would be hoisted like a flag above our house, where our family could claim its honor. That honor that rested in those streaks of maroon blood.

Tonight the men screamed out in joy. My father, my uncles, my cousins. How they all cheered in celebration. The women, their wives, their daughters, and their sisters stood back, like shadows on the edge of the party. The fire would occasionally dance amongst them revealing solemn smiles or proud eyes amongst the darkness. They knew the warning this celebration came from.

I looked into the darkness of their veils. Did they feel it?

I looked back to the fire. It curled and reached out to me. It snaked around me and coiled within me. Dancing towards me it brushed across my cheeks and unfastened the veil further, letting it fall away from me. I looked into the flames, looked at the curves of the flesh, and followed the flames as they danced upon it, engulfed it, and claimed it. The flame flickered, and I found myself looking into those jade eyes.

Those eyes that had shared a room with me. Those eyes that had taught me how to wear my veil. Those eyes I had shared so many secrets with. Those eyes that I had looked up to and grown with. Those eyes that my brothers had looked into and had promised to protect. Those eyes that had wept at our father's feet after they had fallen for a boy from a neighboring tribe. Those eyes of the sister I loved, and the body that now lay sacrificed upon the fire.

In front of me the flame bowed to Nadia as the two began to embark on one last dance. They waltzed around my brothers and tilted on the edge of the knife. They tapped across my mother's eyes and breezed past my father. They encircled one another in dips and lifts. Nadia spun and twirled. Skirts of red flames spun upwards. She kicked up her feet as her partner grabbed hold of her and lifted her up. I watched the two, mesmerized by their rhythm. It cut in fast and jagged. The flame would reach out and whip her back *niqab* one way, twisting and twirling together in a contrast of bright light and that consuming shadow. A light ensnared it as they grew higher and higher, until all at once the flame tossed Nadia up into the night sky where she weaved alone, a dancer without a partner; but it was a concern she cared little for. She continued dancing for me. Her skirts pulled white ash up with them as they spun. Her eyes glistened once more for me in fire, until she shut them away from me forever and she too faded into the black smoke above me.

"Du'a."

The fire lay in small smolders and piles of ash at my feet. The courtyard was empty now, and smoke no longer covered the stars above me.

"Du'a."

Without the high flames, the temperatures had dropped. The wind cut across the yard hitting me, ripping through my dress, but it did little cool me. I stayed seated on the log, watching the smolders in front of me.

"Du'a." My mother now stood above me. Her voice was firm and rough. "Come inside. The celebration is over, the fire is out."

"No." I replied turning away ashes that had begun to blow free in the wind and began heading towards the house. Deep inside me, in my heart, on my tongue, in my eyes it burned on.

The Beautiful Boy
Shawntae Stillwell

"You're starting to show," my mother said to me today.

I looked at her curiously. I cocked my head to the side and furrowed my eyebrows. I didn't know what she meant.

"Your breasts; you need to start covering your breasts," my mother exclaimed.

I looked down at the two small bumps in my shirt. I hadn't noticed them until now. I guess they weren't that important to me. Mother was always open and honest with me; I knew I could confide in her.

"I…" I paused. "I started to bleed, Mother," I said hesitantly. "Yesterday. I don't know how to stop it!" I was scared. I didn't know what a period was.

My mother looked at me in awe. Her mouth opened slightly and she quickly closed it again.

There was a loud knock at the front door.

"Don't tell your father!" she warned me, and hurried to dress her hair and answer the door.

It was Abdulla, Father's long-time friend. Mother let him in and showed him to a seat in the living room next to Father. She came back to the kitchen to fix our company some tea.

She kissed my forehead. "Here," she said to me, handing me a thick white cloth. "Put this inside you. Change it every time you use the bathroom." The teapot whistled and Mother quickly brought my father and our guest some hot tea.

I stood in the kitchen with the cloth in my hands. Mother didn't come back in. She went to her bedroom instead.

Father's friend Abdulla was expecting his wife to have a baby soon. His family had known our family for as long as I could remember. He confided in my father, asking for advice on childbirth.

"Pray for a son," my father said to him bluntly.

I flinched.

He saw me standing in the kitchen, but he didn't seem to mind me hearing their conversation.

"Would your wife like to be our midwife?" Abdulla asked my father. "If that's not too much to ask," he added quickly, aware of my father's wishes.

My father sat silently for a moment, and looked at me through the doorway of the living room where they were sitting. I was still standing in the kitchen, watching, listening. "Of course," my father replied at last. "I'm sure she'd love to help deliver your child."

So my mother went. She packed up a suitcase and left with Abdulla that same day. She stayed at their house day and night, waiting for the baby to arrive.

My father stayed home and watched after me.

* * *

I quickly adjusted to Mother being gone, although I missed her comfort and nurture dearly. Father didn't have the gentle voice or touch that Mother did. He never asked me about school or how I felt. He just told me to do my chores. So I did, every day after school.

Solia, Abdulla's wife, was due any day now. I had talked to Mother a few times over the phone. She checked in on my bleeding. It had stopped now. She reassured me that everything was okay, and that she would be home soon.

In the meantime, I cooked dinner, washed the dishes, and the laundry, and hung it outside to dry. My schoolwork was the least important chore on my list according to Father. So I rarely got it done anymore. He had me do all of Mother's housework so he didn't have to. It's a woman's job and I was the only girl in the house.

Father had married my sister off last year to our cousin Murad. She was only thirteen. Father said that she was well-developed, and it was her time to become a woman and move out of his house. Mother said she had already started to bleed, although the look in her eyes said she wasn't ready to let her first-born leave home yet.

Murad was twenty-seven. He treated my sister very well; he has only hit her once since they married. I guess she didn't pleasure him when he asked. She told me she hadn't felt well that night, but she said it was her fault. She said she deserved it.

I recalled that I hadn't talked to my sister in months. I guess she was busy with her new married life. I was sure I would be doing the same soon. The thought scared me.

My father hated that I was a girl. He despised that I had an older sister. He hated that my mother only gave birth to girls. So he married my sister off to send her away, and hoped to be able to do the same to me as soon as possible.

A strong churning, knotting feeling overcame my stomach. I felt sick. I sat on my bed holding my stomach, nursing it back to health. I couldn't bear to think about how young my sister was when she left, and how I was going to be next. I was hot and sweaty. I walked to the sink and washed myself.

Father walked into my room. "Shouldn't you be hanging the laundry?" he asked me with an aggressive tone. He didn't like it when he had to ask me to do what was expected of me.

I nodded.

* * *

The boy next door was beautiful. His dark brown eyes matched his dark hair, and his olive complexion. He looked at me every day when I went outside to hang the laundry. His eyes glistened in the sun as they stared deeply into my eyes. He's nine, the same age as me.

Father told me not to look at him. "It's dishonorable to look into the eyes of a man," he said to me. So I obeyed.

Today I went outside to hang the laundry. The boy was waiting in his yard like usual. I focused on the basket of clothes, hanging them on the line one at a time.

"My name is Waseem," he called out to me. "What's yours?"

I stood with my back to him for a moment. It felt like an eternity. "Ismah." I turned towards Waseem slowly.

Father stepped outside at that moment. His eyes had a stern gaze on me. I couldn't look him in the eyes. "What did I tell you, Ismah?" he asked me rhetorically.

I grabbed the basket of clothes and walked towards him slowly.

"Don't talk to boys," he reminded me. "It is dishonorable!" He paused. "Just because your mother is away does not mean you can stop acting like a young lady! Do you understand me? Now finish hanging the clothes."

My throat started to burn and it made my stomach ache. I turned and went back to my chores. It took every ounce of strength in my body not to look over at Waseem. I wanted to know what he was doing. I wanted to know what he liked to play. Where he went to school. I wanted to know more than his name and the gentle look in his eyes. But I was forbidden.

* * *

I saw Waseem walking down the road on my way home from school today.

"Ismah," he called me over to him. He remembered my name.

I started to walk towards him, and soon, I found myself running to get to his side. "Hi." I didn't know what else to say.

"Hi," Waseem said back to me. He smiled. He had a bright smile. It made me smile. "What are you doing this afternoon?" he asked politely.

My eyes got thinner, and my mouth started to droop. "I have housework."

Waseem frowned too. He walked with me the rest of the way home. We didn't say another word until we reached our doorsteps.

I smiled at him, thankful for the walk home together. He smiled back at me.

When I got inside Father was standing in the kitchen. He was silent. He didn't look at me.

"Hi, Father," I said to him quietly.

Still no response.

"What's wrong, Father?" I asked hesitantly.

He turned and looked at me straight in the eye. He just glared at me. He grabbed his chin, disgruntled. "What did I tell you," he began, "about that boy next door?" He took his belt off from around his waist.

My eyes widened. I started to run for my room. I got behind my door and closed it. He was too strong. He barged in and shut the door behind him.

"Get on your bed," he yelled.

I obeyed. If I didn't, I would be worse off.

Father pulled my pants down and slashed his belt across my bottom ten times. I counted in misery as each lash felt even more painful than the last. Normally I got nine lashes for how many years I am. I didn't know why I got ten, but I couldn't ask.

When he was done with his punishment, he put his belt back through the belt loops on his pants. I lay on the bed, waiting for him to leave the room. I didn't hear the door open.

"Go clean yourself up," he said to me sternly.

Tears were pouring down my face. I slowly stood up from my bloodstained bed. A sharp pain went down my legs and back up, resonating in my buttocks. I could feel blood drip down my legs. I cried harder, moans escaping my lungs.

"Go," Father demanded.

So I went.

The soapy water burned my cuts and bruises. I screamed in agony. The fabric of the towel dried my body and pressed deep into my wounds. I flinched at the pain I caused myself. I slowly dressed in clean clothes and waddled back to my bedroom, where I changed my bedsheets and lay down. Face down in my pillow, I cried myself to sleep.

When I woke in the morning, I yawned and stretched like a child. I immediately felt the continuation of the pain from the night before. I did not go to school. I did all of my housework that morning as quickly as I possibly could. All I wanted to do was lay down and cry.

I tried calling Mother, but Solia was going into labor, and Mother could not talk.

I lay on my stomach on my bed and watched out my window. I could see Waseem return from school. He stayed in his back yard, waiting for me to come outside. I didn't. I could see in his eyes how he longed to talk to me. He kept peeping into my yard, scanning, and watching my back door for me. I wasn't going.

Father walked into my room. I turned my head and looked at him, acknowledging his presence. He looked out my window and saw Waseem looking into our yard.

"Are you still talking to him?" he demanded an answer.

"No! I swear!" I said quickly.

"But you want to," he warned in disapproval.

He demanded I strip off my pants. He examined the cuts on my butt. He told me I did a good job of cleaning them.

He asked me if I missed Mother.

I nodded yes.

He told me to lay down.

I did.

"On your back," he said gently.

I flinched, and slowly turned over, feeling my swollen buttocks press against the mattress.

He climbed on top of me, and I screamed. He quickly covered my mouth.

"You look just like your mother," he said to me grinning. And he unloaded his built up tension on me. He told me he missed my mother too. I laid in silence with his hand over my mouth, squeezing my eyes shut so I didn't have to watch him, waiting for it to be over.

* * *

Mother returned today.

"Solia delivered a beautiful, healthy little baby boy!" she exclaimed, smiling ear to ear. She walked towards her bedroom to unpack her things, making herself back at home.

Father looked at her, almost in disapproval. He glared at me. He didn't care to hear the news, but we both followed her to the bedroom.

Mother was glowing; she almost looked as if she had given birth, but Father and I knew she was just feeling the happiness for Solia that she would have felt if the baby were her own. After all, she did help bring Solia's son into this world.

"What did she name him?" I asked, excited to know.

Father grunted and walked out of their bedroom where Mother continued to unpack her things.

"Basim," Mother said to me gently. "He has the cutest of smiles."

Mother had finally finished unpacking. I had been standing by her bed talking with her while she did. She came over to me quickly and wrapped me in her arms.

I jumped in agony from the bruising that Father had caused me.

"What's wrong with you?" she asked me, concerned.

I just stood there, regretting ever flinching to her touch.

She stood back from me, still with her hands holding my arms. She crouched down to my level and looked directly into my eyes. They were full of pain and starting to tear up. I was scared. I didn't want Mother and Father to fight.

"Tell me, my child!" she said, worried.

I moved my hands behind my back and stood silently. Mother turned me around and lifted my shirt. She saw the marks on my lower back, leading further down, covered by my pants. She pulled at them, looking down further. I heard her gasp.

She turned me back around. Her eyes were wet, and her mouth quivered. She hugged me, gently, around my shoulders. She told me to go to my room and lay down. I did.

I heard Mother and Father from my room, disputing my bruises. I heard a loud slapping sound, similar to the sound of Father whipping my buttocks. Mother moaned.

* * *

Weeks later, Mother and I were still in Father's house. She still didn't know the whole story, but what she did know was enough to make her wary. But we couldn't leave. This was our home. If Mother left, she couldn't take me with her. And she wouldn't leave me alone with him again. We had to stay.

Day after day, I would return from school and go straight to my room to watch out the window at Waseem playing in his yard. He was so beautiful.

Day after day Mother watched me watch him. She knew the longing I felt. "I used to do the same thing to your father," she said to me. "I just knew he was the one." She sort of frowned. I knew she regretted saying that because of Father's recent actions.

I looked at her and smiled reassuringly. I knew Waseem was different. If I could just go to him. He wouldn't treat me the way Father treated Mother and me. Waseem was graceful and gentle. He had spoken to me so peacefully. He was beautiful inside and out.

Layover
Hunter Stojak

My first flight left Nantucket at 6:45 a.m. I arrived in Boston around 7:30 a.m. Departed at 8:00 a.m. I was in New York sometime before noon, but I was tired by then and didn't care about the time or where I was. I had some extra time before the long flight and I went outside to the street.

There was a street vendor just outside the airport selling hotdogs and I got in line at the cart behind a young woman with long straight blonde hair. The young woman had on these denim shorts that were *short*—I mean, you didn't have to *imagine* what her behind looked like. She had some really skimpy pink tank top too, and I could see the street vendor's eyes darting downwards the whole time as she ordered.

The man working behind the cart had dark skin and a thick black beard and some sort of headdress or cloth on his head. When he wasn't looking at the blonde woman's chest he seemed to be watching the birds fly from tree to tree in the nearby park. He got started on the woman's order without saying anything. After maybe thirty seconds the man placed a hotdog on the counter in front of the woman and stared back down at her chest.

"Four dollars fifty."

The man had some kind of accent that sounded Middle Eastern. The woman silently stared at the hotdog until the man repeated himself.

"Four dollars fifty."

"Are you fucking kidding me?" The woman slowly looked up from the hotdog at the street vendor. "I must have said I wanted onions, like, three times."

The man said something I couldn't understand.

"Did you listen when I placed my fucking order?" The woman was yelling. "Can you even speak any fucking English?"

The man started flailing his arms and yelling back at the woman. I couldn't tell if he was speaking English. The woman just kept yelling back, and I left the hotdog stand and walked to the park across the street.

I sat on a bench under a tree that was full of squirrels chasing each other, and took out my notebook and started writing.

***

I didn't do much but walk around the park and sit down at various benches and write before I had to head over to the terminal. I had to go through security and take off my shoes and metal objects and step through an x-ray machine again because I had left the terminal, and was therefore a threat. The security screening didn't take as long as I had anticipated.

I walked around inside the airport and just looked at products in store windows and explored some of the shops and bought plenty of food to eat on the plane. None of the shops had anything real to read, but I flipped through the pages of a few magazines hoping to find something smart to look at on the flight; all I found was advice on how to shed pounds after my pregnancy. I bought a magazine that had Jennifer Anniston on the cover posing in a bikini, thinking I might laugh at it later. I decided I would write for most of the plane ride.

It gave me hope in a weird way. Of course I hated to see the world so content with shitty writing. It *did* make me feel good about what I was doing though—like I actually had a chance to be someone in that world. I grew up idolizing literary celebrities and fantasizing about my own words being printed in a book. As F. Scott Fitzgerald said:

Nobody ever became a writer just by wanting to be one. If you have anything to say, anything you feel nobody has ever said before, you have got to feel it so desperately that you will find some way to say it that nobody has ever found before, so that the thing you have to say and the way of saying it blend as one matter—as indissolubly as if they were conceived together.

I grew up feeling that the world could be mine if I simply worked hard enough. I had every opportunity at my disposal.

As I paid for the magazine and a bottle of water, the airport intercom announced that my flight was boarding. I hurried to the terminal and boarded the plane. There were no other passengers in the seats next to me and very few on the plane at all. The plane began its takeoff, and I took my notebook out of my bag and continued my writing.

***

I have to write a piece about an Arab woman writer. Don't know her name yet. She's a woman certainly—she's an Arab certainly. I just need to capture what it is to be her. Or what it means to exist in that world.

I can only see her world by comparing it to mine. To decipher the unique code of her life I must present my own world in juxtaposition to hers. I must translate her cultural tongues and provide her with the tools to translate mine; I must make art—a slice of my life for a slice of an Arab woman's life. Our humanity and our similarities will manifest in our stories. Our writing will bring us together.

***

The plane hit some turbulence and I woke up with my notebook still open on my lap. I must have slept a long time; the flight attendant said they could no longer serve alcohol when I tried to order a drink.

The flight was nearly over, but my story still needed plenty of work and the deadline wasn't far off. I jotted down some ideas I had been thinking of before

I fell asleep earlier, and the pilot spoke on the intercom in a language I can only assume was Arabic. A few moments later, he said the plane would be landing shortly and thanked everyone for flying with Delta Airlines. This time he spoke in English.

***

I have never left the city of Tehran. Planes are always flying over my house on their way to Imam Khomeini International. They make such loud noises and I wonder how the passengers can stand to hear it for so long. I look up at them and daydream about the places they flew in from.

I woke up today before the sun came up in the hope of getting some last minute ideas for the book. I climbed out of bed and walked over to my husband's bed and looked closely to see if he was asleep. I quietly walked into the bathroom and turned the shower on. When the water was hot, I looked behind me and peered into the bedroom to be sure no one could see, and I removed my nightdress and stepped into the shower. I heard a creak in the house at one point during the shower and quickly reached for a towel and prepared to cover myself. A few moments passed in silence and I was sure that no one was there. I turned the shower off and dried myself and put clothes on and put my robes over my clothes and my head.

I quietly stepped past my husband's bed and entered the kitchen and washed the dirty dishes. When the dishes and the house were all clean and the food I prepared had nearly finished cooking, I sat near the window overlooking the yard and waited for my husband to get out of bed. I took out a pen and a piece of paper and tried to write.

***

I managed to get a few simple paragraphs on the page before I heard my husband getting out of bed. I stuffed the paper under my robes as he entered the kitchen and filled a glass with water and sat down at the table. I stood up and put food on a plate for him and set the plate on the table in front of him. He ate in silence while I sat at the other end of the table looking down at the floor. He finished the last bit of food on the plate and looked up at me.

"Eat. If you want."

"Thank you. I'm not hungry."

My husband stood up from the table and went into the bathroom and I heard him turn on the shower. I picked up his plate and silverware and cleaned them in the sink. Then I went back to the window and continued writing about that morning until I heard the shower stop.

***

My husband entered the kitchen where I had been writing and I quickly hid my papers under my robe again. He approached me, looking at me strangely and closely.

"You were writing again?"

"No."

He reached his arm towards me suddenly, causing me to flinch. He grabbed the pen I had accidently left on the table and held it up in my face and stared at me silently, expecting me to explain. My mind went hopelessly blank and neither of us said anything for an eternity it seemed. He slammed the pen down hard on the table and the noise caused me to flinch again.

"Swear on the Holy Quran." He was staring down at the floor in front of me anxiously rubbing his fingers through his beard. He repeated himself and I remained silent so he screamed it at me again. I kept quiet still. After a few moments he threw a chair to the floor and walked out.

I was afraid and angry but much more afraid. I thought about a quote from an American writer that my father showed me when he taught me to read:

Nobody ever became a writer just by wanting to be one. If you have anything to say, anything you feel nobody has ever said before, you have got to feel it so desperately that you will find some way to say it that nobody has ever found before, so that the thing you have to say and the way of saying it blend as one matter—as indissolubly as if they were conceived together.

I reached for the papers I had hidden in my robes and continued writing in another room.

***

My husband caught me writing and immediately struck me before I could even notice him enter the room. I am certain I passed out for a while, but my husband did not destroy my papers; he knows they might be worth something. I found him on the couch reading newspapers. He apologized for hitting me without looking away from the paper he was reading. Still, he assured me it was completely justified.

***

"Will you still bring me today?"

He kept reading the paper.

"We will need to leave soon to get to Imam Khomeini—the man is returning home this same afternoon."

My husband folded the newspaper up and left the room. He returned several minutes later with his jacket and shoes on and told me to prepare myself to leave. I went into the bathroom and added to my written account of the morning.

***

I left the house with my husband and he drove me across the city to the airport. There was only one American that I could see and he was holding a notebook and folders. My husband watched from the car as I went to talk to the American man. The man introduced himself and reached for my hand, but I shook my head at him and we sat at a nearby bench. We began to make small, talk but I interrupted him to quickly finish writing in my notes.

"I see you're a procrastinator too," he said and laughed. "I tried to get some last minute writing done on the flight, but that didn't happen—just have to wait for the right material to come along."

I handed him the finished manuscript of my book, and we told each other how the day had been going.

Home
Alexandra Sturges

Ghufran closed her eyes and turned her face into the wind, allowing tendrils of her long, shadowy hair to whip freely behind her. It was the third night this week that the restlessness of her dreams had brought her up here to the roof. It was early spring in Paris and when the wind stilled, for a brief moment, Ghufran pretended that she was sitting in the courtyard of her family's home in Yemen. But the wind picked up again and she inhaled the moist, fragrant city air and her consciousness was brought abruptly back to the rooftop. Opening her eyes, she stared down at her palms in the dim light and noticed how they had softened in the months since she had arrived in Paris. The thick and abrasive callus had begun to dry and peel away. *Like a lizard*, she thought, and it made the corners of her mouth curl up into a smile. A'dab loved lizards.

Ghufran gasped as guilt and distress swelled in her chest. She pulled her jacket tightly around her and swallowed her sobs. Auntie had told her not to dwell on her sister but every night the same dream came to her when she closed her eyes. They were outside their home in the desert, Ghufran could see A'dab's bright, round face laughing and dancing in the hot sun when the wind begins to pick up. Ghufran looks around and the wind blows so hard that she must squint her eyes. She looks frantically for A'dab as the sand begins to pick up with the gusts and she must pull her cloak up to shield her face.

"A'dab!" she calls out over and over before she sees a dark figure through the dust. The sand showers her and makes her eyelids heavy but the face of the figure becomes clear and she screams but nothing can be heard over the howling of the storm. For a fleeting moment Ghufran catches a glimpse of A'dab's little face, and she pushes against the wind and sand to get to her. She grasps her little sister's hand and pulls her close but Ghufran only falls to her knees. She looks down and sees A'dab's feet encased in the ground, immovable. Ghufran screams and rakes at the sand to free her from the trap but her futile hands only scrape and bleed before she is swept away with the wind.

In the morning Ghufran went down to join her cousin for breakfast. Auntie was talking rapidly in French on the phone but smiled warmly at her when she sat. Fatima was reading and nibbling on her breakfast as she normally did in the morning. Within the year, Auntie said that Ghfuran will be able to join Fatima at school each day but for now she would help Auntie at home for a few hours before she practiced her reading and writing.

"Your writing is sloppy today, Ghufran. Have you been up on the roof again at night?"

She looked up at her Auntie and then down at her hands again.

"Ghufran, you will see your sister again someday, God willing." She reached out suddenly to Ghufran who flinched instinctively, but let her Auntie cup her cheek softly before she rose to answer the telephone. Ghufran sighed as she surveyed her writing. Perhaps she would never be able to join Fatima and the other children at school.

Frustrated, she went upstairs and climbed through the bedroom window to get to the roof. The sun was still high in the sky and it was warmer today. Ghufran could smell pollen in the air. With her big toe, she brushed away the small gravel pebbles on the rooftop and wondered what school was like. Would she have to talk to the other children? They would undoubtedly ask her questions. Would she be able to answer them? Ghufran sat down on the gravel and traced her favorite word out in the pebbles. HOME.

"Where are you from?" Auntie's friend's face was very close to Ghufran's as she crouched down with her hands on her knees. The woman was white, and she had long nails painted crimson red. Ghufran could not take her eyes off them. She blinked and remembered the question. She opened her mouth to answer but found herself unable. Auntie spoke solemnly to the woman in French. The woman touched Auntie's arm lightly with her adorned hand before walking away. Auntie grabbed Ghufran's hand and they continued down the busy street.

"Why did she ask me that?" Ghufran asked and looked up at her mother's only sister, sometime later.

"People like to know where other people are from. It helps them get an idea about who the person is and what they are like. Sometimes it is comparative."

Compared to whom? Ghufran wondered what the woman thought of her, the lost girl, whose mother died young.

That night on the rooftop, Ghufran thought about what the woman had asked, and how where you are from makes you who you are. She thought and thought about her village in Yemen. How her hair never saw the sun, how cold the nights got, and how she would hold a wet rag to her bruises to ease the aching. She missed the feeling of the warm sand, the quiet of the desert, but what she thought about most was the corner of the rug in the living room. That was where she would fix her gaze when he would start to yell. Ghufran would stare so intently at that corner of the rug that she imagined that she and A'dab could become part of it. That they could shrink down to a tiny piece of thread and weave themselves safely into the pattern alongside the other threads and that the yelling would stop because they would just fade away into the intricate pattern. Perhaps that is where Ghufran could tell people she was from, the corner of the rug in the living room. Her throat tightened, and though she tried to run from it, she knew that A'dab still had to suffer at the hands of their father. A'dab knew no other home than the tiny house in the desert with a courtyard and an angry father for whom nothing was good enough, but was a bad home better than never feeling at home at all?

Auntie had reminded her many times when she first arrived to "make herself at home." Ghufran did not know what she meant by that. Fatima had made room on the shelves in their room and encouraged her to put her things there. Is that what makes a place your home? Where you put your things? Ghufran owned nothing except the things Auntie had bought her since she arrived. Her and Fatima's room didn't feel much like home. The city of Paris bustled around her and Ghufran wondered, was she a Parisian? She didn't have long red nails and tall-heeled shoes like the woman. She didn't have straw-colored hair and blue eyes like some of the children she saw when she walked with Auntie. Ghufran began to wonder if she had a home at all. The thought made her shiver despite the warm night breeze.

The next morning Ghufran could sense something was different. When she returned to her room after washing, laid out on her bed was a crisp school uniform, like the one Fatima wore each day. At first Ghufran thought that Auntie might have laid it on her bed by accident, but she saw Fatima in the doorway already dressed. Her heart beat faster in her chest and her breath came short and fast. Was today the day? Sure it couldn't be today. Ghufran felt a gentle hand on her shaking shoulders.

The uniform felt starchy. It made Ghufran itch and fidget as she followed Fatima down the busy street to school. She couldn't stop smoothing and adjusting it. She had never been to the school and had just began to imagine what it could look like when Fatima tugged her sleeve. They had arrived.

The building was bright blue, and the doors made Ghufran feel very small. When they reached the classroom, Fatima marched inside with a smile, and scurried over to a group of girls, but Ghufran was frozen outside the classroom door. She could see the colorful walls of the room, the pictures, charts, and shapes. There were even more books than Auntie had—lined up next to each other, they seemed to go on forever. The windows let in the light of the spring day and it spilled onto the floor of the classroom, the children darted in and out of it making shadows dance around. Ghufran thought of the way she played with the shadows in the courtyard with A'dab, using their hands to make a little scene. At that moment something struck her. A calm swept over Ghufran as though the world itself had finally wrapped its arms around her. Ghufran looked down at her feet and smiled, for she had realized something amazing. It is the same sun. The sun in the courtyard, the sun on the rooftop, and the sun on the floor of the classroom, it is the same sun. *Wherever I go, it will follow me, and I will feel at home.* For the first time, Ghufran knew that her feet were exactly where they belonged.

I Am Me: My Own
Carly Svetlik

I feel as if my feet are stuck in the mud with nowhere to go. I have the desire to learn, the eagerness to read every book, and the urge to see new things. I see the path that every girl has to follow in our village and I am scared. My sister is looking forward to the day she can marry, so that she can cook our mother's recipes and have many children. She doesn't know who her husband will be, but Father said Alika's beauty deserves the strongest of men to take her hand. I am not as beautiful as Alika; I do not carry the urge to marry, and I definitely do not want to live this life.

My brother Asad is the warrior of the family. He goes out and gathers food for the family with Father. He is only fifteen years young, but acts as if he is much older and wiser than he really is. He helps Father with everything, and is very much prepared to take over the village when the time comes. He brings home books from the village schoolhouse and practices with Father, chanting large words that I have never heard before. He gets stronger and smarter each day I see him; I only wish I could follow.

And then there is me. I am Adira; I am my father's daughter. I wish to run with the wind and be a free spirit, but instead I am stuck here. I spend most of my days inside with Mother and Alika learning the trades of a woman. We cook and clean every day, we are forbidden to talk to any male outside of the family, and I am no longer allowed to play outside. What I am the saddest about is the fact that I cannot go to school. The village only allows boys to learn to read, write, and practice mathematics. I have looked over Asad's shoulder at times when he is doing school work and have been so intrigued by the numbers and patterns I see.

Asad is not interested in school; he wants to become stronger and prove to Father that he is the warrior of the family. He will protect us all in times of evil and despair; he will be the provider when Father can no longer take hunting trips. Asad will take care of our family no matter what. When he marries a young girl and creates his own family, he will provide for them too, just like Father has prepared him. In the meantime, Father expresses the importance of school, and the value of education. He states no father will want his daughter to marry Asad if he does not know how to read or perform math.

I want to read and write just like Asad. When I try, Father pushes me away to fetch tea or something to eat. When I show interest in Asad's mathematics I am told "Adira, mathematics is not for girls. Go help your mother and sister." I strive to spend more time with my father and learn the skills he teaches Asad. In our village, it is not usual to have a strong-headed and independent female. Most of the girls I see are quiet and hide in their cottages as they tend to the list of chores their husbands or fathers have left. I do not want to live this life. I want to learn and explore; I want to make a difference.

I am sometimes allowed to go out and do some shopping at the village market when Mother and Alika are too busy. I take my time during the long walk and take in all the fresh air and sunlight. It is such fun to look at the beautiful nature that surrounds my village. One time I snuck away from the path I am told to stay on and found a beautiful winding river. It was a hot day so I decided to undress and go for a swim. I knew I would be punished if my family found out but I could not resist the glistening water. To my luck, nature was on my side that day as it started to pour on my way home. Mother had no idea I went swimming as I came home drenched from the rain. She scolded me anyway because I was outside for too long and soaking wet in public.

That night I heard Asad and Father practicing English while I was in the bath tub. I listened so carefully to the lesson plan and repeated every word they practiced very quietly so no one heard. The next day I found one of Asad's reading books on the table. Father and Asad were away hunting for animals, while Mother and Alika were outside gathering herbs. I was all by myself, which was very uncommon. I held the book and stared at the cover. It was the most beautiful thing I had seen in a long time. We have a few paintings in our cottage, but I had never seen such a detailed hand drawing like the one on the cover of Asad's book. I flipped it open and there it was filled with magical words and beautiful drawings; it was like a whole new world that I could escape into. It was only moments after I entered this stunning world that I heard Mother and Alika getting closer to the cottage door. Mother would be so angry to see my chores paused and Asad's school book in my hands. I nervously set it back exactly where I found it and started back up with my rag.

As I tried to fall asleep that night all I could do was think of the endless possibilities of Asad's story. Although I could not understand everything in the story because it used English words, I saw the detailed pictures which were enough to let my brain wander. My dreams that night got caught up with the pictures from the book. My mind wouldn't stop and I couldn't wait to wake up and hopefully get another peek into how the story finished.

That next morning Father and Asad were gone, as were all of Asad's books, paper, and pencils. Mother said they were preparing for Asad's journey to adulthood. I felt sadness that I didn't get to see them off, but mostly I felt sad because the books were gone. All I wanted was to continue my dream and the journey the book provided me. Now with it being gone I felt a loss of hope for my adventurous life. Would I be just like my mother and Alika? Will I always be the one who cooks and cleans and stays inside every day? I am my father's daughter. I wish to run with the wind and be a free spirit, but instead I am stuck here, forever.

The Cycle
Kyle Tellers

It feels like just yesterday I was out playing with the others. I remember thinking "Why did this have to happen so soon? The other girls my age are still outside, able to run freely, feel the wind in their hair and chase after the football." That was seventeen years ago. The day I was veiled.

Now I am twenty-seven years old, a wife and mother, with a daughter who is about to go through the same experience. I do not want her to go through the same experience, but her father and his mother insist on it.

"How will she ever find a husband? Men only want a woman who is pure," they argue. While I know this to be true, I also remember the day it happened to me.

It was a beautiful day in mid-April, sunny but not too hot. I had worn jeans and a shirt out to play football with my friends. We lost the match, but it was okay because we were playing again next weekend. I walked into my home and saw my father and uncle talking. I thought it was strange because I had seen my uncle the day before and we normally only see him once every other week.

I overheard the last of their conversation. "She is ten years old now, she is becoming a woman. It is time she started dressing as one," my uncle had said to my father. My father looked as if he was going to reply then he saw me and became silent. My father said his goodbyes to his brother and began walking him out. On his way out, my uncle just smiled as he passed. He did not say a word. The look on his face worried me. He looked at me as he had never done before; it was like he was judging me.

After my uncle left, my father went to speak to my mother. I could hear the loudness of his voice, but not the words. All I could tell is that he was not happy. A few minutes later my mother came out looking upset. I did not understand why she was upset at first, but now I do as I am about to have the same discussion with my own daughter. My mother slowly came towards me trying to hide something behind her back, but I saw it. It was a *hijab*, entirely black. She told me that it was time for me to begin wearing the *hijab* everywhere, that it would keep me pure.

I was excited the first time I put it on. I felt like a grown up. The next morning when I put the *hijab* on over my head, and went toward the door, my mother stopped me. The excitement faded as she explained I was no longer able to play outside with the other children—I had to stay home when not at school. It was a suffocating feeling, I could only live at home and in school, but at least when we had guests I could see new people, or at least that was how it had been.

I found out later that week that I was no longer allowed to be seen or heard by guests. Previously my father had allowed me to bring food and drink to his guests, and I would always try to have a small conversation with them. I would find out their name, how they knew my father, and they would ask me my name and maybe something about the school, and if I knew their daughters. However this time, I was instructed to stay in the kitchen with my mother and help. We would leave the food on the floor just outside the door, knock to let my father know it was there, and then retreat back into the kitchen. I cannot do this to my own daughter. I want it to be better for her, but I fear that I am powerless to stop it.

A few years later men started asking my father to marry me. I had never met any of them; thankfully my father would turn them away saying I was too young. It seemed odd to me that I was not allowed to meet them and be a part of the decision. I was told by my mother that this is how it is. Because I was a woman, I had no say in my life. When I put on the *hijab*, I had handed over the little control I had. And now as I walk towards my daughter to do the same, I can only think of how much I hate these restrictions, these veils.

When I turned sixteen, I was married off to the neighbor's son. I had not met him before and he was five years older than I am. Soon I had our daughter Amani, aspirations. I insisted on this name with the hope she would live up to it, and that she would aspire to greater things than I. Now I feel as if I am dooming her to the same life I had been forced to live, never being able to chase her dreams.

As I hand Amani her own *hijab*, I am filled with regret because I cannot break this cycle. My mother handed me the *hijab*, just as I am now handing my daughter the *hijab*, and she will hand her own daughter the *hijab*. It will never end. I regret not having the means to get away from here and take her with me to Paris. That is where we would go. I know it is too late for me. The veils have already broken me, but she still has a chance to truly live. But we do not have the money to make the move, and so the cycle continues.

The *hijab* is now in her hands. She has an excited smile on her face. Soon she will realize just what I have done to her with this veil. It is only a matter of time before these thoughts are hers as well.

My Sweet Nanu
Karly Terrio

I remember the day like it was yesterday; the day I took my daughter's life away. My mother had been pressuring me for the better part of a year, and I finally gave in. I realized I did not have a choice. I woke up my innocent little Nanu from her sleep with a kiss on her forehead.

"Wake up, my sweet Nanu. Your grandmother is coming to visit."

She opened her eyes and smiled. As we sat in the kitchen and ate our breakfast, Nanu's eyes wandered around.

"Where is Father, and my brothers?"

I replied, "Oh Nanu, do not worry. They just went on an adventure today. They took a trip to go see your uncle in Cairo. Your father said that they are going to find a beautiful gift to bring you."

"But why didn't I get to go with them?"

"Sweet Nanu, you are growing up so fast and the streets of Cairo are no place for a young lady." The truth was that she was not a young lady. She was only nine years old. She was still a sweet, innocent child full of wonder and joy. "Now eat up, your grandmother will be here soon."

I washed the dishes as Nanu played in the other room. I kept telling myself that this was the right thing to do, that my daughter must be pure. I finished cleaning up the kitchen and lay on the couch in the living room as she played on the floor.

"Grandma!" Nanu exclaimed as her grandmother walked through the door, an even older woman trailing behind her.

"Nanu, I want you to meet my friend," my mother said, motioning to the woman standing next to her. The scarf tied tight around her face seemed to frame her age. Her skin was dry and deeply wrinkled. Her dark brown eyes sat deep in her face. I remembered this old midwife; however, it was many years ago when we met and she had not been quite as weathered. This woman stole my life, as she would soon do to my daughter.

I picked up my daughter and carried her to her bed. She looked at me in confusion as her grandmother stripped off the garments underneath her dress. "Do not worry Nanu, we are going to make you pure," her grandmother assured her.

The old midwife said a prayer as she unpacked some things from a black satchel that hung from her shoulder. That is when I saw the blade. I kissed my daughter's forehead, "Close your eyes, Daughter, and hold my hand."

The midwife walked over to the bed and rubbed some paste on my half-naked daughter.

"Mama, what is going on?" Nanu questioned.

"Shh. Do not worry daughter."

All it took was one fast cut with the blade. Nanu screamed at the top of her lungs and her eyes shot open, tears pouring down drenching her face. The midwife rubbed some ash on my daughter, which caused her to scream even louder and start kicking her feet. I watched as the blood pooled between her legs, knowing that she was losing something just as vital as blood. As the blood left her body, I watched the life drain out of her eyes. With that blade, the old woman cut out my daughter's dreams, hope, and desire.

"Why, Mother? Why would you do this to me?" Nanu cried as her grandmother tried to hand her pieces of candy and a new toy.

I started to feel dizzy and had to hold onto the wall to keep the room from spinning.

"Mother. Mother, wake up." Nanu looked down on me as I lay on the floor. "You fell off the couch. Is everything okay? When is grandmother going to be here?"

At that moment, I knew that I did have a choice. This is my daughter and it was my responsibility to save her from the suffering that I had experienced. "Nanu, go to your room. You are to stay in there until I come to get you, and do not make a sound."

"Why, Mother?"

"Because I love you, sweet Nanu. Now go on."

I paced back and forth trying to think of what I would tell my mother. I could not tell her the truth, for she would never accept my decision. She would rather do it herself while I was not watching than have a granddaughter who was uncut.

Then came the knock I was dreading. "Come in," I answered the door and watched my mother walk in, the old midwife followed behind her.

"Where is Nanu?"

"Oh Mother, I am so sorry. I thought you were coming next week. Nanu is in Cairo visiting her uncle with her father and her brothers."

"Layla, how could you forget? We have been talking about this for months. It took us nearly three hours to get here. I should have expected this from you. You were always so scatterbrained. Now you expect me to leave and come back next weekend?"

"I am so sorry, Mother. I have been so distracted lately. With the kids out of school for the summer, they have my head running in circles." That wasn't a complete lie after all.

"What are we going to do about Nanu? You can't wait much longer. She is getting older and will soon start having impure urges if we do nothing."

"You are right. A friend told me that there is a midwife just a few towns over that has taken care of her daughters. I am sure that I can arrange something with her."

"You better Layla. I cannot believe you wasted my time like this. We are leaving."

And just like that, it was over. I thought I did not have control over my own daughter's fate, and now I realized that I did all along.

A few days later, my husband and sons came home, and life returned to normal. My husband gave Nanu a beautiful silk scarf and thanked her for being such a good girl while he was away. Nanu thanked him and smiled as I had instructed her to.

I know that someday when Nanu goes to marry, her secret will come out. I just hope that by then it will not matter.

Torn
Tyler Uhlendorff

"Wake up."

I jumped awake, completely startled by the commotion my sister Tahira caused as she shook my mattress.

"What?" I grumbled as I flung my arms forward, attempting to catch the culprit. She always did this.

I never understood where her energy came from; it was as if she were powered by the sun.

"Let's go, we're going to miss it," she persuaded me, motioning her eyebrows like ropes, lassoing me towards the door.

"Why do we always have to go?" *It's only a sunrise*, I thought.

Her eyes said otherwise as they sparkled towards the window. "Because, Salim, it's morning." Her cheeriness was beginning to rub off on me.

"Alright, I'll meet you by the garden in two minutes," I sighed.

As she sprung out the door she ignored the shriek her scarf made as it snagged on a nail, tearing its flawless landscape. It seemed nothing could hold her down.

I fumbled my slippers on as I ruffled my way out of bed. As I hurried I noticed a piece of fabric had been filched by the nail. Lifeless and dull, it now wilted around the nail, forfeiting its energy as I swung my door closed behind me. I made my way down the hall past my parent's room, which luckily fell silent, despite the commotion we'd caused. I fetched a roll from the basket as I handled my way out the back door. I couldn't hike on an empty stomach.

I trampled through the grass clenching my jaw closed as I took a bite. I could only see Tahira's head as the sun glowed around her. With each step I grew closer to her and our secret spot. I heard a familiar bellow as our uncle's quails shrilled from across the pond. I sat down beside her.

She had grown a lot in the last few months; her shoulders were now broad like our cousin Nura. "Isn't it pretty?" she whispered.

I nodded, as I felt the dew dampen my bottoms as if I'd wet them. We were both changing. I had begun to see hairs under my chin, and often dreamed of mountains covered in silk. It was hard to believe we were the same age, although she often reminded me that she was two minutes older. We were best friends.

The next hour we spent rolling through the grass, tunneling our way through the field. Our parents would be up soon, and my father would expect help in the barn. We retreated to the house, rushing to discard our filthy garments. My mother undoubtedly knew of our shenanigans, yet removed the stains quietly without ever a mention to our father. She was good at hiding things; in fact, I'd never seen her cry, even when they'd fought.

It had been years since they last tried; the doctors said they were lucky to have been blessed with us. Yet it was we who gave them hope for more. It was just the other day I overheard my uncle persuading my father to marry a second wife. It took but a second for my father to say no and that he believed that Allah would grant him more children when the time was right. He was a good man.

I secured my last button as I heard their bedroom door close. Tahira had disappeared to help Mother some time before I had finished changing. It would be a few more minutes before my father emerged, yet the sizzle of the skillet was already chiming from the kitchen as my mother prepared our breakfast. It wasn't long before I heard familiar footsteps enter the den where I was waiting.

"Good morning," I offered, as he grinned toward me.

"Good morning to you as well, my son," he replied, caressing his fork to take a bite.

Once finished, we made our way towards the barn. By now I was used to the routine: change the water, spread the feed, and clean the waste. I knew he was grateful for my help. My uncle's four sons had already taken wives and were off living in the city. I was all he had. It took most of the day; it wasn't until I began shoveling the last stall that the thunder began to crack. *It was supposed to be a nice day* I thought; *after all it began so well.*

Dinner came and went and I found myself perched by the windowsill while Tahira hummed in sync with the patter of rain coming off the roof. Our parents were whispering in the other room as if they disagreed. Fragmented by the rain, it sounded as if my father was upset about something. If only my ears were bigger, I would know the rest.

He went to bed early, while my mother silently found purpose in cleaning the already spotless kitchen. She had always been good at hiding things.

My body suddenly felt weakened as if it was anticipating a cold; I decided to lay down. As I tossed and turned I recalled the day. Despite my protest I loved waking up with the sun. I knew how much it meant to Tahira. I loved her, and the bond we had. Before long I had drifted into a heavy sleep, abandoning all thoughts.

My eyes shuddered open as I peered across the bedroom at the clock. 8:45 it read, but how? Where was Tahira? I looked towards the window to find the sky cold and gray. The air was silent as I opened my door to the dark hallway. *Where was everyone?* I thought, as I investigated the house for any signs of life. *Was I dreaming?*

It was then that I heard my uncle's quail screech from across the pond. Hoping for an answer I rushed to find my shoes. The cries grew louder as I made my way across the field towards his house. With each step the foul sounds became more human.

It was Tahira. I panicked as I reached the window. I had only heard her cry once before, but somehow I knew it was her. All I could see through the window were what appeared to be feathers; dozens of scarves tangled the room as Tahira's cries shivered against the glass. I shuffled for a glance, trampling the freshly budded roses outside the window. It was no use. What felt like hours passed until finally it stopped. I stared uninterrupted as the room cleared, revealing something different than the girl I'd remembered; the hope was severed from her eyes.

She lay still on the cold dark floor, withered from the mysterious nightmare that had just ended. *What had they done to her?* I thought, as I ducked beneath the porch. Women began spilling from the house, like hens from a coop. As soon as they left I sprinted inside to find the room empty. Her torn scarf was all that remained in the now lifeless space. As I scooped it up, I recalled the cries. A shiver rushed through my veins as I sat on the floor. I dozed off for a few minutes, consumed by confusion.

When I awoke, I returned home to find my father in the den with my uncle, while mother prepared lunch. "Where is Tahira?" I asked.

"She isn't feeling well. Best we leave her alone," my father commanded.

After lunch I retreated to my room, examining the scarf she'd left behind. It was my mother's, a gift Tahira had received on our last birthday. Woven with the finest silk, it was now tarnished, scarred by the rusted prick of a nail. Perhaps my mother could mend it, I hoped; she was always good at hiding things.

As I walked into the kitchen, I could tell she was upset. Had the fight from last night really bothered her this much? Did she know what had happened to Tahira? Without hesitation I held the scarf at arm's length. "It's ruined," I cried.

"No, no," she assured blankly, "I will stitch it up as if nothing ever happened."

If only the same could be said for my sister.

Saleema, the Faultless
Pablo Valentin

She sits up in bed crying out of frustration. It is not fair to her and it is not fair to him. He leaves the room. This isn't the first time this has happened. She can't get in the mood; he respects her but has to leave the room sexually frustrated. He's smoking a cigarette outside. She is still in bed crying. She doesn't understand why they cannot make love. She doesn't understand why she cannot separate past experiences from her life right now. She wants to forget the past and enjoy life right now.

When she was just ten years old she was fooled and swindled into believing that she had to be cut. She was told it was the will of Allah. She was told by her mother and aunts and their friends that it had to be done. She didn't understand but agreed. It all happened so fast, but to her it took so long. What only took a few minutes felt like hours. She never experienced so much pain. She never saw so much blood. She thought, *Are they trying to kill me?* She cried and yelled and begged for them to stop. She just wanted it to be over. Before it was over, she passed out. Everything faded to black.

He comes back into the room and sits next to her on the bedside. He wipes away her tears. She feels lucky to have married a man who respects her as an equal. She has always heard stories from friends of their husbands forcing themselves on them when they had no desire. She is very happy to have married a man who doesn't force himself upon her. He kisses her forehead and tells her he loves her. She loves him too. She feels happy.

They lie in bed again. They kiss. She enjoys this. Knowing him and his patience makes her feel comfortable. The kissing progresses and they begin to disrobe each other. She is starting to get in the mood. They continue to kiss each other and he begins to feel her body. She enjoys feeling his hands all over her body. He rubs her back and her waist. Everything is fine. He touches her inner thigh and everything fades to black. That feeling from that day when she was ten years old has returned to her body; the day they changed her forever.

She wakes up sweating, her husband once again sitting by her side. She asks him how long she was out of it for. He responds, "Only a few minutes, dear."

She tells him it felt so long. That she was dreaming for so long. She tells him it was terrifying.

"Just relax. Return to sleep, my love," he tells her.

It's been a year since that night when she passed out due to her husband's touch and her old horrifying memories. She's a mother now and has never been happier. She and her husband created a beautiful young baby girl. They named her Saleema. Saleema's mother would never allow her to go through the horror that is female genital mutilation. She would never make her endure the pain that she had to endure. Seleema, both flawless and faultless, will remain that way forever in the eyes of her parents.

Limbo
Natasha Weinstein

I'm stuck.

I see the world outside, a world I long to be a part of, but I'm stuck. I hear my mom calling for me, to teach me responsibility, but I'm stuck.

I'm in this world, not yet an adult and no longer a child. I'm forced to long for a time I can no longer be a part of, a time when everything was so easy. I miss my friends, playing with my friends, being carefree. I love my mom, but I miss my friends and being young.

Every day it is the same routine: wake up, do my chores, stare out the window until I'm yelled at. My mom tries to teach me, but I can see the pain in her eyes, a pain that I am developing as I watch the world go by. I am sure that when she was little she had friends, she played outside, she knew what it was like to fall and cut her knee on a rock, and then get back up not caring about a single thing that happened. But that is not the woman I see. I love my mom, but she hurts.

Every day my dad tells me the same thing: "When you grow up, you will marry and love your family, but no matter what you will always be my little girl."

I am not his little girl though. He treats me differently than others. When I'm upset he'll still hug me; when I burn my finger trying to learn to cook, he'll still hug me—but I am not his little girl. When I was his little girl he would take me on walks and watch me climb trees. He would carry me to bed when I fell asleep during dinner. When I was little my dad cared. I don't think he cares anymore since I am not his little girl.

I'm forced to watch interactions through a veil. When I was little, I could bounce around, but my veil forces me into a different place. I might be home, but there is a veil over my house. I am the only daughter, but daughter is only a word. My mom teaches me how to wear a *hijab* and about my role in our world. I don't like it. When I'm alone I pretend I'm anywhere else but here, that I get to play with my hair in the middle of a park and not be gawked at. I like to dream about being carefree, but my dad taught me girls are not allowed to dream. I am not his little girl.

I try to fit into this new role, but it's not me. My mom doesn't know but I see her cry. I can hear her talk to herself as she cooks, while I'm cleaning the house. I know she loves my dad, or at least I think she does, but I know she isn't happy with her role in life. She told me about when she was young and could play with friends and about how she had to transition into this new role: adulthood. But no matter what she says my mom doesn't convince me it gets easier. If it got easier, then I wouldn't dread being married. If this "adulthood" thing got easier, then my mom wouldn't cry. She tells me she loves my dad, but what is love?

Love is such a weird word. When I'm alone dreaming about other lands, I wonder what love is like there. The only world I know is the one I live in, this place where I'm not allowed to play with friends because of these....things on my chest. I don't like it. How can my parents say they love me when they are forcing me to wear the *hijab*, to do my chores, to not let me express myself? How is that love?

And yet, I still try. I want to please my mom. I want her to see that I can do what she does, and that even if I am resentful, I can still be happy because that is what she wants. And that way maybe she won't cry. Maybe that's love, but I don't know. No matter what I try, I still feel stuck. I hear stories, folktales really, of girls traveling to other worlds. These girls get to be free and daydream, but what makes them different than me? Why can't I travel? Because my father says girls aren't allowed to dream. A folktale must be a fancy word for myth then, something that doesn't actually exist. Maybe my childhood was a folktale, and in reality, I was being trained to be a "proper" woman, whatever that means.

These are the times I miss my brothers. They're older than me and left years ago. When they were still around my mother seemed happy. At least I don't remember anything else. I must have been happy too. Even though I am a girl they would let me tag along when they met their friends, and they would pick me up when I cut my knee on a rock. They loved me. I am more their little girl than I ever was my father's. They still care, but they're long gone. One married, and the other died before I was old enough to understand what death was. I still have one brother, but I lost him, like my mom lost him, when work and marriage took him away from us. That must be why my mom cries at points. Because all she is left with is me, this girl who wants nothing to do with anything she is teaching me.

I still try. I want to please but I keep messing up. I stare out my window, longing for the world I used to be a part of. I watch girls younger than me run past my house while I'm stuck inside. I think I might be slowly disappearing. Every day I go through the same routine, and every day the same thing happens: I care a little less. Is it possible to still exist and yet, not be there? I'm stuck in between two worlds and I just want to be free.

I'm stuck and I can't get out.

I see the world I long for and can never be a part of.

I'm stuck and I can't find my way.

I try to be a part of the world I am meant to live in.

This is my limbo.

Lady of the Desert
Shannon Welch

Hedaya gazed out the window at her desert surroundings, her usual routine by now. Everything had changed since Father died. Mother hadn't been able to get out of bed from the grief for two months. Hedaya's aunts had to come and help around the house, to cook, to clean, and to nurse Mother back to good health. However, this had been Father's second heart attack, even after the doctor had told him to take things easy—after all, he was fifty-eight years old!

But there was so much to be done for the family. Between Hedaya and her three younger sisters and two even younger brothers, there were loads of mouths to feed. Everyone was running in and out of the house, yelling, jumping, and playing. Hedaya was used to the daily hustle and bustle of the household.

But ever since Mother got sick....silence, quiet...the frantic air of not know- ing what would happen next to the family. While the aunts took turns caring for Mother, Hedaya, as the eldest sibling, was naturally in charge of making the younger ones behave. But just a glimpse at noontime by her bedroom window, Hedaya looked out at the vast desert and the sun. *How I wish I could be as open and free as the desert! No one to take responsibility for...just to feel the sun on myself and be able to go where ever I please!* Hedaya thought to herself. It wasn't that she didn't love her siblings, aunts, or Mother. In fact, she felt closer to all of them than ever and wished each one of them the greatest happiness. But Hedaya sometimes felt that her head would explode with everyone else to care for and never having a moment to herself except for her noontime window watch. Her heart was broken at the sight of her frail, sad Mother. Hedaya reflected some more. *Mother and Father adored each other! I wonder if I will ever have a marriage that lovely!* Before Hedaya could finish the rest of her thoughts, Aunt Rana called for her downstairs.

"I'm coming!" Hedaya shouted as she ran down the rickety stairs into the kitchen.

Aunt Rana shook her head in disapproval but there was no time for lectures. The children needed their lunches! Aunt Rana and Hedaya worked side by side to prepare the large lunchtime meals. As they worked, the children laughed and told jokes with each other. Hedaya couldn't help but smile and laugh along with their antics. One day she wanted to have a family as well, but maybe or maybe not with as many children. Being only sixteen, Hedaya hoped that she wouldn't have to worry about that for a while. There was a lot of strain on her already.

When the children finished up their meals and all was cleaned up, Aunt Rana led Hedaya into Mother's room, where Mother and her other aunt, Aunt

Grace were. Hedaya gave them all confused looks; this was not part of the daily household routine.

"Sit down, Hedaya. We have an announcement to make." Aunt Grace said, trying not to show any emotion in her face. "Before your father died, he was in the middle of negotiating a marriage contract between you and Mr. Esam. Now, we all know that Mr. Esam is a few years older than you, but he can provide well, has a house, a budding farm and. . ."

"*Wait!* What? I'm sixteen years old...Mr. Esam is...thirty-two. What about what I want?" Hedaya yelled.

She had never really rebelled in her lifetime. There was no reason to. Hedaya couldn't believe that they had sprung this on her. And her own Father, Allah rest his soul, didn't even give fair warning that he was looking for suitors for Hedaya. Hedaya had never felt so betrayed before. This felt wrong and sketchy. To marry for family honor, to marry an older man she barely knew, or to run away?

All the women stared at Hedaya in shock at her yelling.

Mother reached out a shaking hand to her oldest daughter. "Now...my child. This is for your future. Without Father around, what will we do? Bills need to be paid and figured out and Mr. Esam has already paid a more than generous amount for your dowry. Please. Just give him a chance...."

Hedaya's willpower fought with her heart in that very moment.

As she watched her mother's already heartbroken eyes, she thought, *Hadn't she suffered enough? Can't I at least pretend to have a happy wedding and marriage... at least for Mother's sake?*

These thoughts circled Hedaya's mind like vultures waiting for the kill. But she couldn't do it. She wanted a deep, true love like her parents had and the only way to do this was to choose her own husband when she was old enough and ready for him. Hedaya tried to explain this to her aunts despite their brushing-off.

"You're sixteen.... What would you know of the world?" Aunt Grace yelled at her.

Eventually, night fell and everyone went to bed. But Hedaya couldn't sleep. She had other, bigger, worldly plans. She could go out into the desert. Run away and be free, even if it kills her.

"*My freedom is my only option for my own honor.*" With these last thoughts, Hedaya packed what little she had and walked off into the never-ending desert, following the path of the moonlight.

Sunshine
Mary Zemina

The sky was raining bubbles. Leila spread her arms out over the soft grass beneath her and stuck out her tongue. A bubble bounced lightly on the tip, spreading a sweetness like honey over her taste buds. It drifted until it struck her nose, causing her to sneeze. The bubble burst, spraying sweet drops of rain over her face.

A few feet away, her younger sister Nur ran through the meadow, her arms scattering rain-bubbles and her feet kicking up sunshine. She spun, and her long, silky black hair trailed behind her like a river made of the night. When she stopped moving, the sun particles by her feet settled back into the lush green grass.

Amira was still not back yet.

Leila propped herself up on one elbow and looked toward the village. Did her other sister realize how late it was getting? It was nearly bedtime back home. They had to return so their father would not discover the Door.

Nur turned and met her eyes, as though reading her thoughts. She gathered up her cloak and headscarf, but spent several minutes searching through the grass for the covering for her face. Leila watched her stir more sun motes until she finally pulled it out of the grass, shaking off the bits of sunlight that still clung to the heavy black cloth.

Leila stood, watching as the bubbles of rain bounced off her clothes with each of her movements. She'd left her own dress and *niqab* by the Door when they'd entered this world. She found it much easier to keep track of things when she used landmarks. So while her youngest sister scrambled to make sure that her garments were all accounted for, Leila stretched her shoulders and her back, feeling the slippery material of her Eshraqi clothing. Every time she left this world, she missed the clothes. People here dressed in bright, loud colors with intricate patterns, whereas at home, she and other women and girls dressed in monochrome.

As she rose from her final stretch, Leila's eyes fixed on the horizon. Just beyond the illuminated skyline of the village were three figures. They grew as they approached. Minute by minute, the rain of bubbles lightened and she could see clearly. The one in the center was Amira. Finally. To her left was a short and slight girl called Aisha. Leila and her sisters had met Aisha in the village many years ago, when their mother still traveled with them to the Mysterious Worlds. Aisha, despite being closer in age to Leila, had become close friends with Amira, and the two were nearly inseparable whenever Amira visited.

And to Amira's left was Selim, Aisha's brother.

Leila double-checked that her scarf was pinned tightly around her face, covering all her hair. "Put your scarf on," she hissed out the corner of her mouth at Nur. "Amira's bringing Selim."

Nur rolled her clothes into a bundle and stared at Leila with molten brown eyes. "I don't have to do that here. Eshraqi people say it's optional."

Leila held Nur's hand loosely and met her eyes. "Mother and Father would want you to. You're not a child anymore, Nur. You're old enough to follow modesty rules at home, so you should follow them here as well."

Nur shook her hand off and skipped across the meadow in the direction of the Door. The sunlight flared under her feet with each step.

Shaking her head and sighing, Leila turned around to watch Amira again. She and her companions had stopped just inside the meadow. They appeared to be talking, or, rather, arguing. At least Amira and Selim seemed to be. Leila rubbed her arm and took a few steps forward. There were now only a handful of bubbles raining down, and they drifted aimlessly in the gentle summer breeze before they popped.

A voice came on the intercom in the village, carrying on the breeze just as the bubbles had done. It was almost time for bed at home, but here in this world it was time for *Asr* (evening). At the sound of the call to prayer, Selim stopped speaking. He and Aisha looked toward the village and then back at Amira. Aisha pulled her into a quick hug before running home. Selim rested his hand on Amira's shoulder and looked into her eyes, which were the only part of her face he could see through her blue and purple swirled *niqab*. He kissed her on the forehead and then he, too, held her close for a moment before running for the village.

Leila and Amira both watched the sunshine he'd kicked up in his haste as it returned to the grass. Keeping her face pointed toward the village, Amira walked backward until she was within arm's reach of Leila. Taking her younger sister into her arms, Leila smiled and led her toward the Door.

They walked through the bright and flowery meadow until they reached the grove, where a stone wall covered in vines hid the entry to their own world, the Door their mother's family had kept hidden in their old house for generations. Leila touched her hand to the vines, but before she could pull them away to reveal the doorknob, Amira stopped her.

"Leila," she said, grabbing her hand.

Leila looked at her. She'd removed the covering from her face and slipped her black dress on over the bright clothes she wore whenever they went to Eshraq. Leila held her own clothes under her arm, still bundled tight.

"What is it?" she asked.

Amira cast her eyes to the ground. "Selim wants to ask Father for my hand."

Leila dropped her bundle to the ground with a heavy plop. "Father doesn't know him," she said. "He can't ask."

"Of course he doesn't know him. Father doesn't know about Eshraq at all." Amira placed her hand on her hip and looked up at her. "And he'd destroy the Door if he ever knew we were traveling without his permission or guardianship."

There was a fist squeezing her stomach, batting away all the rest of her organs so they hit the sides of her ribcage.

Leila drew in a labored breath. "Does Selim know that he cannot ever be with you?"

When Amira was silent, Leila looked over at her. Selim had set his eyes on Amira from the moment they first met. Even as a child, he'd been determined to marry her. Leila bit her lip. It would never work. Their father would be furious that they'd become so familiar with a man who wasn't a relative.

And I'm the oldest, Leila thought somewhat bitterly. Amira wasn't even sixteen yet. If she got married first, Leila would be a spinster at eighteen. She didn't know if she could live with that, on top of Father's repeated refusals to allow her to go to England for college.

But Amira stood before her now, tears beading at the corners of her eyes. She loved Selim. Leila had no doubt of that. But he was older than them both, just barely entering his twenties. As much as he wanted to marry Amira, pressure from his family might not allow him to wait long enough for Leila to get married before her sister.

Leila picked her clothes up from the ground, shook out the sun particles, and draped an arm around Amira. "Tell Selim he must come to live in our world and get to know our father first." She pushed the vines out of the way, revealing the secret Door that allowed them to travel between their home and six other worlds. Pulling the door open, Leila said, "Then maybe Father will allow you to marry him someday."

***

The world of the lizard people always had something new and strange to discover. Leila settled herself on the wall of the fountain and observed. The city around her buzzed and pulsed—literally.

The frequency at which the pulses in the ground came was directly related to the air traffic, where the magnetic hover vehicles flew over the heads of everyone living on the ground. The more frequent the pulsing, the more careful people had to be when passing landing sites.

It was the first lesson Leila's mother had told her when she'd brought her here as a young child. If the ground is beating like your heart after a race, look up before walking.

The ground was pulsing so quickly now that Leila couldn't count how many times it pounded each minute. So she gave up and decided to watch the people walk by instead. The people of this world were brightly colored, their bodies covered in scales from head to foot, and tails swishing under their loose robes.

It was the clothing that had surprised Leila the most when she'd first traveled here with her mother nearly ten years ago, rather than the fact that lizards walked on two legs and talked just like people. The women who passed her dressed just like those at home, with a billowy, solid-colored dress, a scarf wrapped around their hair, and one covering their faces, leaving just their bright, jewel-like eyes visible.

Leila had sat on her mother's lap at this very fountain, watching the veiled women walk past them without a male guardian. She had only ever seen her mother do that when they traveled to the Mysterious Worlds, though one of her aunts often traveled alone to go to her job since her husband worked on the opposite side of the city.

She remembered watching the bright flash of color as one of the scaled hands or bare, scaled feet came out from the loose cloth. And then she saw one of the lizard people stop by the fountain and remove the face covering for a few minutes to get a drink of water. And then she realized it was a man.

Leila smiled now, watching the passersby. She could tell the men and the women apart now, even though they both wore the same clothes. But in that moment, when she'd been just eight years old, she'd realized the strangest thing about this world wasn't the fact that it had two suns in the sky, neither of which ever fully set, or that its people were reptilian in form. It was that she'd seen a man dressed like a woman.

In the pressing crowd of reptile people, a girl in black wove her way through the streets. Leila hardly had to look to know it was one of her sisters. The lizard people were all much taller than humans. The black-clothed girl rushing toward her now looked as small as a child in comparison.

The girl came to a stop beside Leila, gasping for breath. It was Amira.

"You didn't tell me you were coming here today," she said, fingering a stitch in her ribs.

Leila traced her finger through the cool water of the fountain.

"Mother doesn't want any of us going to these worlds alone. What if something happened to you?" Amira sat on the stone next to Leila. "There's no guarantee the Door would even open to the place you'd gone. You could have been in Eshraq, or the floating city, or the—"

"The Door will bring you wherever you want to, if you ask politely," Leila said, swirling her hand in the water again. "You didn't know?"

Amira pursed her lips.

"I suppose I'm late, then? Is it time for prayers?" Leila patted the bag she'd brought with her. "I forgot my watch at home."

"I know," Amira said, holding it out. "It's not time for prayers, though we've got an hour until dinner."

It was hard to keep track of the passage of time when she was in this world. Unlike in Eshraq, where they could stay for many days without missing more than a few hours of time at home, time passed much more slowly here. A few hours under their two suns could mean missing an entire day in her own world.

When Leila didn't take her watch, Amira placed it in her lap and played with it. The two sisters sat in silence, letting the tall lizard people pass them by on their daily tasks.

Leila followed a pair with her eyes. One was a man and the other a woman. They both wore the deep red clothing of university students. She'd learned the importance of colors in their society years ago. Red was for students in tertiary education, blue for children, green for single adults in the workforce, orange for government officials, and white for married people. Black was worn only by those mourning the dead, or by the human visitors.

Looking down at the heavy black clothes she wore, both at home and here, because it was easier than trying to buy from the locals when they could not understand each others' languages.

"Father says he will never allow me to go to England for college," she whispered.

Amira cast her gaze sideways. "Did you at least convince him to allow you to study in our own country?"

Leila's eyes felt like they would burst out of her face. She closed them and allowed a single hot tear to slip out.

"Leila," Amira said, covering her hand with her own.

Leila opened her eyes and looked at her sister.

"You must keep trying," Amira said.

Leila wiped her eyes and held the back of her hand to her forehead. "Why? What's the point? He's the head of the family. His word is final."

Amira looked out at the street. She pointed to a woman who walked close to them, leading her young daughter by the hand. The woman was dressed in splendid robes of burnt orange. Leila had seen this woman many times on her visits to the Two Sun World. She was the speaker of their parliament, and the city was covered in ads asking for people to vote for her as their president.

"If these people could understand what you were saying, they'd never forgive you," Amira said.

The larger of the two suns dipped below the horizon, dimming the world around them into the twilight that constituted night on this world.

***

Amira had always thought that Eshraq, the world that bled sunshine, was most beautiful at night. She stood in the grove by the Door with Nur, watching the breeze rustle the leaves, which glowed a bright blue against the inky blackness of the sky. The moon was only a small sliver in the sky, as though it were protesting the inevitability of tomorrow night's new moon.

Leila had always thought night in Eshraq was beautiful, too. But she wasn't there. She had stopped traveling to the Mysterious Worlds nearly three months ago. Instead, she spent every free moment locked in her room, refusing to talk to anybody.

Nur tugged on her hand. "It's time to go home," she said. "We need to get a good night's sleep. Leila's getting married tomorrow. Do you want to fall asleep during her wedding?"

Amira pulled her hand away from her little sister's. "You go back. There's something I want to do first."

She looked up at Amira with narrowed, cunning eyes. "You and Leila always say that when you're about to do something fun and don't want me to see."

"I promise you I won't have any fun, Nur. Go back through the Door. Don't worry about me."

Nur hesitated, pulling at the black dress she'd hastily pulled over her brightly colored Eshraqi clothing. "Don't take too long. I don't want Mother to get angry with me for coming back without you." She swept the bioluminescent vines out of the way and stepped through the Door.

Amira placed her hand on the hard wood separating her from her family. Through that door was Leila, shut up in her room all alone ever since their father announced he'd accepted a marriage offer for her. One of his co-worker's sons had just graduated from medical school and was settling down into a life as a doctor, working in the trauma unit of the local hospital.

It was a good match. Hazim was well-educated, with a job that was very promising. He would be able to take care of Leila and their future family very easily.

She would never have to worry about money or lack of food, like their family did now. They were so poor that they couldn't even afford a house of their own, not after their grandfather had squandered his family's money and left their father penniless, with a ruined reputation. The work he could get never paid well, and they lived in their house only at the generosity of their mother's older brother, who'd inherited it after the death of his parents.

Leila would never worry as their mother did. Their father couldn't imagine a better future for his daughter.

But Leila could. And Amira could. Leila had always loved school, and she was always at the top of her class. She'd dreamed of going to college in England ever since she was a little girl.

A glowing vine fell against Amira's hand. She pushed it away and stared at the dark wood Door, trying to make out its features in the semi-darkness. Leila hadn't spoken since their father announced her engagement, except during the daily prayers. She'd accepted his announcement, as any obedient daughter would.

Amira stepped away from the Door. She grabbed a heavy rock from the ground and threw it at the Door, watching the wood splinter. She threw it again, and again, until the Door lay at her feet in a pile of dry wood fragments. A solid, stone wall spread out behind the vines where it had once been.

Her family would no longer be able to travel to this world. And she could never return home. Amira pulled her swirl-patterned *niqab* tighter around her face and walked out of the grove and through the meadow, heading for the village. Heading for Selim.

As she walked, sunshine flared at her feet.

A Grain of Earth
Miriam Zizza

Layla hated not being able to breathe in her own backyard. The *niqab* chafed against her cheeks, trapping the air from her lungs with its fibers. Her fingers itched to tear it off and let the warm rays of the sun run through her long black hair, over her skin, and to let it fill her pores until they overflowed with golden light. But her father would have had a fit.

They will see that you are different and they will take you.

Layla always wanted to ask him what was wrong with being different, but she never did. As soon as he was done talking, the fevered light in his eyes would blink out and they would become dead and dark, just like they did whenever she asked about her mother.

So Layla remained quiet. She kept wearing her *hijab* and *niqab* in public, even if it was just for stepping outside to sneeze. It was only for a few hours, only until the heavy sun dropped its weary head below the horizon. Only until the world fell asleep and the creatures of the night seeped from the cracks in the roads and the corners of the alleys. That was her realm. There she could be free.

But for now, the sun still beat down, suffusing her black clothing with heat until she felt the sweat running down by her ears. Layla dug her fingers into the earth, glancing back at the windows of the house. They watched her, her father's silent guardians. She stared defiantly back at them, knowing their vigilance could have been worse. Layla had fought and haggled her way out of true imprisonment by those windows, those walls. Her father had wanted her to stop going to school.

The more people see you, the more they will begin to realize you are cursed, Layla.

But they couldn't see her. Not like this. Not with her entire body and soul shielded by dark cloth. Nothing but her eyes were free. She'd had to call Uncle Kazemde to make her father see it would be okay. He was the only one who had any sway with her father. And that was only because he was her mother's brother.

Layla's fingers brushed a hard surface. Her heartbeat quickened, rattling around her rib cage. She reached into the uneven hole in the soft earth and removed the metal box. It was small and square, the lid a little rusty. Red-brown flakes drifted away beneath her touch. With a shaking hand, she reached into her pocket and removed the key she'd stolen from her father's bed stand drawer. He never opened it anymore and wouldn't notice its absence. Or so she told herself. After she'd taken the key, Layla had sat cloistered in her room for a good ten minutes, reassuring herself that he wouldn't know, before she had mustered the courage and gone outside. Her father was on a business call in his office. He wouldn't be out for hours.

The key fit reluctantly into the lock, as if trying to convince her that it didn't belong. Layla stilled her trembling fingers and the key went in. She lifted the lid and a few crumbs of dirt trickled inside. At the bottom of the box were four sets of eyes. Brown eyes. Warm eyes. Joyful eyes. There was a depth to them that made Layla stare and feel empty as though everything inside her had been scooped out, put in a box and buried in the ground. Her mother and father had their arms around each other, looking down at their children with smiles as pure and gentle as moonlight. Layla envisioned her father's coffee-stained teeth and wondered if this was the same man. Kasiya and Layla had their arms around each other too. But her brother was pulling on her hair and she was sticking out her tongue. The thumping of her heart began to hurt. She wished he hadn't left.

Layla dropped the box in a panic as the front door slammed. Her father wasn't supposed to be done with his meeting until three. The *hijab* became a strangling weight on her shoulders and neck, the *niqab* sucking tight against her mouth as she gasped. Layla's gaze remained fixed on the picture. She knew she would break in half if she buried it again. Burying was reserved for the dead. Layla snatched the photo and tossed the box back into the hole, scrambling to her feet and kicking the soil back into place.

"Layla? What are you doing out here?" her father asked, heavy brows low over his eyes.

She slipped the picture into her pocket, accidentally smearing it with the stripe of dirt on her thumb, and smiled tightly. "Nothing. Just reassuring myself the world is out here before I spend the rest of my life finishing schoolwork."

"Your clothes are filthy, Layla." He looked away down the road like he always did. As if waiting for that missing half of himself to return. The half that would make him more than a shadow. "I don't want to see you again until you've finished your homework."

"Don't worry," said Layla. "You won't."

***

She could sense the night before it came. All the white noise buzzing in her body from the stress of daytime hours went silent. Peace flooded her mind and her bones. The *hijab* and the veil became a dream easily left behind. They lay discarded on her bed right now as if she had sloughed her skin, shed that daylight identity and donned the night. This was who she really was. The fire started in the tips of her toes and worked its way up her legs and into her stomach, curling there like a great, flaming lion, ready to rise and burst out of her chest.

Layla expertly escaped her house, opening the front door without a sound to the anthem of her father's snores. She left her shoes behind. Then she could truly feel the earth, feel her freedom, and feel the Strength coursing through her unchecked. It wasn't a curse. It was a gift. The same gift her mother once had. But her father had never believed this. He had always worried. And now he was blinded by bitterness.

The moon beamed down like the smiles of her parents in the photo. Layla smiled back at it. That light was the only love she'd felt for years. Glass shattered somewhere in the distance and ugly, abrasive shouting broke out. She ran. Not because she was frightened, but because she was free. Because she was meant to. Because this was the only way she could truly live. The night air was pure adrenaline, burning through her lungs, through her entire system. Layla couldn't have moved with swifter steps or more grace if she'd had wings. The darkness was her wings.

She ran through the waiting streets, the glowering, leering eyes unable to track her progress. They were all left behind, covered in dust and defeat. Layla knew they couldn't touch her. They would suffer if they did.

A crack and the sound of more glass raining to the street. Layla ran toward the screams. Somewhere in the dark, a girl's voice had responded to the volley of low, angry shouts. Her words were indistinct, but her fear was not. Layla's muscles felt hot, energy and Strength mingling like molten lava in her veins. She pounded around a corner and stopped.

Her hair whipped around her in a gust of wind, blowing into tangles in front of her face. Layla stepped forward, feeling the gritty street beneath her, and its scarred surface was an anchor to her soul. The road seemed to pulse, and with each of those pulses the fire inside Layla burned brighter. A man stood with his back to her, arm raised, a broken bottle glinting in his fist. Pressed against the wall of a small shop was a girl of about Layla's age. Her short, dark hair was matted with sweat and a livid cut stretched across her cheek. Wild eyes locked on Layla, and she suddenly realized she knew this girl. She had classes with her at school.

"Nuru, what are you doing out so late?" Layla asked.

Nuru's already wide eyes grew larger. The man turned around, pointing the broken bottle like a sword.

"This time is reserved for ugly beasts like him so we don't have to see their faces in the light," Layla said.

The man snarled and spat on the ground. With a roar he came toward her, weapon shining with moonlight as though the glass wasn't empty at all. Layla ducked his swing and jabbed him in the stomach. He grunted, staggering, and lashed out again. She stopped his arm inches from her face, fingers locked tight around his wrist. The Strength inside nearly scorched her from the inside out. Layla twisted his arm down hard and pried open his fingers. The bottle hit the street in a thousand shards. Layla kept pushing on his fingers until she heard one crack.

Cursing, the man finally pulled free and swung a heavy fist at her. Layla sidestepped it easily and kicked him in the back. He flew and hit the ground palms down. The man slowly picked himself up and turned toward her again with a growl.

The smell of beer came off him in waves. She wondered how well she'd be able to fight while holding her breath. The man's beady eyes narrowed and he lunged, catching her off guard as he tackled her straight to the ground. Layla's head cracked to the earth and the darkness filled with stars. He grappled with her arms, trying to pin them down. She wrenched to the side and bit his hand. The man jerked back in surprise and enraged pain. When he next leaned down, his eyes were full of deadly intent. Layla lurched, jamming her head into his jaw. His neck snapped back and she squirmed free. She scrambled to her feet and yanked his arms behind him while he was still stunned.

"Leave her alone or I snap one of these off," she hissed.

Her only answer was his ragged breathing.

Layla pushed on his shoulder. "Sometimes asymmetry makes things look better. It would certainly be an improvement for you." She looked at Nuru, still cowering against the wall. "Don't you think so?"

"Alright!" the man said.

She pushed harder.

"I said *alright!*"

"Actually, it's not alright." Layla pivoted, feeling the dirt from the street in-graining itself in her skin. She hauled the man to his feet. "If I see you again, I'll change my mind about the asymmetry and snap them both."

His lip curled and he swore at her, calling her several names that she was sure he'd just created on the spot. The man didn't even glance at Nuru before limping away. The girl was frozen, pasted to the bricks behind her.

"Go home," said Layla. "I'll make sure you get there safe."

Nuru's mouth dropped open in a silent question. She stayed that way for a full minute, but the words wouldn't come. Her eyes narrowed as she regarded Layla, but she'd never seen her without her *niqab* and without the veil she was not the same person. Nuru shook her head and the suspicion left her eyes. She pulled her sweater closer around her and finally peeled herself from the wall.

Layla became Nuru's shadow until she reached home. When her classmate stepped inside, she was already gone, the unlocked lion inside her restless with freedom. And though the Strength would continue to roar in her bones when the sun returned, it would be trapped by her father's law, the *hijab* and *niqab*, its wildness smothered until darkness came again.

***

Layla was bored out of her mind. So bored that she might as well not have been present. Normally she loved school and soaked up every word that fell from the teacher's mouth. But the teacher was out sick today and had been replaced by a rotund, balding man with a sweaty, red face and nasally whine. Layla wanted to jam her fingers in her ears. But the frequency of his voice would have still penetrated her skull. Even the thickest of heads wouldn't have held up against this auditory torture.

The door burst open and everyone in the room turned toward it, thankful for the diversion. Nuru stood in the opening, heat in her cheeks and rage in her eyes. Layla had noticed her seat was empty and had thought she was taking the day off to recover from the incident. Apparently she was more resilient than Layla had given her credit for. Nuru was a very independent girl whose strength was in words, not physicality.

"The posters are gone," Nuru said. Her arm shook, even as it continued to hold the door open.

"Posters?" the substitute asked, sniffing and mopping his forehead with a white cloth.

"*My* posters."

Everyone knew about Nuru's posters. Originally, they had just been small, slick fliers she'd handed out herself. It was safer to promote her values and goals that way, but it reached only a small population. The posters had been a bold move, and the entire school was whispering about them. About what it would be like not having to wear the *hijab* or the veil. Not everyone did, but those who knew the strange, suffocating isolation of the coverings stared at the posters in awe. Nuru had never worn the *hijab* or *niqab* and she never would. She told any female who would listen that they shouldn't have to either.

Layla itched to remove the coverings right now. But her father's face surfaced in her mind. Those empty, dull eyes accusing her. She stared at her desk instead.

"Of course the posters are gone, Ms. Hamadi. You didn't have permission to put them up. And anyone in their right mind would realize they were preposterous and demonstrated nothing but naivety," the substitute said.

"Demonstrated?" Nuru's eyes grew dark, her lips very thin. "No. I'll *show* you what they demonstrated."

The entire class held its breath as she took five steps across the room. Each one took a lifetime. The clock on the wall stopped. Nuru reached out, her long fingers brushing Layla's headscarf. Then both the *hijab* and the *niqab* were gone. The silence was sickening.

"Oh," Nuru breathed. The head coverings fell to the ground in a pile, the sound of the rippling cloth like an avalanche in the stillness.

Layla faced her classmates for the first time. They all stared at her, but none so much as Nuru Hamadi.

"You," she said. "Last night." Her hand slowly traveled up until it covered her mouth. "Layla…you stopped that man from…." Nuru burst into tears.

***

Her father's fury was cold. "I knew it would come to this."

Layla suppressed a shiver and fiddled with the zipper on her jacket. A million responses chased themselves around her mind, but her throat remained dry and her mouth closed. She slipped her hand inside her pocket and briefly touched the photo she'd put there. Those smiles seemed like a dream now.

"All this time you have willfully and deliberately gone out against my wishes." The anger was worse because he would not look at her. He stared out the window, a hand to his square jaw. He'd turned his back on her the second she'd walked inside.

"It's not your wish to make, Father." As soon as she said it, Layla wanted to grab the words and stuff them back inside. But her tongue ran on without her, untamable, out of control. "Mother used her gift all the time. To *help* people."

"What Zahra had was no gift. It was a curse that stole her from me. And now you are determined to abandon your family? Why?" Her father grabbed the windowsill, knuckles shiny and white. "Why is death so important to you, Layla? Because that is all you will find if you continue down this road."

"Everyone dies eventually, Father," Layla whispered. "Mother died doing what she loved. What right do you have to say that is wrong? She did it because she wanted to. She knew what she was doing. As do I."

"No. You don't." Her father's back stiffened. "You are still a child. You are blind to reality. Now that they know, they will never stop looking for you. You will never be able to marry, to have a family of your own. No man will take a cursed woman. You have cut off your future before it has started and you have betrayed me by doing so."

"Marriage? A *future?*" Layla's hands balled to fists at her side. "Father, you've never wanted me to leave the house. What future could I possibly have had? And who are *they?* You want me to feel like a hunted animal, but how can I when the predator doesn't even exist?"

"The world is a predator, Layla. If it sees that you are different, it will take you and destroy you. And now it has seen. You've let it see you," her father said, the muscles in his shoulders tightening. "Which is why I am sending you to your uncle."

Layla shook her head and picked up the two duffel bags on the floor. "I can't stay with Uncle Kazemde forever."

Her father finally turned to face her. His eyes were hollow, two pits set deep in his skull. "You will stay there for as long as I say."

***

Layla had been furious at first. How could her own father force her to leave her home and her friends? But now, standing in front of the mirror in her new room at her uncle's house, she was starting to think that this might be good. It might be better. The mirror was full length and showed her what she rarely saw in the light of day. Herself. Her true self, free of both *hijab* and *niqab*. She didn't need those chains here at Uncle Kazemde's. He was her mother's brother, the only uncle she had. And he understood much more than her father did. Her father would have wanted her to continue covering up, even here in the United States. Uncle Kazemde would lie for her, if only because he knew she was as stubborn as his sister.

If Layla was here to start over, she would start over free. She had heard from Nuru about a thousand times that the people in the West didn't care so much if you were different. Layla didn't know if that was entirely true, but she knew they didn't care whether or not she walked around with a headscarf and veil.

"Layla."

She jumped and turned. Uncle Kazemde stood in the doorway, tall and thin and stooping a little as if he were afraid he'd hit his head. His hands were in his pockets, hiding his musician's fingers. The crooked scar on his cheek puckered when he smiled and the end of his pointed beard went up.

"Can people really tell I'm different just by looking at me, Uncle?" Layla asked, glancing back at the mirror.

"I can," he said.

Layla tilted her head and frowned at him. "You don't count. You're related."

Uncle Kazemde grinned. But the laughter in his eyes slowly faded, and he removed his hands from his pockets only to tuck them away beneath crossed arms. "You are different, Layla. People look at you and know that you are strong. That frightens them. People don't like things they may not have control over."

She bowed her head. "So Father is right." Layla looked at the discarded head coverings on her quilted bed, feeling her stomach plummet.

"No," said Uncle Kazemde, stepping into the room. "They don't see your Strength here." He squeezed a hand around his upper arm. "They see it here." Her uncle put his palm over his heart. "That is what scares them, what scares your father, even more than your gift."

***

That night she almost ripped her *hijab* and *niqab* to shreds. It was her first night out in this new neighborhood, this new town, this new country. She had been looking forward, as she always did, to the moonlight weaving pearly streamers through her hair, the ground firm and reassuring beneath her feet. And then she remembered the eyes. The way her classmates had stared at her when Nuru's story spread. When they heard about what she'd done. Hero or freak? Layla saw no distinction in their expressions. She had vowed to herself never to suffer that scrutiny again. But here, in her new life, the only way she could do that was to wear her coverings at night when she should be free.

If she'd thought this out more thoroughly, maybe she wouldn't have had to. But Layla had been so eager to defy her father, to leap out from under his thumb and throw her head coverings away. She hadn't realized that would mean wearing them was the only way to keep her identity safe. This wasn't hiding, like her father wanted her to. His paranoia was what had allowed her to run free at night without the veil. Now she had to take different measures, make a different sort of sacrifice now that she could walk unveiled during the day. Concealing her identity was just as much for her as it was for the people she cared about. Maybe "they" *were* out there, waiting for this strange new discovery, waiting to drag her to a lab and put her under a microscope. But it would never happen if she left no connection between herself and the girl who roamed the streets at night. And no connection meant she had to cover herself with the very things that she had hoped to leave behind.

The usual thrill was subdued as Layla arranged the *hijab* and *niqab*. Maybe her father had known exactly what sending her to her uncle's would mean after all. He'd known exactly what she would do, that she would remove her coverings as soon as she set foot on United States soil. That she would then have to hide in the moments she felt the most free. That the night would then be tainted. The anger sat uneasily inside her. Usually when she got mad, the anger would mix with the Strength inside, making the internal furnace burn hotter still. This time she felt nothing but regular old fury. Layla closed her eyes, commanding herself to calm down. She wouldn't let her father ruin this for her, no matter how hard he tried. She was doing what she loved, just as her mother had.

Layla picked her jacket off the floor where she'd thrown it on her arrival. She'd still been seething then, wishing her father had been someone else. She hung the white coat on the door and left, passing through the house like a ghost. The air was different here, lighter, emptier. Layla took a deep breath in, but her lungs didn't seem to fill the way they should have, as if they had shrunk. She frowned and wiggled her toes in the grass. At least the moon was the same, even hundreds of miles away from home. Its light spilled around her and it was almost like she wasn't wearing the *hijab* and *niqab* at all.

She ran. There was no wind tonight and the air was flat and stale as she breathed it in through her veil. Uncle Kazemde lived close to downtown, so she didn't have to go far before she found trouble. Layla heard the woman struggling before she saw her. She was crying and shrieking, though the voices of her attackers nearly drowned her out.

Layla entered the side street squeezed between a bar and a hair salon. Trash fluttered from her passing, stuck in the grate of a drain. The red light from the bar's open sign made the darkness burn. One man held the woman close to him, her arms twisted behind her, while the other flipped through her wallet.

"These teams don't look very fair to me," Layla said.

"Are you stupid, kid?" the man with the wallet asked. "Do you want to get robbed?"

She didn't answer. Instead, she ran forward, threw herself into a handspring, and kicked him in the chest. He only stumbled back a few feet when he should have flown across the alley and hit the brick wall. Layla frowned and tightened her fists.

"Crazy witch," the man muttered. He tossed the wallet to his partner and advanced towards Layla, pushing up his sleeves.

Layla bounced on the balls of her feet, waiting. When his hook came, it was too wide. She dodged beneath it and drove a quick one-two jab and cross into his stomach. He flinched and grunted, but that was all.

"Come on," Layla hissed.

Her next punch should have cracked a rib. The man was barely wheezing. He grabbed her arm and the panic finally set in. Something was terribly wrong. She barely managed to wrench herself free of the man's grasp. Layla ran toward the crying woman, slamming her palm into the face of the thug who held her. He released his grip, clutching his bloody nose. Layla eyed the bright red in satisfaction. At least she'd managed something. She grabbed the woman's hand and pulled her toward the end of the alley.

"Get out," she said.

The woman fled, and Layla was not far behind. This time there was no joy as she ran. Her limbs felt weak and rubbery. She stared at her hands, unable to understand. She should have been able to toss those two men like throw pillows. But she'd barely been able to hurt them. The constant fire of the Strength seemed to have gone out. Layla's heart thumped fearfully and she did not stop running until she had reached her uncle's house.

She was surprised to find him waiting for her in the kitchen. He looked up at her entrance, taking in her gasping breaths and haggard appearance. "I knew you would come back. I would have stopped you, but I knew you wouldn't listen until you'd seen it for yourself," he said.

"Stopped me?" Layla put her hands on her knees. She shouldn't have been so out of breath. "Uncle Kazemde, I don't understand. I thought you supported my gift."

"I do, Layla. I do." He stood and guided her to a chair. "But here you will find it does not work."

Layla stared at him, wondering if she should get her ears checked. "It can't just not work, Uncle."

His black eyes were solemn. "It can and it does, as soon as you leave Egyptian soil." He sat down across from her. "Your Strength is connected to the land, Layla. It comes from the earth, the very heart of Egypt. Without that soil beneath you, the Strength cannot flow and you become just like the rest of us."

"No." Layla was shaking. "It can't be true. Uncle Kazemde, what am I supposed to—My father knew. He knew this whole time, didn't he?"

"Yes."

She cradled her face in her hands, trembling. "What do I do? How can I do anything?"

"Talk to him, Layla," said her uncle. "Talk to your father."

"I can't." She struggled to keep back the sobs. "He won't care. He's always hated this gift."

"I know," Uncle Kazemde murmured. He pushed a mug of hot tea across the table, as if he'd been preparing for this breakdown. He probably had. "Asim made sure everything was pristine at Zahra's funeral. Not a single grain of earth." He studied the grainy whorls in the table. "Your mother used to say that was all she needed to be herself." Uncle Kazemde raised his head and the lines of his face carried sorrow. "I'm sorry, Layla. What else can you do? Egypt will always be a part of you. When you have been away as long as I have, you learn to carry it in your heart."

Layla nudged the tea away. "Well my heart's not good enough." She left the kitchen and pounded upstairs to her room. Flinging open the door, Layla threw herself inside. She stared hard into the mirror, but there was no difference. The Strength was gone, but her reflection had remained the same. Some part of her felt that shouldn't have been possible.

Movement caught the corner of her eye and Layla turned slowly. Every motion felt weighed down by lead, by her father's unfairness. He'd known what sending her here would do. He'd wanted her to be powerless. The movement turned out to be her jacket, still swinging on its hook on the door from her explosive entrance.

Her jacket. Layla glanced back at the mirror and met her own brown-eyed gaze. Brown eyes. There were four sets of brown eyes in the photo. In her jacket. Layla's pulse became thunder in her ears. Each of the four steps to the door was like crossing a canyon. She reached inside her coat pocket and removed the picture.

It was still smeared from when she'd dug it up in the backyard. Smeared with a single grain of earth....

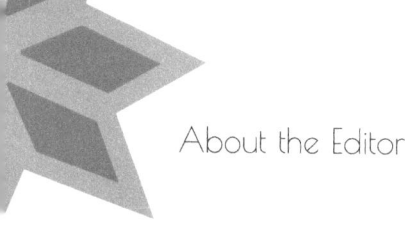

About the Editor

Rula Quawas is a professor of American literature and feminist theory at the University of Jordan. She was the founding Director of the Women's Studies Center at the university, and she was also the Dean of the Faculty of Foreign Languages. Rula's research focuses on feminist readings of American and Arabic texts written by women writers. She has written and published numerous essays in English on American and on Arab women writers. She has co-authored three communication-skill textbooks, a book on Jordanian women writers and a book on intercultural communication. She serves on many editorial boards such as Studies in Literature in English and the International Journal of Arabic-English Studies. Rula was honored as a distinguished international scholar, and she was also awarded the Meritorious Honor Award for Leadership and Dedication to the empowerment of Jordanian women. She was recently nominated for the International Women of Courage Award. Her dream is to forge new pathways and to see women fulfill their aspirations and become what they are capable of becoming. Rula Quawas strongly believes that dreams do come true.

www.ingramcontent.com/pod-product-compliance
Lightning Source LLC
Chambersburg PA
CBHW051258250626
47155CB00009B/3336